THE

CURSE

OF THE

MAYA

A Truth-Seekers' Story

JOHNNY PEARCE

AND

ANDY LONERAGAN

The Curse of the Maya
Copyright © 2019 Johnny Pearce & Andy Loneragan
Reprinted 2020
Published by Loom

This is a work of fiction. Names, characters, businesses, places, events and incidents are either the products of the author's imagination or used in a fictitious manner. Any resemblance to actual persons, living or dead, or actual events is purely coincidental.

Cover design: Loom

Trade paperback ISBN: 978-0-9935102-4-3

LM 08/26

ABOUT THE AUTHORS:

JOHNNY PEARCE

Johnny Pearce is a teacher and co-head of English at his school. Part of this project is to show to his pupils a reason for learning about writing: writing with a purpose for an audience. They can become writers, too. He is also a philosopher who likes to think a lot. Hopefully, this has seeped into this book. Perhaps there is fuel for some good P4C (Philosophy 4 Children) sessions within these pages. As one famous thinker once said: the unexamined life isn't worth living. Examine your lives with big questions! Pearce lives in Hampshire with his partner and twin boys and loves writing all sorts of things, from fiction to non-fiction, poetry to geekery. He hopes the readers both enjoy this book and become inspired to write their own, either for themselves or anyone else.

ANDY LONERAGAN

Andy Loneragan is also a teacher in Hampshire. He worked alongside Johnny Pearce for a number of years and despite this experience, agreed to write this book with him. This is Andy's first foray into writing and he wants to show his pupils that writing and hopefully reading too is something everybody can enjoy.

ACKNOWLEDGEMENTS:

The authors would like to thank a whole host of people. Firstly, several younger readers who have been our willing guinea pigs, including Libby and Ginny Pellatt. Geoff Benson (he's not a younger reader...), as ever has been a great help, and, most notably, Rebecca Bradley. Thanks for all of your input! The students at our various schools also deserve some appreciation for being involved in the early drafting of the book.

PRAISE FOR *THE CURSE OF THE MAYA*:

"Both entertaining and thought-provoking, an exciting journey through danger, and philosophy, bugs, betrayal, sibling rivalry, and an awesome archaeological puzzle."

Rebecca Bradley, author of *Cadon, Hunter*

To searchers everywhere:

You can find it

and you can do it.

Prologue

The Guard

The jungle night was silent; *well, as silent as the jungles of Guatemala ever got,* thought Carlos as he trudged round the empty camp. The buzz of cicadas and the almost inaudible squeak of bats hunting the large cricket-like creatures were now so commonplace to him that Carlos barely even heard them. This was his fourth night out here on his own. Now that the ground crew had left, having cleared a substantial area of the jungle, ready for the scientists, archaeologists and who-knows-who-else to arrive, he was alone.

Carlos didn't mind spending time on his own. Normally. He had been an independent security guard for many years; Guatemala was not the safest of places for foreigners. Many of his jobs were along similar lines: keeping people (or, as in this case, places) safe before the main event began, whatever that might be. A vague job description for sure, but Carlos liked it this way - he liked not knowing what the next job may entail. Normally.

This job was different.

The beam of Carlos's torch cut through the darkness of the humid night air, revealing the site around him - tents, boxes of equipment, and caches of food that he'd been forbidden to touch: sights that were very familiar to him. He turned to his right. The blade of light faltered as he turned, failing to illuminate the imposing, roughly hewn stone steps of the recently discovered temple that towered over him. He knew it was because of the distance between himself and the monument, but Carlos couldn't help but think the temple *wanted* to remain in the darkness and was somehow overpowering his attempts to see it more clearly. *Estas loco,* he thought: just craziness. But the thought would not leave him.

On his previous nights, Carlos had stayed in the camp, but tonight he would not allow silly fears about ancient temples to defeat him. He took a number of strides towards the crumbling stonework, his determination evaporating as the light of his torch rested on a set of glyphs clearly depicting an ancient human sacrifice. *Well, perhaps tomorrow,* he thought to himself.

Just as he turned to walk back to the pile of hessian sacks he had formed into a sort of chair, a light flickered at the top of the temple stairs.

Impossible. There was nobody else out here. If there was, he would have heard them coming from miles away as the only way in and out was by helicopter, or four-wheel-drive jeep.

There it was again. Definitely. A light.

An uninvited, unannounced visitor to the camp, to the temple? Carlos knew he had no choice but to investigate. After all, that was why he was here. With one hand on the butt of his pistol, he headed up the rocky steps. The entrance to the temple met him at the top. It was not particularly grand - simply a large, rectangular hole in the otherwise unbroken walls of the square room set at the summit of the stone pyramid. Carlos tried to pierce the deep black of the ancient building with his torch, but, once again, the darkness seemed to be impenetrable. And yet, from somewhere within, the light flashed again. This time, red.

Without thinking, Carlos stepped into the dark, almost expecting it to weigh down around him, to surround him, to consume him. But nothing of the sort happened and he let out a long breath. He hadn't even realised he had been holding his breath. To his left, the light pulsed again. Carlos felt for the video capture device attached to his cargo waistcoat pocket and fumbled about, finally switching it on. He couldn't be too careful.

"*Hola*?" he called into the tunnel-like corridor that ran downwards from the entrance chamber. Nothing. Not even an echo. The light pulsed again and Carlos felt a strange pull. He longed to turn and run, but the red light burned once more and he felt his feet begin to shuffle down the cramped passageway.

Black then red, black then red. All other details forgotten, Carlos was drawn forward by the mesmerising throb. Around how many corners, down how many passageways he went, he did not know, but the light grew stronger, stronger.

Finally, he emerged into a vaulted chamber, deep in the heart of the temple. Just as he was about to curse his curiosity, his impetuousness, the red light burst into existence once again, though this time he could see what he thought was its source. There, in the middle of the room was a podium, on top of which was an object unlike anything he'd ever seen. He knew it was ancient, hundreds, thousands of years old. A shiver ran down his spine. Was he the first to see this for over a millennium? How was it creating that light? Why? Why now, after all these years?

He took a step towards the podium. Black. He took another. Red. Black. Red. Black. The light became too powerful, the changes too rapid. He shut his eyes tightly but there was no escape. Sudden pain, like a spear, shot through the centre of his forehead. He covered his eyes with his hands but the strobing light searched for and found every crack. He felt a trickle of blood on his upper lip and traced it to his nostrils. Something was wrong, very wrong indeed.

Something gave way in Carlos's brain, incapable of making sense of the barrage of light. His hand, smeared with his own blood, stretched forward to the podium, to the strange object that sat atop. Centimetres, millimetres from the artefact, Carlos slumped backwards.

Red...black

Red.........black

Red...........

Black........................

1

Verity

"Vee? Where's your passport? Have you found it yet?"

Her father's voice had a ring of frustration to it, like he wanted to be out of the door in the next ten minutes. *He needed to learn to relax*, she thought. They had a good hour.

"Vee? Did you hear me?"

Her name was Verity, but everyone called her Vee. Verity didn't roll off the tongue easily, but she liked the name. It meant "truth" and Verity had taken her name as her lifelong mission in everything she did. Life was like a puzzle, and she was there to solve it. She could complete Sudoku puzzles quicker than her father, and relished a good detective book, a real whodunit mystery story.

Right now, the problem to solve was the whereabouts of her passport. And, so far, the solution had eluded her. The truth of the matter was…she didn't have a clue as to where it was. As a result of this conundrum, her bedroom was in a complete state, like a tornado had whipped through it with no concern for anything but causing havoc.

The clock was ticking. Her family had to get to London Heathrow airport to catch a plane to Central America. This was the first time, now that Mum was gone, that they had accompanied Dad on one of his trips. Ethan said they were boring trips, but he was a *boy*, so what would he know? Being the sibling who read books, Verity felt she knew more than Ethan. A lot more.

Verity's bedroom door opened.

"Hey, Vee, Dad's getting pretty irate. Have you found it yet? Why have you even got it? It should be in the drawer with the others. You always have to do things differently!"

Brothers were bad at the best of times. But *twin* brothers? They were worse than bad. They were *detestable*.

"Okay, Ethan. Keep your hair on. I suppose *you're* ready?"

"Yes. I have been waiting downstairs for ten minutes. We are *completely* ready," replied Ethan.

Twins are funny things. Sometimes they love each other and are inseparable. Other times, they hate each other, and can't stand spending time in close proximity. Then there are those occasions when twins can love and hate each other in equal measure. They can wind each other up until they explode, but also depend on each other in ways that other siblings of different ages very rarely do.

Verity and Ethan were that sort of twins.

Right now, she hated him. Not real hate, of course, but brotherly and sisterly hate that comes when you see the other one giving you a smarmy grin, like teacher's pet.

Ethan swept his hand through his dark brown hair, and shifted to his side. "Oh look, Vee, here it is," he said as he pulled the passport from under a pair of dirty jeans on the dresser.

"That was never there! *You* had it, didn't you? You little..."

"Vee! For goodness sake, girl, come on!" came Dad's voice, thundering from downstairs.

"Some weasel just 'found' it for me!" she shouted back, before snatching the passport from Ethan's hands and storming out of the room.

6

She liked puzzles, but she hated tricks. Tricks were what people were able to do when they *weren't* being truthful. Ethan was good at that. At tricks *and* not being truthful.

Dad was waiting for them downstairs, his tall, thin frame leaning against the front door, tense and tired (already).

"Right, your bags are packed in the car, everything in the house is turned off, and the airport is waiting for us," he said, running his hand through his sandy-coloured hair. Sometimes, he really reminded Verity of Ethan. No, sometimes, Ethan really reminded her of Dad.

Her father was a very careful man who didn't like to take risks. "Plug sockets can cause fire," he always said if they were going away for anything longer than a weekend, before turning each and every one of them off. The house became a dead zone where all living technology was put briefly on hold - frozen in time – to be resurrected upon their return.

Parts of Verity, like her father, were careful: her thinking about puzzles, her homework, when she was making things in Dad's shed. Parts of her weren't careful; these were mainly the parts responsible for cleaning her room.

After a last check around the house (Dad liked to check again, just after a good check, and then once more, to make sure), the three of them piled into the car, to set off to the airport. Their destination, Guatemala, a country squashed snugly between Mexico, Belize, Honduras, El Salvador and the sea.

The trip was going to be exotic. It was going to be surprising. But most of all, and unbeknownst to the twins and their father, it was going to be very dangerous indeed.

Verity, though, was not aware of this. She was excited. She loved airports, at least the few she had been to. There was so much opportunity to people-watch, guessing where they might be going, and why. There were people everywhere: families, groups, people on their own, couples in love, couples out of love, children, workers, holidaymakers, businessmen and women, the old and the young. Airports were feasts for her eyes. They delighted her.

2

Ethan

Ants scuttled around on their never-ending errands, almost bumping into each other, yet keeping to their swift journeys from here to there, arranging themselves in single file columns with occasional bursts of speed around the edges in attempts to overtake slower movers. Some stopped, drawn in by lights, or shelves covered in attractive goods, or departure screens, or the realisation that one of their children was missing. Most, however, had places to be, causing flowing rivers of movement, cascades of motion at all levels of the large building. The departure hall was like two river deltas moving in opposite directions crashing into each other. Except, there was no crashing: all these people, on all of their different journeys, had, without thought, arranged themselves into an efficient network of flowing bodies and minds so that it was as if the hall itself had come alive, its veins and arteries ebbing and surging in constant flux.

Ethan hated airports. Here they were, in the huge departure lounge, in its flowing busy-ness, and all there was to do was shop, and shopping was boring. There were no games to play, and by games, ideally what Ethan wanted was football, rugby or cricket. The things he loved school for. And karate, at the weekends. But here, all he could do was wish he had his hand-held games console, but Dad hadn't let him bring it. *What was the point of going on holiday if you couldn't take things like that?* he thought. He had read his football magazine already, and Verity didn't want to play Uno.

With a giant *hurrumph*, Ethan stood up and announced, "I'm going to that shop over there." Vee was reading a book, and Dad was reading a science magazine. Both were being as fun as watching paint dry.

"Don't wander too far," said Dad without even looking up from his reading.

Ethan sauntered across a busy walkway, stopping in the middle because...he could. Ethan loved damming channels at a beach he used to visit on the Isle of Wight that had a small river running down through the sands. He would block channels with sand and stones, small rocks and bits of driftwood. Now, himself an unmoving boulder in these currents, Ethan stood stock still and took in the motion around him. After a minute of affecting all those around him, he moved on and into a shop, one that sold a whole range of things that people might want on their holidays, or might have forgotten to bring.

After ten minutes of absent-mindedly scanning a whole range of different items, something caught his eye and stoked the fires of adventure in him. After all, the only fiction books he *did* read were spy books. He would surely put these to good use in Guatemala.

"You spent how much? Well, that's all your pocket money for the first two days gone!" Dad said in an irritated voice upon Ethan's return.

No one seemed quite as excited about his binocular and compass survival set as Ethan was. Oh well, their loss.

Ethan proceeded to spend the next twenty minutes of mindless waiting staring at random people through his binoculars. This included Verity at very close range, scaring

10

her as she looked up from her book to be confronted with the two massive, shiny alien eyes of his new purchase.

"These'll be well useful in Guatemala, when we're in the jungle, looking out from that new temple they've found," Ethan said excitedly to his sister.

"Shhh. You know we're not supposed to talk about it. They're keeping it secret whilst the experts look at everything. They don't want the press and TV stations getting all excited and ruining the site before they've done all the proper work."

"Calm down, Vee. You're so uptight, sometimes. Look, maybe we'll be able to see some orangutans with these," Ethan replied.

Verity looked up from her book, and right down the other end of his binoculars, into her brother's eyes. "Orangutans live in Borneo, in Asia, Ethan. On the other side of the world. We're more likely to see spider monkeys. Fingers crossed, we'll even encounter an ocelot. Or maybe, if we're really lucky…you'll be eaten by a jaguar!" she raised her eyebrows and gave him a side-ways glance. "This is why you need to read more books."

"Geek."

After looking up at the monitor above their heads, their father interrupted the testy twins. "Right, kids, we're going to be boarding soon. Make sure you've got everything. That includes your passport, Vee."

"Ha, ha, Dad. Very funny," she sarcastically replied.

Dad began collecting his own belongings together before turning back to the children suddenly, as if only just registering the twins' conversation.

"Vee's right though, Ethan, we shouldn't go shouting about this temple. It's quite a find, and the world's press will go mad for a story like this. The British Museum knows and they are very excited, which is why they have let me go and help. They're even paying for me. I expect they'll want an exhibition in return. I've always had expertise in Mesoamerican history–"

"That's the area around Mexico, Guatemala and El Salvador, Ethan. You know, between North and South America," Verity interjected, with her own smarmy, knowing "smile".

"Yeah, I knew that, thank you very much Miss Hume. We're not at school now, *teach*!" Of course, Ethan didn't know that; or, if he had once, he had since forgotten it. He only held on to useful information, like football formations that his favourite teams used, or who had transferred to where, and for how much money. Or how to get onto level nine in his latest computer game, *Trail of Oblivion.*

"Anyway, I want to know if there's going to be another Mayan prophecy about the end of the world. The Mayans sound cool!"

Verity looked at Ethan in that way that made him feel he was about to be corrected. He was going to be taught something. He hated that look.

"Actually," and he hated it when Verity started her sentences with *actually*, "people often make the mistake of using Mayan as an adjective to describe things to do with the Maya, or to name the Maya themselves. But you should only really use the term 'Mayan' to refer to the language. All other times, it's best to use the term 'Maya'."

"OMG. Hashtag no one cares, Vee. You're so dull," Ethan reacted.

"Oh, so I'm a loser for *knowing* things? That's really childish, Ethan, even for you!"

"I know something, Vee. I *know* that you're a complete–"

"-ly awesome sister. Thanks Ethan." Verity gave her brother a smug look.

"Children, I'm not putting up with this for the whole journey. Cut it out!"

Their father had spoken, but how much good it would do was another question.

The three travellers were soon seated on the aircraft, buckled in with excitement growing, the two children hijacking their father's three weeks of work for a holiday of their own. No one could look after them for that final week before the beginning of the summer holidays, so he had received special permission to take them with him. He had been hoping that they wouldn't get in his way - as he had often reminded them over the last few weeks.

However, they would end up doing far more than get in his way. Far more.

3

Verity

Getting out of the automatic doors at the front of the airport in Flores, Vee could tell they were in a different country. More than anything else, it was the air. Hot and sticky, heavy and close, the air felt foreign, almost alien. She had been to a couple of hot countries before, but the air there had been dry; here, it was different. Straight away, her skin and clothes felt a little damp as the cumbrous, moisture-laden air consumed her. Already, she yearned for the air-conditioning of the plane that now felt hours ago.

The morning sun was out, and beaming down on everything around, making the cars shine and glass glint; even the concrete of the buildings seemed bright. The noise of the engines and the occasional beeps of the car horns had their own aural flavour, much like the packet of nachos she had just eaten. Verity felt that everything out here was going to feel different. She pulled the sunglasses down from the top of her head and onto her nose. Wearing sunglasses and not being in school uniform could only mean one thing: the summer holidays had truly started.

At first Verity was disappointed that the three of them had spent so little time in the airport at the capital Guatemala City, but the connecting flight on to the airport at Flores, in the north the country, proved to be excitement enough. They didn't fly on a jumbo jet like they

14

did from London, but a small, fixed-wing plane that was barely big enough for them, their pilot and their assorted luggage. The small craft had shuddered, bounced and then, like a bird taking to the air for the first time – or the last, she thought to herself – seemed to wobble in the air before finally settling into a steady, rhythmic flight. She had scrunched up her eyes and swallowed hard during take off but then remembered her brother was sat across from her and forced herself to look around her. Vee noticed Ethan glance in her direction, before returning his gaze to the diminishing world beneath them, his eyes bright with exhilaration. She hoped he hadn't seen her hands, white knuckled, holding tightly to the seatbelt that, fingers crossed, wasn't as old as it and the rest of the plane looked.

They were due to be picked up at Flores airport by Señor Cruzar, who worked at the university back in Guatemala City, where they had first landed. He was in charge of the project: of working on the temple and finding out about its history, as well as registering all the artefacts that they might find. However, when they disembarked from their plane (as Vee tried to steady her heart and her breathing) and walked through the arrivals gate, there was no one there to meet them. There were several people standing with names on placards, waiting for various travellers, but their surname was nowhere to be seen.

"I guess we'll wait out the front," Dad had suggested. "I have a number, but we'll wait for a bit. My phone should work out here – I spoke to the phone company and sorted all that out."

Dad hadn't let the children bring their mobile phones, which had caused a minor eruption, and a few tears. He had said that it would be good for them to spend some time away from technology and social media, to "get back to real life".

"But real life *is* social media, Dad!" her brother had insisted.

"No. And that's final."

And so it was. No mobiles, which had meant the two children actually spoke to each other on the plane (when they weren't watching films on the TV screens that came down from the seats in front).

"Dad?" said Verity. "Are you going to speak Spanish the whole time?" Neither of the twins could speak Spanish, but their father was fluent, having worked out in Central America on different archaeological digs when he was younger, and having studied the area intensely for his university courses.

"No, Mr Cruzar can speak English, so when you're around, I'll try to speak in English. But, knowing how nosey you are, Vee, if we do speak Spanish, you'll know we're just keeping secrets from you!" Dad smiled. There was a glint in his eyes, though, that suggested that he might actually do that. Verity had a habit of asking so many questions about things her father was doing that it drove him barmy.

"You know, kids, one of the great modern Mayanists of our time, David Stuart, was taken as a kid to Maya sites by his parents, just like you two now. He is famous for deciphering Maya hieroglyphs. Perhaps, you could make something of your lives just like him!"

Just then, a screeching sound could be heard. The three of them looked up to the left and saw an old, battered and dirty Land Rover hurtle along the busy airport road to come screeching to a halt next to where they were standing. A man with a dark moustache, in his late forties, Verity guessed, wound the window down further, and smiled.

"Daniel Hume?" he asked in a thick Spanish accent, so that Daniel sounded like *Danielle.*

"Hi! Yes! *Hola!*" her father bumbled back, placing a beige baseball cap he had finally found over his wavy, sandy hair. The twins got their darker brown hair, hazel eyes and lightly tanned skin from their mother.

"*Excellente!* And these must be your lovely children. *Hola!* I am Señor Cruzar, but you can call me Edwin. Or Ed." He pronounced Cruzar as *Crusar* and not as *Cruthar* (as it would have been in Spain, a fact which Verity was aware of, having watched a YouTube video on the basics of Spanish). Always doing her homework, she hated being unprepared. For anything.

Which was why Verity had been furiously reading up about Guatemala and its history, particularly about the Maya, since the temple was supposed to be of ancient Maya origin. She couldn't wait to show off her knowledge about the civilisation, such as it being the only American civilisation with a fully developed written language, or their practice of human sacrifice for religious and medical reasons, or how the Maya calendar worked (she had even brought a small clay one with her that she had made her dad buy off the internet). This would have to wait; she would find the right time to amaze those around her with her fabulous historical knowledge, and her own theory about how the Maya civilisation disappeared: a mystery to many, still, to this day.

"Please, please, let me help you with your bags," Señor Cruzar offered, and he jumped out of the battered four-wheel drive, shook her father's hand, and started picking up their luggage. He had clearly been out in the heat for some time already. His khaki clothing was covered in the orange dust that also coated the jeep. Vee watched him as he swept up a number of her father's heavy work bags with relative ease, his broad shoulders and thick arms showed little sign of effort. Although he was old, she thought, he was still clearly capable of getting stuck in with the hard graft. Because of this, along with his breezy smile and obvious passion for history, decided Vee, he was a man she must impress!

After some small talk, an apology for being late, and packing everything and everyone into the cramped vehicle, Señor Cruzar pulled away from the airport.

"So, this is all very exciting for you, no?" their host asked the children, looking in his rear-view mirror at them, strapped in and bumping around on the back bench-seat.

Before Ethan could mutter a word, Verity jumped in. "Yes. I can't wait to see how this temple fits in with the Maya timeline, and what sort of artefacts there may be. I'm guessing it is from about 200 BC?"

"Wow. Okay Little Miss, you're obviously a bit of an expert."

"Well," Dad interrupted, "We have had a number of conversations about this. Don't worry, no one's mentioned anything to anyone else."

"Good, good. And yes, Vee, we think it is from about that time period. They were building cities around then. We are trying to work out if this temple is on its own, or part of a larger city or built-up area. The problem is, nature is more powerful and, what is the word, *persistent* than we give it credit for. The jungle has grown up everywhere."

Even Ethan seemed interested in what Cruzar had to say.

"Your English is very good, Ed," Verity remarked.

"*Gracias, señorita.* I did my studies at an American university."

Cruzar drove the jeep through the small city of Flores, taking his passengers on a guided tour. The city (more like a town) was situated on the edge of a large lake.

Their host took them across a causeway and onto a small island that housed the city's historical heart.

Verity, more so than Ethan, was all ears as Cruzar explained the history of the small city around them, as they drove past exotic and fascinating buildings that felt so alien compared to what they were used to back in their market town outside of London. The children had spent enough time being taken around the museums and sites of London by their parents, although Ethan preferred the term "dragged" rather than "taken", but everything here was wonderfully different, and certainly a lot smaller than London.

After an hour or so of driving, and a brief pause at a rest stop where they could buy some snacks and food, the jeep set off north, towards the Maya Biosphere Reserve, which covered the north of the country. Deep inside this huge forested area was the hidden treasure that the family were eagerly waiting to see.

"We are hoping," said Cruzar to his passengers in his thick Spanish accent, "to maybe solve the riddle of why the Maya civilisation disappeared. Do you know of this mystery, children?"

Quick as a flash, Verity, with a smile on her face, answered. "Yes, it is one of the world's great unsolved puzzles. Sometime around the ninth century, the Maya just sort of collapsed. There were almost twenty million people in their civilisation, and yet we don't know what happened. Some people say it could have been too much hunting and not enough food or water, some people say they could have been invaded, and others say it could even have been an *alien* invasion. But they would be idiots."

"Cool!" said Ethan, excitedly. "That's what I reckon. Aliens did it. They came down first and took one or two people to do experiments, and when they were sure about humans, they returned and took the rest. I've read about stuff like this. There are cattle in America that have had parts of their bodies removed by aliens after similar experiments!"

"As I said, idiots believe that sort of theory. I was reading online that it was probably due to lots of reasons, including a big drought and too many people to feed. When people don't have enough to eat, it can lead to them going to war about it."

"Your daughter is a clever one, Daniel!" smiled Cruzar. "I think she will find this trip useful. However, we think we may have found some things that lead us to believe something else may have...happened. Something interesting. But you'll have to wait and see. And it's a long way still to go."

The jeep trundled along the road and into the countryside as Vee's mind whirled with ideas and theories, wondering what they had found at the temple.

4

Ethan

Vee was so...arrogant. She thought she knew everything. Okay, so she probably knew more about the Maya than he did, but she could be so...so...*dismissive.*

Other than his spy books, the other things Ethan *did* read were nonfiction books about aliens and the unexpected. They were nonfiction, he had told his sister, because they contained *fact.* He loved learning about conspiracy theories, and weird and wonderful ideas about how and why mysterious phenomena happened. He loved stuff about the Bermuda Triangle, ghosts and aliens. He had recently read a book on the curse of the pharaohs to fit in with his Egyptian topic at school. Luckily, Vee was in a different class, so she couldn't give her opinion about his curse of the pharaohs ideas, and why his classmates definitely *shouldn't* disturb any mummies, if they came across some after taking a wrong turn in a pyramid.

The jeep slowed as the jungle around them became denser, the trees forming an impenetrable wall. In places, the colossal trunks were almost within touching distance, their intertwined branches creating a twisted, mossy ceiling overhead. Without warning, the glaring Central-American sun returned, as the canopy disappeared, with a burning heat that made Ethan reach for a bottle of water by his side.

Even behind his new sunglasses, he squinted in the bright light.

They had arrived at a small, sleepy village – with its huts and other simple buildings – where they were met with an exciting surprise. Their father had warned them to expect something even more adventurous than the adrenaline rush that had been their interconnecting flight earlier that day. When the noisy chug of their ride's engine had subsided, they could hear the steady thrum of rotors and Ethan glimpsed a shining fuselage between the buildings.

"A helicopter ride? Seriously? Dad, you are so *awesome!*" Ethan had gushed. He couldn't keep a small smile from his face as he watched Vee's face pale, despite the heat.

"Where we're going, it would take too long to drive the jeep," Cruzar had said.

Now, they were all packed, squashed into the small, white helicopter like sardines. Ethan still couldn't wipe the smile off his face. It had begun to fade but was refuelled by the fact that his sister's appearance had gone an even paler grey as what must have been the last of the blood drained from her face. Ethan poked her.

"You're such a wuss, sis!"

"Shut up, Ethan."

The rotor blades whirled into a hurricane of noise, whipping up the dust around them. Before long, they were soaring away from the village at the end of the road they had been travelling on, which now looked like a ribbon of yellow in a sea of green, lit up by the bright sun in the cloudless sky.

His father was holding Verity's hand tightly in his. When Verity looked over at Ethan, he balled his fists up and pretended to rub his eyes and make a crying sound. He could make out, over the noise of the thundering engine, and with the help from some pretty easy lip-reading, "Shut up you idiot!" It only made him do it more. After all, that's what brothers were for, surely?

The world from above looked entirely different from how it did down from the ground. Now, it seemed to Ethan like a computer game, a world-building game where he could clear trees here, build something there, and send his armies in to attack way over there. Ethan's mind fizzed with imagination, as carpets of rich green were punctuated with the snaking strings of interconnecting roads: tiny veins in the body of the country, delivering their vehicles from one organ to another.

After a stunning trip over the world below, Ethan could spot (through his newly acquired binoculars that he had made sure were handy) a clearing in the trees up ahead. He placed his binoculars up against the glass as the helicopter began to descend.

The clearing looked to have been manmade, recently, as there wasn't any grass to be seen; the stumps in the centre had been pulled out to give a comfortable landing spot. The helicopter was expertly brought down by the pilot with only the mildest of bumps.

Ethan saw Verity give out a huge sigh, and the colour return to her face.

"Don't worry, Vee, we've only got spiders and snakes to worry about now!" Ethan loved to poke fun where he could. Verity stuck her tongue out.

As the four passengers unclicked their seat belts, they could see a figure emerge from the darkness of the forest at the edge of the clearing, like a jaguar coming out into the open after lying in wait. A man in khaki cargo pants, with a green shirt unbuttoned to reveal the top of a hairy chest, walked slowly towards them only to stop and put his dirty-booted foot onto a tree stump. Resting his meaty forearm on his thigh, he retrieved a thick cigar from his shirt pocket, and a lighter, then rolled the cigar in his fingers to inspect it, before finally lighting it. He took in a few short puffs and remained there, casually looking at the newcomers, dark eyes peering out from beneath the brim of his leather outback hat. Around its brim was a strip of fabric like a bandolier, but rather than a succession of bullets, it held a pointed line of fanged teeth. Ethan had never seen anything quite as awesome.

"Ernesto!" shouted Cruzar as he made his way over to the other man. They briefly shook hands and Ernesto, seemingly begrudgingly, straightened up so that the men could have some quiet words with each other.

Meanwhile, the children and their father took their backpacks from the tiny storage compartment on the helicopter and walked over to meet Ernesto.

Cruzar introduced them as Ernesto stood with his foot propped against one of the tree stumps, puffing on his cigar. "Daniel, this is Ernesto, one of the main men here at the camp. He is an expert in artefacts. Ernesto, this is Daniel Hume from the British Museum, and his twin children, Ethan and Verity."

Ethan's dad stuck out his hand. The other man looked at it for a moment, adjusted his already imposing posture – and the even more imposing holsters slung over both shoulders – and then gripped Dad's hand firmly, looking Daniel in the eyes.

"*Hola, Señor* Hume," he croaked, and smiled out of the corner of his cigar-filled mouth. "Welcome to your new home," Ernesto continued, pointing back behind him with an open hand. "It has *everything* you need. A bed for relief, a hole in the ground for relief, and a big tent full of equipment to study things. *Lots* of things."

24

The gruff and burly man had a glint in his eye, but Ethan couldn't tell what it signified. Regardless, the man was cool! He had a faint scar running down the tanned skin of his right cheek; his chest, too, was marked, this time by a tribal-looking tattoo. Ethan couldn't help but notice that the man was festooned with weaponry, from the two large pistols that hung from the shoulder holsters to the bowie knife strapped to his thigh. He was exactly like the hero from another of Ethan's favourite adventure video games. As if he could feel Ethan's stare, the man turned towards him and fixed him with a peculiar look.

"Just in case of trouble, you know," he said, fingering the buckle that kept the dangerous-looking knife in its place and then pointing at the teeth that decorated his wide-brimmed hat. "You won't be any trouble though, will you?" He smiled reassuringly, first at Dad, then back at Ethan. The smile created deep wrinkles in the skin around Ernesto's mouth. His eyes, however, remained untouched, unreadable.

"Such a character this one, eh? We are lucky to have him," chuckled Cruzar, slapping Ernesto on the back, a gesture that may have toppled a slighter figure; Ernesto seemed not to have even felt it. "And now, to the camp."

The three foreigners were led from the clearing and into the forest from where Ernesto had emerged. At first, the forest near the clearing was thin and sunlight easily penetrated the trees to paint a picture of vibrant greens. Leaf litter covered the ground and crunched under Ethan's hiking boots. Soon, the trees grew thicker and sunlight filtered through the canopy of the entangled branches above, creating a mottled view of light and shade around them.

Ethan hefted his heavy backpack, with his smaller rucksack attached in reverse and worn on his front, along the path that had been cut through the undergrowth. It was a wide and well-trodden path due to the amount of equipment that had been lugged over it.

He wasn't usually one for the wonders of natural geography, but everything around Ethan was alien to him and required closer inspection – an inspection that could never be completed as a result of the unrelenting pace they were being set. The forest, mostly dry and crackling underfoot, was unlike the gentle woods near his home, with its noisy mammals and insects jumping and flying, climbing and creeping. Tiny swattable bugs whined about his ears as larger beetles and spiders scuttled here and there.

He was a mixture of anxiety of the novel and wonder of the soon-to-be known.

Ethan swatted at a fly on his arms. His hands came back a grimy brown with a smear of red. Sweat and dirt hadn't taken long to merge into its own layer that had already coated his arms, his legs and, by the looks of Verity and Dad, his face too. He was sure this was something he would get used to. He had been warned that hot, daily showers were off the hygiene menu. A diet of rain and unrelenting heat, leaves and mud, buzzing insect life and long-dead buildings: this was what his father said the coming weeks would entail. Ethan's grin was back.

Soon, they descended down a gentle hill, Cruzar leading the way.

After a while and through a break in the trees, Ethan caught a glimpse of something. Then he lost it. "What was that?" he asked. "I saw something." He retrieved his binoculars and looked again.

The group stopped and Cruzar pointed to their destination that could be seen in the near distance, across on the next hill. Stone peeked out, here and there, barely visible through the forest cover, blanketed in green – a mixture of both foliage and moss.

"I'm not surprised it has remained hidden for so long," Ethan remarked. "It's all so green. I can hardly see it."

"Yes," said Cruzar, "even Google Earth only has distant views of this part of the world, and those stones are quite camouflaged, so you just can't make it out. Believe me, I've tried!"

Ethan could just about make out a pyramid shape – not the classic, smoother Egyptian style of pyramid, but the South American style of huge stone steps zigzagging their way to the summit. Verity had made a point of showing him pictures of the Maya pyramids, such as the one at the ancient Guatemalan ruins of the Maya city of Tikal. That pyramid, Ethan thought, whilst peering across from one hill to the next through his new favourite toy, was much steeper than the one he was now looking at. The one at Tikal was more open, now surrounded by grass. This temple was at one with the forest, having itself become almost natural in its secretive hiding place.

"Come, we have more walking to do," and Cruzar beckoned them on.

5

Verity

The huge construction loomed out of the forest floor like an ancient island out of the sea, except that this was surrounded by crowds of trees acting as an ocean of green. Vines trailed across the huge stonework; plants and bushes sprouted from the face of the temple, obscuring and camouflaging. The sun broke through the canopy near the base of the pyramid, here and there, to shine broken light on stones here, and greenery there.

The whole sight that met Vee and her family was thoroughly impressive. Not in the sense that you would see a pyramid in Egypt in the distance grow impressively bigger, sitting out in the open desert. This was impressive in the way it suddenly appeared as they started to walk up the next hill, looking out of the undergrowth and breaking out above the trees. Unlike Tikal, and perhaps many other pyramids, this one was built into the side of a hill and the central stone staircase that ran up the outward facing side followed the angle of the incline. It was as if the hill and the pyramid were part of the same structure, working together to give the same impression. It was as though the Maya gods themselves had built it at the same time as the world was made. The Hero Twins, after winning their epic ball game, rose into the sky to become the sun and moon that would look down on this temple for hundreds upon hundreds of years. *Would it be here for thousands more years? How much longer will the sun look upon it, now we have found it?*

Verity was hot and sweaty, tired and uncomfortable, but still her breath was taken away by the looming magnificence of this building, erupting out of the earth in front of her. Even with her dark brown, shoulder-length hair tied tightly back in a ponytail, Verity had to wipe sweat from her face as she gazed up at the temple.

It was big. Not as steep as the one at Tikal, but wide and imposing. An ascent of steps led her eyes up the middle of the pyramid to the top, flanked on either side by larger stone blocks that went up in giant-sized steps to the zenith. It looked like there was a small stone building at the top of the steps, with a shadowy doorway. The top of the pyramid, and certain parts of the side in different places, were bathed in the afternoon sun.

"Wow, Ethan. This is pretty similar to Lam...Lam...Lamanai, that's it. Some of the Maya pyramids are set on hills like this." She turned to Cruzar. "Ed, what have you named this place?"

"Well, again your knowledge is brilliant. Lamanai, over the border in Belize, means 'submerged crocodile'. We are not sure what to call this yet, or what it might have been called before by the original Maya. There are glyphs on the temple–"

"Glyphs are those picture symbols, like the ones you see in Egypt," Vee explained to Ethan, who was standing next to her, mouth agape.

"Yeah, I'm not stupid," he replied.

"–that we are yet to fully decipher. And the exciting thing is that there are a couple of other ruined buildings nearby that we know of. But we are yet to investigate more. We think this could be a whole city."

"A *city*! Wow!" Vee exclaimed.

29

"Yes. It's also why we didn't want to contact the media yet. We would have all sorts of people round here and there could even be looting. No, we keep it quiet for as long as we can while we get some work done. Your father will help us with the glyphs and the artefacts that we find."

"I can't wait, Edwin. This is…*magnificent!*" her father said, a wide smile on his face.

"But first, we must get you settled into your new home." Cruzar indicated a campsite that had been set up to one side of the temple's base, amongst the trees.

There, the ground had been cleared of undergrowth, and tents had been erected, shaded by the canopy above. In the middle of the camp was a communal tent that had open sides, like a massive gazebo. This had a horseshoe of tables set up, surrounded by other tables here and there, each with equipment or artefacts on them.

To one side of the communal tent was an open area, a small clearing that the sun could get to. There, above two cubicles, hung various containers of water: large, transparent plastic "bags" with tubes trailing down from them.

"What are they?" Verity asked, pointing.

"Those," said Cruzar, "are your showers. The water is collected from the river and heated by the sun in those bags. We can't waste our water here, unless you want to drive for hours to get some more, or roll it down from the helicopter clearing in big barrels?"

"Er, no thanks," she replied.

Cruzar led the three of them to their tents. Verity and Ethan were to share one, whilst their father had one to himself.

"How come yours is bigger than ours, Dad?" Ethan complained.

"Because, young man, I'm not a holidaymaker. I'm not a tourist like you. I'm here on work duties, so they need to be...nicer to me!" And with a cheeky smile, their father unzipped his tent, and started unpacking his belongings inside.

The children's tent was big enough that they could stand, albeit with a bent back. Inside were two foldaway camp beds made of thin, rusted metal.

"First things first, Ethan: insect repellent," Verity stated as she plonked her bags down and rifled through the pockets to find a squirty bottle.

"First things first, Vee: melted Mars bar!" Within seconds, Ethan had located his hidden treasure and was getting sticky fingers and mouth in attacking it.

Verity rolled her eyes.

After unpacking their belongings, laying out their sleeping bags, and blowing up their inflatable pillows, the pair sprayed themselves liberally with insect repellent in a probably vain attempt to escape the mosquitoes. They emerged from their tent to find their father was already in the central tent of the campsite, busying himself with talking to experts and looking at finds.

Verity looked about the camp as they walked towards the middle. There were a good twenty or so tents, perhaps more, dotted around, some more secluded than others. She looked at the people working here, walking there. *I can only see...one, two...two women. That's all. Out of, what, twenty? Twenty-five? One day...one day, I'll change that.*

"*Holá!*" came a voice from their left. The two children turned to see...another child.

"Well that's unexpected," said Verity, more to herself than anyone else.

"H-hello!" A boy with slightly messy brown hair and olive skin, slightly shorter than the twins (who, though they often fought over who was taller, were pretty much the same height), bounded over to them. He was dressed in a pair of cargo shorts and a faded football shirt. "Hello. I have been...er...waiting for you," he said in a thick Spanish accent.

"Hi there. I wasn't expecting to see anyone else our age here. Pleased to meet you," said Verity holding out her hand. The boy shook it.

"I see you're a Barcelona fan!" said Ethan.

"Oh great, we're already talking football," Verity moaned.

"Yes, I like them. And Chelsea. You are from England, no? I was told you might be coming. I am so happy. I am so, what is the word? Ah yes, I am so boring."

"I think you mean *bored*," Verity helped.

"Yes, yes. I am Leonel. Or Leo. Whatever you want to say." And he shrugged his shoulders. "My *papa* works here. My *mama* is...she's...she's not here anymore. She died. So I have to be here with *papa*. No one else in camp, they no like it, me being here. But hey, I am here."

"Oh my goodness, Leo, that's exactly the same as us. Our mum died last year. From cancer. And Dad couldn't get anyone to look after *us* for that long, not even our grandparents. So here we are, too. We're like peas in a pod!"

"Eh?"

"It just means we're the same. Except you're from Guatemala. You speak good English, though," Verity said, as they all walked towards the centre of the camp.

"Yes, my father made me learn it. He says it will be useful for when I am older. I do most of it on the internet, and we watch movies and things. Also, I have a teacher once a week."

"A tutor? Ethan could do with one of them, then perhaps he'll speak proper English!"

Ethan shot her a withering look. "Ha ha, Vee. You're *hilarious*... At least I have manners: Leo, I'm Ethan, and this here is Smellity. Sorry, Verity."

"I see you two are very...friendly together," Leo remarked with a smile.

Verity looked at Ethan with a smart-alec grin. "Oh, we love each other *very* much."

Verity suddenly bumped into someone, someone who wasn't there before, someone who had appeared out of nowhere. She staggered back and looked up. There, standing brutishly in front of her, looking coolly from under his dark leather hat – like one of the stones of the temple – was Ernesto, cigar smouldering in the corner of his mouth.

"*Holá*," Ernesto's voice was pure gravel. "Welcome to camp, kids. One thing to tell you. You have fun here, but you must keep away from the work."

"Er, okay, Ernesto. What do you mean by keep away from work?" Verity asked.

There was no emotion in Ernesto's eyes. He looked from Verity to Ethan, and then to Leo.

"You keep away from the equipment here in the *laboratorio de campo–*"

Verity didn't understand this last bit, but he was pointing to the central tent, and used a word that sounded like "laboratory." *Campo* must mean...*camp*?

"–and you keep away from the temple. No go in."

Ernesto wagged his finger slowly, menacingly.

"Sure thing, mister. Sure thing," said Ethan. "But where can we go?"

Ernesto nodded his head in a couple of different directions.

"You play. Here. There. Forest. Make a play place."

33

Having said his piece, Ernesto slowly turned away and made his way towards the centre of the camp, to the *laboratorio de campo*.

"He was talkative! I suppose we should go and make our own *laboratorio de campo*," said Vee, and led the other two over to an area on the edge of the campsite where they arranged some logs into seats, clearing some of the dry leaf litter to provide bare earth.

Whilst they were clearing and organising, moving logs and creating a makeshift table (of sorts, from some empty wooden pallets), Verity was thinking. She finally concluded: "Do they really think we would ruin their work? I have to say, I don't much like that Ernesto man. Why can't we get involved in the work? We could be really helpful."

"Yeah," said Ethan, "the way he told us to have fun was particularly...un-fun-like. I wouldn't like to sit down and play Monopoly with him."

"Probably because you would get bored within five minutes and walk off to play on your console," Verity said, giving Ethan her usual sisterly look.

After getting their own new headquarters ready, the three children sat down and proceeded to chat, to get to know each other better. They took a wander around the camp, and then returned to their base.

"Do they have jaguars or anything like that around here? I mean, could we get eaten? Are we safe?" Ethan asked no one in particular.

Leo piped up in reply. "We should be safe. They don't really attack humans."

"Well," it was unsurprising to Ethan that Verity had something to say on the matter, as she could see from the rolling of his eyes, "they normally eat capybaras. But where humans have encroached on their habitats, there can be a little danger."

"What, like we're doing here?" Ethan responded.

"No, I doubt it. There's enough forest out here. They'll probably be more scared of us than we of them," Verity said.

"Oh, that old chestnut. Tell yourself that next time you are squinnying over a spider in the bathroom, Vee."

"The jaguar was an important animal for the Maya and there probably *was* some encroachment on their habitat as their cities were out here in the forests. They used to wear jaguar skins, and there are some accounts of shamans being thought to turn into jaguars to eat people," Verity explained.

"And I thought my card tricks were pretty nifty..." Ethan quipped. "Anyway, isn't it time you went to the staff room for a break *Miss Hume*."

"Ethan?"

"Yes, *Miss*?"

"Shut up."

The afternoon was closing in, and the sunlight was losing its strength like tired prey giving into the inevitable demands of the daily hunt. The Guatemalan night would soon have its victory. And in the dying embers of sunlight, straining weakly through the trees, the children gazed up to give the temple another enchanted look.

The pyramid, earlier in the day a monochromatic black and white, was now a shining bronze statue, a glinting treasure in the darkness of the surrounding forest. Each of the many tiers of the temple shone brighter (where nature hadn't covered it), more golden than the last as the fingers of shadow that gripped the lower steps failed to reach those above. The glyphs cut into the rock many hundreds of years ago were transformed into a spiralling inky river: cascading words, phrases, songs and stories just waiting to be understood. It was a marvel of engineering and art combined, a sight that mesmerised the three children.

As Verity looked at the temple, natural light fading and the lights of the camp twinkling on, it was as if the temple itself was looking back at her.

"Come in, my dear, come in," it beckoned, mysteriously, "for I have secrets."

6

Ethan

The children, all three of them, had been enjoying the five days they had been at the camp at the foot of the temple. Ethan's father had taken them up to and around the temple several times, and Leo's father (an expert in biology and zoology) had taken them for a few trips into the forest to look at the wildlife. The flora and fauna had fascinated them as much as the temple, especially since Ethan and Verity were only used to seeing, at best, wild deer back in the UK (and that had been once, on a school trip).

Leo's father, who was working with the team on the historical connection to zoology – what evidence there was onsite about the food that the Maya people might have been eating – had shown them capuchin monkeys and toucans, spider monkeys and basilisks. To Ethan's slight disappointment, these were not the enormous, quite-literally petrifying creatures of ancient myth, but rather passive, quite harmless lizards no longer than the children's forearms; what these creatures had in common with those in the legends was beyond him.

The children discovered that the forest noises were loud in the mornings, loud in the daytimes, and loud at night, all with different sounds. Insects, birds and mammals all contributed to the soundscape of the Guatemalan forest.

One morning, the twins had even resorted to arguing about when a forest became a jungle and what the difference in definitions between the two was. Without Google to defer to, such discussions never had the resolution that they did when everyone's friend and general expert was called upon in a given conversation. They realised that Google had a lot to answer for in society, in life, but Google always had that answer.

But still, five days into their Maya experience, they had yet to enter into the temple. "It's just that we have to do some investigation first," Ethan's father had said.

"You no go in. Not now. Not tomorrow. Maybe later," Ernesto kept saying. "I'm sorry, kids. Soon. I promise," Edwin had repeated.

Ethan's father had been particularly busy poring over a certain artefact that had been found before the children had arrived at the camp. He had shown it to them, and it was something that Ethan wouldn't forget in a hurry. Daniel had ushered them into the tent with a reverence that made Ethan feel like he was entering a church rather than the mud-encrusted marquee. The twins and Leo had quietly gathered around a trestle table laden with trays full of half-cleaned and part-labelled objects: all forgotten, forsaken in favour of whatever it was that lay beneath the only pristine-white piece of cloth that the children had seen in days. Without speaking, Daniel had slowly removed the veil, revealing a green head made from carved jade.

Ethan's breath caught in his throat and the silence that filled the tent told him that the others had been similarly affected. It was not the gleaming, polished surface of the mask that had stolen his ability to breathe, nor the size of the artefact – the combination of the two would ordinarily have impressed Ethan because of the value they implied. No. Firstly, it was the eyes. Where the majority of the object was the same shade of green, gleaming in the rays of sunshine that pierced through the gaps in the rough canvas of the tent, the eyes were startlingly white with bottomless, pitch-black pupils. As the sides of the marquee shifted, so too did the light and as it danced across the eyes, they seemed to move too. The shape of the eyebrows gave the eyes a sad, even mournful look that was only made more real by the gaping mouth. The lips were stained red and in the darkness of the open jaws, Ethan could see a tongue; the face looked like it was about to scream. And for good reason. Curved, knife-sharp ivory teeth seemed to burst from beneath the very surface of the jade skin. Some came from within the sides of the mouth, curving around and over the lips – stretching the lips into a silent, open-mouthed cry. More erupted through the cheeks and forehead as if a brutal creature made from nothing but vicious fangs and violence was trying to rip its way through the stone face. The whole thing was horrifying.

After a few moments, Ethan realised that the artefact was not a solid sculpture, but a mask – a thought that was accompanied by an immediate desire to pick up and place the cool stone over his face. He had known feelings like this, the way he felt that he *needed* to pick things up to experience their realness in his hands. This time though, he felt different. Maybe it was the excitement of simply being at the dig-site, maybe it was the stories of masks that gave their wearer super-human powers but Ethan felt a powerful craving, an undeniable longing to hide his face behind that of the screaming stone. It was an urge perhaps powered by childhood dreams but one that filled him with a sense of dread, one that Ethan would resist at all costs.

"It would probably have been worn by someone important during a ritual ceremony. Perhaps even a human sacrifice!" Dad had told them as he picked up the mask and held it gently in both hands. "We're not sure what to call it. It's amazing, eh?"

Where Ethan was all "cool" and "awesome", Verity was silent, letting her eyes do the excited talking.

That had been on the second day. The next day, they had seen their father deep in highly energised discussion with several people about something. They had obviously found another artefact, or seen something in the temple that had raised their heart rates.

Someone had been brought into the camp, and they had seen their father talk to him; they had both been excited and animated. Because the other man seemed (from a distance, anyway) not to speak English, Edwin was there to translate. The man had been pointing up to the top of the temple, indicating with his head, and moving his arms about eagerly as he spoke. Then he pulled them over to an item he was holding, somewhat like a camera. Some of the men, including his dad, crowded round and watched in silence.

Something had happened. That much, Ethan was sure of. Something important.

A few nights later, Ethan's father had spoken to them at some length. He was equally animated as he spoke then, eyes shining with wonder. Ethan remembered it well.

***

"One of the archaeologists has found some glyphs, some symbols, carved into the rock inside the temple. I've taken a look at the glyphs over the last day, and it seems...it seems that they tell us something."

"What, Dad?" asked Ethan, intrigued.

"Well, it seems like they say, or indicate, that the jade head is or has some kind of curse."

"Cool!"

"No, this is perhaps...super-cool."

Ethan rolled his eyes.

His father continued, with Verity spellbound. "We think that the jade head might well be cursed in such a way that it brought about the decline, the end, even, of the Maya people. At least, that's what the people who lived here must have thought."

The excitement was contagious. Ethan's eyes widened. "So this head thing was the reason the Maya civilisation ended?"

"It seems that way. Or, it seems to be that the *Maya* thought something like this. Which makes that head of enormous interest. Priceless, really, in terms of Maya artefacts. Everyone is buzzing right now. It's–"

"Are you telling me that you think this head is cursed enough to have spelled the end of the Maya?" Verity interrupted. "That the head has...magical qualities?"

"Well, not necessarily. I *am* saying that the people who lived here *thought* that. As for magic or curses, there is no evidence yet. Apart from on my laptop...but..." he trailed off.

"But...?" Ethan couldn't let this drop. He had a feeling that this was linked to whatever the adults had been watching earlier. Dad seemed to realise what he had said and quickly changed the direction of the conversation.

"What is certain," he cleared his throat, "is that this could be a real part of the history of how the civilisation ended!"

"That's amazing, Dad. Man, I can't believe it. Do you reckon it was like the curse of the pharaohs? Maybe it's diseased. Maybe it was left here by aliens with some kind of weird device inside it, or some kind of substance that we can't even detect coating it and everyone who comes into contact with it is cursed. Oh no, maybe we shouldn't even touch it ourselves! We could all be doomed! Have you thought of that, Dad? Are we in danger, Dad? Are we?" Ethan's voice moved quickly to a panicked pitch as he rattled off his theories.

"Calm down Mr. Aliens-did-everything-including-giving-us-ancient-batteries!" Verity smirked.

"Shut up, Vee. No one can explain the Baghdad Battery. I reckon it was aliens who showed those guys how to use basic electrical technology."

"Come on, Ethan, we've been through this. No serious academic believes it was an ancient battery. You need to stop watching crazy TV shows. Don't believe everything you see."

"I see you, Vee."

"Come on, kids, give it a break," their father said, exasperated. "Look, all I can say is that if this pans out, and we need to do some checks, then this is an amazing find. Together with the glyphs, this is one of the most important Maya discoveries for years. Heck, maybe ever. Edwin is beside himself with excitement. This place is electric. I've got to do some tests and research tomorrow, but I have to admit, this could be the highlight of my career."

"Wow. What a great start to our holiday, I mean, your work, Dad! I was wondering, though, who was that guy you were speaking to the other day?" asked Ethan.

"Ah, yes. I wasn't going to tell you. I didn't want to worry you. He was a guard here, before we got here. Before most of the team had visited here. He, er...he had an experience."

"An experience?" Vee was intrigued.

"He noticed some lights, from in the temple, he went to investigate, and he saw, we think he saw, the jade head. And weird lights. And then he...well... he fell unconscious. Anyway, don't worry about that. You just stay safe and keep having fun."

"But Dad–!"

***

That sense of awe and discovery, excitement and dangerous adventure had remained with the children. So they hatched a plan. On the fifth morning, they had been taking their breakfast, as they normally did, at their HQ, as they called it. Between them, they had agreed that they must go into the temple. There was no negotiation here. It was going to happen.

Their plan involved asking to go the river, about a twenty-minute walk away, which they were allowed to do on their own, to go and "look for wildlife". They would be down there for a good few hours (or, at least, this was what their fathers were to believe). This would allow them perhaps three hours in the temple, if they were not seen by anyone.

The three children packed some equipment in their rucksacks and met at their own camp HQ. Just as they were about to set off, they heard some raised voices from the middle of the main camp. Looking over to the centre, Ethan could see his father embroiled in an argument with Ernesto. The bulky man took off his hat, waved it around and then jammed it back on his head. The "conversation" was in Spanish, so Ethan couldn't make out what it was about, but it was clearly pretty important and a little heated. There was a lot of hand and arm waving, raised voices, and pointing at one of the tables in the central tent.

"What's going on?"

"I don't know, Ethan," said Verity, "but since our dads know that we're going to the river, I guess now's a good time to get out of here."

"I didn't like Ernesto, anyway. I like him even less now, He gives me the creeps," Ethan complained.

The trio turned, leaving the twins' father to fight his battle, and walked out of the clearing and away from the pyramid.

7

Verity

Of course, they weren't really walking away from the temple. Once they were safely out of earshot and sight, the three children doubled back on themselves, giving the camp a wide berth, to circle back around towards the temple.

Because they were not using established paths, the three friends had to occasionally beat the bush back with sticks that they had collected over the days. Vee hadn't taken her stick as seriously as Ethan, who had whittled away all the notches with his penknife to give himself a smooth bush-beater. Verity's was a nobbly affair, but it did the same job.

Before long, the explorers (for that's how they felt) had reached the foot of the imposing temple. Standing at the bottom, full of awe and excitement, the children looked up the massive stone stairs. The day was overcast. Rain was expected later. But this didn't stop the temple from looking otherworldly. Magnificent.

Strong and regal, proud yet comfortable, the pyramid sat there, presiding over its kingdom with a sense of majesty. Whether the power that the pyramid commanded over its buildings and lands was earned through peaceful ruling and respect, or from the fear of sacrifices and the human and animal blood that once flowed from its summit, only those ancient buildings would know.

Once, when this had been a bustling city of Mesoamerican culture, of trade and work, gods and mere mortals, the pyramid would have ruled it all, visible from every street, from every corner, from every living quarter. This impressive monument to ancient Maya culture was both the head and the heart of that newly discovered society, and it felt to Verity as if was still beating now, to this day. Its lifeforce, she could almost sense, was reaching out to the other buildings, crumbling as they undoubtedly were, trying to keep them alive and to ward off the threat of time, the attrition of the weather, the chaos of life that had nestled in every crack, nook and cranny, all trying to wear those city bones to dust and earth.

What secrets did this building hide? What memories of long forgotten history was it holding on to?

Verity was lost in her imagination.

"Come on, Vee!" Leo's excited voice broke her out of her dream.

"Oh, yes. I was just thinking. You know these people didn't have horses or mules, or even metal tools. And yet, they built things like this. It must have been so tough."

The stone steps up the height of the temple were large and required big lunges from their legs to get up. They had to stop several times to rest their muscles. The twins and Leo, with their thin, almost scrawny frames, were dwarfed by the huge stonework around them.

Verity wondered how it must have felt to have been a Maya prisoner of war, maybe a rival chieftain, to walk up these steps to meet their death. Would it be having their head chopped off, or their heart removed? *What a terrible choice!* Either way, those gods needed the blood, or so the Maya thought. Verity imagined the poor man, painted blue to represent sacrifice, maybe wearing an ornate headdress, being led up to his gruesome death.

Not just humans, she remembered, but crocodiles, dogs, jaguars and even turkeys were sacrificed. Those gods sure were bloodthirsty!

Every so often, the children stopped to look behind them, at the impressive shallow valley, forest and hills in the distance. The view from the pyramid was stunning. Every now and again, birds alighted from their resting place in the trees for one reason or another. Either they needed food, or they didn't want to be food for something else, Verity decided.

Finally, and not without a lot of panting and sweating, the children reached the summit of the temple. They were just above the canopy of the tallest trees, but bushes and small hardy trees clung on to life on the temple, in places. *Life is determined to win, no matter where.*

After a few gulps of bottled water, Verity did her usual thing, and tried to educate her brother.

"There would have been an altar here. Look, I think this is the where it would have been. I wonder why it's gone. Anyway, four men would have held down the victim over it, with his chest pointing up. Then the priest, with an obsidian knife – you know, that shiny black rock stuff – would have taken his heart out."

"Eurggghhh! That's disgusting. Why would they have done something so *evil*?" Ethan asked.

"Well," said Leo, "I guess they thought it was good. They were pleasing the gods, no? That's a good thing, right? For them."

"Not for me. Imagine being the guy getting sacrificed. I hardly think he would have liked it!" protested Ethan.

"Actually, in some civilisations, it was a...what is the word – yes, that is it – an *honour* to be sacrificed."

"Yes, Leo's right, I've read about it," added Verity. "I'm not sure that was the case for the Maya. I know that sacrifice was sometimes linked to their ballgame."

"Yeah," Ethan's eyes lit up, thinking of sport. "The ballgame is cool. There must be a court around here somewhere. I was reading in your book on the plane, Vee." Verity smiled to herself, thinking of Ethan secretly reading her book when she was asleep. There was hope for him yet. "The court was in the shape of a capital 'I', and they bounced the rubber ball, without their hands or feet, trying to get it through these stone hoops on the wall. They'd wear these kneepads and elbow pads. The bummer was that sometimes the losers were sacrificed."

Leo made a grim face. "And sometimes, they think, the winners."

"Holy moly. When we won the footie tournament last month, we all got a McDonald's meal as a treat. That's *way* better than, you know, losing your heart. Or your head..."

The three gave a last look over the Guatemalan forest about them, and moved towards the dark opening in the wall of the large, square, stone building crowning the top of the pyramid.

"Let's get our torches ready," Verity suggested, and they rummaged through their bags. Ethan edged his way in front of his sister, and Leo took his place at the back of the line of three. With a deep intake of the humid forest air about them, Verity tried to calm her excitedly beating heart. "This is it," she said, and nudged her brother into the dark doorway that seemed to cross civilisations and time to welcome them into another world. Or did it warn them of another world that awaited them beneath their feet?

8

Ethan

Ethan's heart bumped and churned, thumped and fizzed. This was seriously exciting. He looked about him, eyes adjusting to the darker surroundings. The room at the top was largely empty and let in a lot of sunlight. There were glyphs similar to those found on the stonework around the temple and on the way up: hands with finger and thumb touching, faces, crosses, and a lot of shapes and pictures that he just couldn't work out. The scientists would no doubt be documenting every single one of these symbols.

"These word pictures are amazing. You know they would sometimes have fifteen pictures for the same sound? They liked to combine them and use their own artistic skills, putting pictures within pictures, to say what they wanted to say. It's why it has been so difficult for the experts to decipher," explained Verity.

"Thanks *Doctor* Hume," replied Ethan.

There were two passageways that descended from the sides of the room. Ethan picked the one on the left.

Being at the front gave him an extra thrill. His light flashed around, followed by the scanning beams of the two behind him. The field scientists seemed to have cleared the passageways as they were easy enough to walk down, if a little narrow. The musty smell of an age of dust and moisture clogged his nose. Ahead, coarsely cut limestone bricks paved the way forward with occasional empty alcoves breaking up the explorers' walk. Ethan ran his hand over the rough stone, imagining the hundreds, perhaps thousands of hands that had come before him, doing the exact same thing.

After zigzagging back on themselves downwards, there was eventually no remaining natural light to be seen from outside.

"I hope everyone packed their spare batteries," joked Ethan. "It's just us and our torches."

Darkness surrounded them, fought off only by the beams of torchlight that created prowling shadows in their wake. From the corner of his eye, he could see Verity steal glances behind her. In other circumstances he, would have given her a hard time, but, as he worried at a fraying edge of his cap, he knew she wasn't the only one who felt a little nervous.

They shortly came to another room with what looked like a sort of altar or podium. Over to one side were some dusty pots and jars. Ethan moved closer and touched one. *How old must this be? Maybe a thousand years. Maybe more!* Each item had a small white card with a number written on it in thick pen. The archaeologists and team-members below must be in the middle of recording all the things they had been finding. They had a big job ahead of them, that much was certain.

The dust covering the closest item was crusty and hard, untouched as it was for the best part of a millennium or so. In the torch light, colour from the tall, thin pot-like container fought to be seen through the years of grime on the outside. Around the top were some small, painted glyphs, telling a story that Ethan could only wildly guess at.

"It's like *we* are now the archaeologists," Leo said, excitedly. He shone his own torch at the walls. "Wow, guys, look at this," Leo added in his thick Spanish accent.

The children's eyes followed Leo's torch beam as it snaked across the smooth walls of the room. Pictures were painted in blues and reds and browns. The scenes from the murals told more unknown stories, involving people with flamboyant headdresses, some with cloaks of white, all involved in some action or conversation that was a mystery to the children.

"This is like a museum. It's incredible," said Ethan, and he looked over at his sister to catch her eye but she was too busy, standing against the wall, poring over the pictures with her torch. She was mumbling to herself.

"I wonder what this stand-thing was used for," Ethan inquired, looking at the smooth stone podium at the far end of the room. He moved over to inspect it more closely.

"Let's move on," suggested Leo. "We maybe have lot to see."

The next room they came to, spacious and rectangular, housed something quite large, and very macabre, surrounded by further murals.

"A sarcophagus!" Verity squealed.

"A what?" Leo asked.

"A stone coffin. There will be a dead body under here. Or at least some bones. We'd better not touch it – Dad and the others will surely be wanting to look at it properly. We do not want to be the cause of any damage," Verity said with authority.

The sarcophagus seemed over-sized – big enough to fit two or three bodies in. On top, the limestone lid was engraved with yet more glyphs depicting what looked like a large number of events or ideas. Ethan remembered his

Egyptian studies – was whoever was in there "accompanied" by his servants? Or maybe his gold?

"I wonder if these tell the life story of the person, or people, inside," Verity mused.

Ethan smiled. "C'mon, Vee, let's see if we can budge the lid. I fancy chatting to some skeletons, though I hope this isn't cursed..."

"No!"

"How about you, Leo?"

"Err, okay." His new friend grinned back at him.

Both boys put their torches in their mouths and moved to shift the huge lid. Struggling together at one end, the pair failed to move the heavy stone slab.

"Serves you right," Vee said, with her typical "smile".

"Whatever, Vee. You need to start taking risks in life," Ethan suggested.

Verity turned and continued to look over the murals on the wall behind her. Ethan decided to do one of his favourite things: scaring his sister.

Whilst she was mumbling away to herself, hand carefully brushing the wall art with awe, Ethan crept silently up behind her.

"BOO!"

"Arrgghh!" she screamed, dropping her torch. She stamped her foot and thrust her clenched fists to her sides. Picking the torch up hastily, Verity turned round and slapped Ethan's arm. Hard. "You're such an idiot, Ethan, you really are."

"And you're such a wuss!"

Ethan turned and moved on. Out of the room, a steep staircase ran down into the looming darkness. Here, the way was not so easy: the steps were slippery, wet with moisture, and there were odd rocks, fallen from the ceiling above, littering the staircase. Ancient cobwebs hung in the corners. The tell-tale signs of the adult explorers were noticeably absent here. The three faces peered from behind their small torchlights.

"Shall we go down?" Leo asked.

"Does a one-legged duck swim in circles?" Ethan replied, mimicking his father's favourite saying.

"Eh?"

"Don't worry, Leo," Verity added, "he means 'yes'."

Carefully, step by slow step, the three children made their way downwards.

Ethan made a spooky *whooh* sound to see if it would echo, but the tunnel down which they were walking was too close and ragged and the sound simply stopped as if trapped by the webs that fluttered faintly as the children crept by. This was somehow more unnerving than the ghostly echo he had anticipated. Even sound was dead down here.

After fumbling and stumbling down the staircase, they came to yet another room, this one considerably larger than the last. There were a few statues, pots and other artefacts littering the room and stuck in various alcoves. There were possibly some further exits from the chamber at the other end, but Ethan's torch failed to properly penetrate the stifling darkness.

"Does anyone get the impression we are quite far down now?" asked Verity, an edge of concern in her voice.

"We are in pyramid heart, I think," replied Leo.

The children spent a good half an hour checking everything in the room. Although initially they stuck together, their confidence grew, allowing their curiosity to take control. They looked at pots, jugs, statuettes, and what looked like masks, talking amongst themselves in enthusiastic whispers. Each item had a numbered card next to it, like in the earlier room.

At one point, Ethan saw that Verity had to change her batteries, her torch shining at full brightness once again. His own torch kept on going. After that, he moved out of the room and into another passageway, leaving the other two behind, wandering further downwards. He wanted to find more things, seek more treasures. *He* could be the one to find that priceless jaguar amulet! Ethan leant against the wall in a small room he had found, dreaming of greatness.

It was then that he heard the scream.

And then again, but for longer.

He knew that voice, that scream. It was Vee, for sure.

"Verity!" he called back up one of the stairways he had descended. "What's wrong? Where are you?"

"Help!" came the faint reply, shouted from elsewhere. "Please! Help me!"

And then: "Ethan! Where are you?" It was Leo.

"I'm coming!" And with that, he sprang into action. Leaping up the steps, two at a time, Ethan was like a spider monkey jumping through the trees. Even though the beam of the torch he was holding in his hand was bouncing wildly off the walls as he vaulted up the steps two or even three at a time so that he could only briefly make out where he was going, something automatic took over his body. His brain switched onto auto-pilot and steered him accurately on.

Zipping round corners, and jumping over fallen stonework, Ethan flew back to the room they had all been in.

Except there was no one there.

"Ethan, please help me!"

His head turned, picking up her calls from through another doorway, a different one. Without hesitation, he sprang through it. Following his sister's distraught voice, he raced through passageways and down steps until he found the other two.

At the sight that met him, Ethan's heart pounded in his chest and his lungs matched the frenetic pace. Indeed, it felt like his heart had leapt out of his body, but without the help of a Maya ceremonial priest.

Vee was there, in front of him. Well, some of her: her head and shoulders. Ethan found himself in a passageway at the bottom of a long, roughly hewn staircase. In front of him, Leo was teetering on the edge of a gaping hole in the floor that threatened to swallow his sister. The stonework had fallen through. What was underneath was anyone's guess, though Ethan thought he could hear some water. He didn't know if it was two metres below the hole or twenty-two.

Verity had fallen through, but had managed to hold on to the ground around the edge, as well as finding a handhold in the wall to one side. She was on the other side of the opening with her back to him, hanging on for dear life. Leo was next to Ethan, staring on.

"What to do, Ethan? What to do?"

"Hold this," said Ethan, and gave Leo his torch. "Shine one torch at each wall." He didn't want to admit it to Leo, but he was just about to try something he had only seen in a computer game.

He had to clear the hole to get to Verity on the other side, easily two metres. He took several steps back. "Hold on sis."

Just then, her right hand slipped from its hold and she hung there, in the hole, gripping desperately on to the wall hold on her left with one hand. Verity's eyes were wide. Her mouth hung open. Her fingers seemed to slip, millimetre by millimetre. He had to do something. Anything.

Ethan took a short run-up, accelerating to a fast pace in a few steps. Launching from just before the hole, he flew through the air, first to his left. His foot came out and he pushed, with all the strength he could muster, onto the wall and fired himself back the other way, where his right foot came out and met the other wall. Glancing off one wall and then the other, the fleeting shadow that was Ethan soared through the air to land deftly on the other side of the hole.

"*Dios mio!*" exclaimed Leo in admiration. "Way to go!"

Ethan skidded down onto his side, lying with his feet down the passageway and his head next to Verity. With great urgency, he grabbed for Verity's dangling arm and pulled her. She was able to help by grasping the stony floor, fingers desperately clinging to whatever they could reach. Together, the siblings scrabbled about until Verity was able to scramble to safety.

She lay on her back, panting, rubbing her sore hands.

"Th...Tha..." she attempted.

"I'm sorry? I didn't quite hear that... It's okay, Vee, I know you appreciate me. And...you're welcome."

"You two – I have a plan."

"Good, what you thinking Leo?" said Ethan.

"Yes. We get out of here. Back up to the day."

"That's quite some plan. I like it," said Verity, matter-of-factly.

Leo was one side of the hole, with the other two now the far side. Leo threw Ethan's torch back, which he shakily caught. The unsteady beam twitched across the walls as he drew deep breaths. He felt an arm, a hand at his back then around his waist. He closed his eyes and leant against his sister. Without saying a word, the twins moved off down the passageway to investigate whether they could get out. Sometimes, words just weren't necessary.

Thanking their lucky stars, they soon found that one of the doorways led back up some other stairs to meet back in a room near to where they originally were. They breathed a big sigh of relief to reunite themselves with Leo. A three-way hug ensued in the dusty darkness.

"Two things," Verity said, eventually turning to Ethan. "First of all, you were really great down there. *I* couldn't have done that. Thanks. Really. But that's the last time I'm going to say that, so savour it."

"Aw, thanks sis," Ethan replied, a smile on his face. *This is indeed a rare occasion!*

"And secondly, I've had enough of *here*, and I want to be *there*," she said, pointing up.

With that, the three adventurers turned their torches to returning to the surface of their new world. It was a thrilling place, but not somewhere they wanted to spend too long. Some thrills they could do without.

9

Verity

The sunlight burned Verity's eyes as she walked out of the mouth of the head of the temple. It was as if the temple had rejected them as a meal, a sacrifice even, and regurgitated them back out into the real world. It took a good minute for her eyesight to return to anything like normal under the burning intensity of the sun

It was mid-afternoon now, and the birds were still singing in full glory, the noises of the abundant wildlife all around them creating a blanket of sound. The trees of all their varying sizes, some huge and stretching out over their lesser neighbours, others, in pockets, smaller and fighting for their own sunlight, seemed greener now that Verity had come out of the depths of the pyramid. *What a beautiful world we have. We need to do a better job of looking after it.*

The children carefully descended the first twenty or so large steps to sit down for a rest. They took their bottles from their bags and drank refreshingly. Clouds were gathering not too far off. *Rain's on the way. I hope our tents won't leak!*

For now, though, warm sunshine bathed the children when the clouds broke.

"That was close," Leo said, breaking their silence.

"I don't think we should go back in there in a hurry," Ethan added, to everyone else's nods.

Verity looked out and imagined a Maya city below her, with its different buildings. A ballcourt, a palace, a plaza, observatories for looking to the skies, wells, houses – all could still be hidden under the trees and undergrowth, waiting to be discovered. The fieldworkers had said that they had evidence of some other structures, but they were waiting until they had given the pyramid a good look over, before calling in further teams, and, with them, the media.

Breaking the natural sounds of the forest around them, the engine of a jeep could be heard. The three children looked down the pyramid. At the bottom, they could see the twins' father in his khaki and green clothes, walking towards the base, looking up and waving.

"Excellent, it's Dad," Ethan remarked with a smile.

"Oh no, it's Dad... He's going to be so angry that we've been in here when we shouldn't have," retorted Verity.

"Oh bum." Ethan's smile faltered.

But as they were just raising their arms to wave back, the jeep that they heard pulled up behind Daniel with an abrupt halt. Two men got out of the front and jogged towards their father, one of them wearing a large cowboy hat - Ernesto. There was a short and angry-looking exchange, before one of the men grabbed at the English scientist.

"Hey," Verity automatically reacted, instantly seeing that something was wrong.

To her amazement, she saw Ernesto seize her father and wrestle him to the ground. The children could hear grunts, and short, sharp shouts.

"What the heck is going on?" spat Ethan, dismayed at the scene playing out below them. What came next was very unexpected.

The other man took out a pistol from a holster on his belt, and smacked the butt of the gun over her father's head. Instantly, he stopped struggling and his body went limp.

Ethan was on his feet, eyes bulging, veins in his neck throbbing. "What are you doing, you crazy fools!" he screamed.

Ernesto, legs astride their father, sitting on his torso, looked up. He pushed up the brim of his hat to get a better look up the pyramid.

The day was full of unexpected surprises, it seemed, and not many of them were good. This was no exception.

Ernesto's next move was to remove one of the guns from his own holsters. He pointed it up at the children, all three of whom were now standing, muscles tensed.

The shot that rang out scared birds from trees and sent strikes of lightning through the young explorers' hearts. The bullet ricocheted off some stonework only a metre from Verity, causing her to yelp.

The children turned and ran. Verity scrambled with all of the agility of a panicked chicken with a fox in its henhouse. They made it to the top only to hear another shot, making a dusty impact on the stonework of the building at the top next to the entrance. The three darted inside, and fumbled in their bags for their torches. Verity chanced a furtive look out of the doorway to see Ernesto lumbering up the steps of the pyramid in hot pursuit.

"What's happening?"

"I dunno, Leo, but we need to run, and the only way is down. Down there," said Verity, grimly, pointing down the passageway they had only just emerged from.

For the second time that day, and all too soon (as far as Verity was concerned), the three children entered the pyramid.

Except, this time, they were running.

Fast.

10

Ethan

The torchlight shook and bounced off the rough stonework as if the photons of light were themselves panicking. Ethan was last behind the two others. His heart was thumping twice the speed it would normally, and his ribcage was fighting hard to keep it back in its place. *What is going on? What have they done to Dad? Why would they want to harm him? Or us?*

But soon, after jumping down stairs and round corners, Ethan's mind was free of thoughts and his brain was spending all of its energy on running, turning corners and jumping. Together, they passed through the rooms that they had already been in.

However, it didn't take long for disaster to strike.

Whilst sprinting across one of the ancient chambers, Ethan dropped his torch. It spun across the floor, before dimly coming to a rest. He took a few steps to pick it up. When it was in his hands again, the blasted thing faded. It had run out of batteries. The light was extinguished like, he felt, their chances of escaping unscathed from this maze of tunnels and stairways.

Leo and Verity had not stopped. They hadn't even noticed he was not behind them.

"Hey, you two!"

He could hear their footsteps some way off, down...down...

"Guys!"

There was no answer. To his dismay, he could hear some faint sounds from behind him. Ernesto must have entered the pyramid now. He would be upon him soon. Sooner than he cared for.

Ethan had spare batteries in his bag. Without a working torch, he had no hope, no chance of escape. It would be like a blind person looking in a dark room for a black cat that wasn't there. Kneeling down, he unslung his rucksack and felt for the side pocket. Quickly locating the batteries, he placed them on the floor in front of him. With trembling hands made worse by the ever-nearing footsteps, Ethan unscrewed the torch.

I have to put the batteries in the right way!

As he slowly tipped the torch up to let the batteries slip out, he felt them. *There* was the nobbly bit at the end of the first battery.

I've got to put the negative end with the flat face in first, with the positive end sticking up.

This was now an urgent race against time. Time had stood still in this place for over a thousand years. Things inside had happened slowly. Dust had settled, spiders had spun the odd web, the years had passed.

Now, there was panic in the air, with hearts pulsing, feet thudding and minds racing. Ethan managed to get the first battery in the right way, but he fumbled the second and it bumped out of his trembling fingers to fall into the dust

Come on! You can't be serious!

Ethan felt blindly about on the dusty ground, shuffling gritty sand this way and that until his fingers found the battery. Relief coursing through his veins, he grasped the battery and felt for the end. He rammed it home. The end of the torch seemed to take an age to screw back on, but when the circuit in the torch was finally fully connected, the light that shone forth, as puny as it really was, felt like the burning hope of a thousand suns.

He pounced to his feet just as the heavy, clumping booted steps of Ernesto burst into the room.

The man stopped.

Heavy breaths came from behind his own shining light.

"You. Boy. Stay just there."

But as he – or indeed, the shining torchlight that was Ernesto – started towards him, Ethan turned on his heels and sprinted out of the door right next to him.

He was alone with a madman with no one to help him. And he had a sinking feeling he knew exactly where he was.

Taking the them two at a time (he had a feeling history was repeating itself), Ethan bounced down the stony steps, echoes of booted feet behind him.

Down at the bottom of the stairway, he rounded a corner, and his fears were realised. Yes, he was right.

There, in front of him, lay the gaping hole from which he had earlier rescued his sister. He had no time to think or worry. He had no choice.

It was do or die.

With a sharp intake of breath, a step back for a run up, and a mighty launch forward, Ethan threw himself straight into fifth gear. By the time he reached the edge of the hole, he was in overdrive. He only had the pitiful light of his small torch to go by, but still he managed to get his timing right. In one, superhuman feat of athleticism, he sprung from one side of the hole and vaulted through the air to land on the other.

With his efforts, Ethan surely would have won the gold medal for long jump at his school sports day. His landing was less than graceful, and he felt his knee slam against the cold, hard rock beneath him. He glanced quickly back to see Ernesto round the corner. The man ran to follow Ethan, but skidded to an ungainly and abrupt stop.

"Whoah!"

The hole had been unexpected, and he must only have seen it at the last second. Ethan used this pause to his advantage and shot off down the corridor, limping only slightly.

It didn't take long, he heard, for Ernesto to clear the hole, with his longer legs. He heard the big man's heavy landing and grunts. *Where to now? Just onwards. To anywhere.*

Ethan rounded another corner to be met with another corridor, with alcoves (or were they doorways?) set off on either side. He ran on.

Half way down the low-ceilinged passageway, he turned back to see his predator.

This was a bad decision.

His feet catching quite a sizeable rock in front of him, Ethan went flying, torch spinning out of his hand to smack against the wall and die instantly.

There was no light except the oncoming brightness of Ernesto, the blinding glare promising who knew what. The torchlight grew brighter as it lumbered at even greater speed towards Ethan, joined with grunts of exertion or excitement or perhaps, fury.

This was it. He was done for.

11

Verity

It was a risk and there was no guarantee it would help or buy them any more time, but she had to do something...

Verity and Leo had run through a labyrinth of rough stone corridors, each looking just as the one before. Occasionally they had seen flashes of light and it was these that they tried to follow. Verity kept stealing glances behind her, terrified of seeing the bulk of Ernesto behind them. And so it was that they fled. *Run. Turn, check. Run again.* After one turn, the light became constant: a pinprick of white in an otherwise impenetrable ocean of darkness. It was getting bigger. It was getting closer. Someone was approaching. Fast. *Ernesto or Ethan?*

Verity pushed Leo into a roughly chiselled doorway and out of sight and gestured silently for him to remain hidden. Meanwhile, she ventured up to near a fallen hunk of masonry, a chunk of the ceiling that had fallen away and now lay in the middle of the passageway. There, she concealed herself in an alcove of her own.

Verity had never been one for thrill-seeking. She much preferred a museum to a theme park. A theme park might give someone a few short-term thrills, but what could they do with that? No, she preferred adding something to her life and so spent her time looking at as many placards and artefacts in a museum as she could. That's why she was here, in Guatemala: to enrich her life and learn more things.

Ethan, on the other hand (she often reflected), was very much an "in-the-here-and-now" sort of person. He loved his sports, his thrills, his theme parks. He would be down the park with his friends having his kind of fun whilst Verity had her head in her books, having her kind of fun. Okay, so he had more friends than she did. Well, so what? Life wasn't just about having as many friends as possible and being liked by other people. Or was it? Sometimes, Verity wondered about life. What was its purpose? Did it have a purpose? All these people who lived in all these countries believing all of these different things – did they all have the same purpose? How about these Maya? Did they have a meaning to their existence? Did they get it right? Was there even a "right" or a "wrong"? Was this question even the "right" sort of question? As to the Maya, was all of this that was left over, all of these pyramids and evidence of human sacrifice, was it all in vain?

Of course, this was *not* what she thought about when she was hiding in an alcove waiting to trip up a dangerous man chasing them for some unknown reason, but what she thought about when she was lying on her camp bed in her tent at night.

She was a thinker, all right, but now her thoughts were being clouded by the hammering of her heart and the pumping of adrenaline around her body. She shook herself out of her stupor in time to pick out not one but two beams of light cutting through the darkness. It was not a case of Ernesto or Ethan but both at once!

A blur shot past her. In the ever-growing beam of a torch, she clearly recognised the panicked prey as her brother. She opened her mouth to shout out his name and reached out her hands to pull him to her, to keep him safe, but much to her dismay, her brother fell head over heels and into the dirt. His torch spun away from him, suddenly strobing the tunnel; first illuminating Ethan's horrified, pain-filled face and then spinning to temporarily blind her from the scene playing out in slow motion before her. A loud *thunk* echoed around the stone walls and the light died.

Ethan, lying, mouth agape, terrified, was illuminated by the oncoming torchlight of Ernesto.

The hulking man pounded his way forward at pace, as if readying to launch himself onto the boy ahead of him. In his speed and greed in catching his prey, Ernesto didn't notice Verity concealed in the darkness of her alcove. She stuck out her leg as he ran past, caught his heel, and sent him sprawling.

Thud!

The sound of a solid impact mixed with a shudder-inducing wet splash rippled through the corridor. Ernesto's head made contact with the rock over which Ethan had tripped.

Silence.

Ernesto's torch had crashed against the wall, pointing back towards the man's head. Verity could see blood trickle down his scalp to drip off his nose. His trademark hat had flown off and lay bent at his side.

In the dim light, Ethan looked over at Verity.

"Vee...Vee..."

"Oh, Ethan. Oh...what have we done?"

"What you had to, sis. What we had to."

12

Ethan

Reunited with Leo, the twins made their hasty way down the next corridor, leaving Ernesto to whatever fate the ancient pyramid had in store for him. *There must be another way out of here. There must.*

Ethan's inner hopes were realised, but not until they had wound this way and that, deep within the darkness at the very base of the ancient building.

The dim lights of their torches were finally outdone by some cracks of light, allowing the outside world to filter in. Where there was light, there was also moss and growth. Life was tenacious, finding a way to survive in every nook and cranny possible. The children followed these tendrils of light till they came upon what was once a grand opening at the rear of the pyramid. Ethan let out an exasperated, exhausted breath: their exit seemed to be blocked by collapsed masonry from somewhere above. He leant against the cold stone that barred their way. The stonework surrounding the doorway – many times higher than Ethan could possibly reach – was chipped and rough but still conveyed the original artists' message. Intricately carved skulls, row upon row, glared down at the children as they collapsed against the boulders that denied them passage. The faces in the rock seemed to smirk at them.

"This must be something to do with the human sacrifices, maybe where the priests entered the temple?" Vee said, unable to ignore the historian's voice in her head.

"Well, we might be next if we can't get out!" responded Ethan. Before the conversation could continue, their attention snapped to Leo. Uninterested in the ornate carvings or indeed the siblings' conversation, Leo had been scrutinising the mound of rubble piled in their way. Although mostly made of pale limestone, the obstacle was dotted with patches of green, vegetation which had grown between the gaps. It was through one of these gaps that Leo suddenly plunged his hand. He felt blindly around the hole, touching the strong vines that seemed to act like a net, holding the boulders in place. He pulled his arm back in but thrust it immediately at Ethan.

"Have you got a knife?" Half question, half demand. Ethan patted his pockets. He knew he had brought his penknife with him but had it fallen out in the earlier panic? No. There it was – safely in its pouch in his shorts' pocket. He handed it to Leo who, without hesitation, flicked open the blade. His arm once again disappeared into the pocket of green.

"I think," he spoke hesitantly, "I think, if I can cut vines, we can push out rock."

"But, what if it collapses...?" Vee's voice quavered. The thought of causing tonnes of temple to crash down upon them was almost too much on top of what they had already been through.

"The vines, they are old and strong, should hold the rest in place. If I do this right-"

He broke off midsentence and fell forward slightly as a large slab of rock was released from its mossy moorings. Sunlight flooded in, illuminating the twins, who had grasped at each other, ready for the sudden rumbling roar of falling stone. When nothing happened, Ethan flung his sister's arm away from him, coughed and looked away sheepishly. Leo's mouth, which was already cracked with a smile, widened revealing a stretch of white that seemed to glow against his grubby, dust-darkened face.

After a few more minutes of sawing at carefully selected rope-like vines, and with one last shove from Leo, a final stone was dislodged, revealing a gap big enough for the children to get free.

The three escapees squeezed through, breathing in but still felt the sharp edges scrape at their shoulder blades and chests. One by one they emerged, bathed in sunlight, the humid air of the jungle drawing around them as if in a welcoming embrace.

"Yes! *Por fin!*" Leo exclaimed as he managed to struggle through the final vine.

The three sat down on some nearby stones and had a drink from their bottles. It was only now that they were able to take in what had just happened. Ethan was in shock, his face having lost its usual colour.

"What...what do we do now?" he asked.

"Right," said Verity, "we need to work out why Dad was taken. And I need to think."

Ethan sat silently watching his sister as her brow furrowed and she was lost in deep thought. After a short while, she continued.

"This must all have something to do with the argument Dad was involved in. There's something going on here."

Ethan added: "And I bet it has something to do with that mask. I bet it does!"

"Yes. I think we need to get back to camp and see what Dad has on his laptop. We need to see what they were all looking at."

70

Leo looked worried. "We cannot be seen, though. Who can we trust? We can definitely trust my father, but we need to get to him, alone."

Together, the children formed a plan: they would get back to the outskirts of the camp and then sneak into their father's tent to retrieve his laptop. There had to be something on it that could help them work out what was going on. Only then could they work out their next step.

After only a small squabble, the children agreed on where they must be and the direction they needed to go in order to find the camp. With the tribulations of the temple fresh in his mind, Ethan did not argue when Vee suggested she take the lead. He took one final look at the temple, glancing up to its sun-kissed summit, before taking his position at the rear of the trio. They carefully worked their way through the forest, brushing aside undergrowth as they went, moving slowly towards the campsite.

Soon enough, they heard the noises of the camp, and were watchful not to get too close. They worked their way around the site so that they were as close as they could get to their father's tent. The light was now waning and the sun was on its fairly quick descent - afternoon being replaced with evening. As a result, the camp lights were starting to flicker on, accompanied by the chugging sound of the diesel generator that provided the scientists and archaeologists with their electricity.

Crouching behind a nearby bush, the nervous trio of intrepid adventurers were biding their time, waiting for the right moment.

When it was fully dark, which, in Guatemala, (being nearer the Equator) was earlier than they were used to at this time of year, they decided they would have to act. The throb of the generator would cover any sounds they made but the electricity it produced powered a bank of floodlights, surrounded by clouds of buzzing insects, that lit up swathes of the site in harsh, white light. This was still a dangerous task.

"I'll do it," Ethan had said, earlier. He felt he could get into the tent quickly and quietly, like a ninja. At least, that's how *he* imagined it.

As it turned out, he was fairly accurate in his prediction. With a quiet but swift step, he half-crept, half-ran to his father's tent. No one spotted him as he quickly unzipped both layers.

Yes!

There it was, on the camp bed. Thankfully, his father had returned the laptop to his tent earlier that day. Ethan grabbed the laptop bag with all of its various bits and pieces inside, and a few snacks he could see lying about. With the nervous quietness of a church mouse, he popped his head out of the tent to survey the surroundings. Just as Ethan was about to exit, twigs snapped to his right. He ducked back in straight away.

Crunch, crunch.

Leaf litter cracked as one of the camp members strolled past, on their way to their own tent across the way from his father's. Luckily, the man was oblivious to anything other than his destination. Ethan felt the pull of temptation to call out to him; to ask for help; to explain what had happened. He closed his eyes and gritted his teeth. They couldn't trust anybody. They had to do this alone.

After the scientist or workman – Ethan hadn't dared to look long enough to discern the man's role - had entered his own tent and zipped it up (as everyone did to stop the mosquitos from entering), Ethan stepped outside his father's tent and slowly zipped it back up so as not to make too much sound and to hide his ever having been there.

With his newfound booty in his hands, he crept back to where the other two were waiting.

"Well done!" Leo whispered. "Let's get to somewhere safe."

"Yeah, I know where to go. Follow me," Ethan suggested.

It was difficult, but there was *some* moonlight to go by, as well as the twinkling lights of the camp in the near distance. Unseen, they made their way through the forest to a small clearing they knew of not too far from the base of the pyramid. They wouldn't be found there as it was somewhere they had discovered and used in secret, to be away from the adults, over the week.

Some people say that there are times in the night when landscapes sleep, when quiet blankets the densest of forests or the driest of savannahs or the quaintest of woods, or even the busiest of towns. Perhaps this happened in the small hours before dawn when night turns unstoppably into day, when the world gets ready to open its sleepy eyes. To the children, though, the Guatemalan forest felt like it never had this quiet time. Neither in the morning, nor the afternoon, nor, too, the night. For the night, in this part of the woods, never seemed to sleep; the forest never dozed; life was truly awake. You only had to listen for it. And that wasn't hard.

Insects buzzed and whirred, chirruped and hummed in their hidden homes, blanketed under the safety of darkness. And those hidden homes appeared to be...everywhere. This was their place: the home of insects; of the small mammals that scurried around catching the scuttling creatures; of the wild cats that made dinner of the agouti and pacas that were not fast enough to escape. This was not the rightful home of three young children. They were intruding upon nature, stealing its timeless innocence, rudely interrupting its routines. The clearing wasn't used to such nocturnal interferences, and yet the hidden world continued unabashed, ignoring the hushed human voices, and crunching feet, earthquakes to the bugs beneath. Humans were of no concern to the clicking conversations of these tiny creatures and their chattering discussions that had lasted here, unhindered, for millions of years.

The children sat on a log and huddled together, taking the laptop out of the bag. Flipping the lid open, they sparked the machine into life. The artificial brightness of the screen, in their present setting, seemed wholly out of place and initially made them squint in discomfort.

With dirty hands that weren't used to operating a mousepad in the dark, in a forest, after being chased out of an ancient pyramid by a crazed man, Ethan managed to fumble the cursor about the desktop. There was a video player open in one of the windows, so he maximised it.

"Let's see what this is," he suggested.

He pressed play and a dark video jolted into life. It displayed a gloomy tunnel lit up by a torch held by a hand and arm that often flashed past the camera.

"This is body camera, no?" Leo said.

"Sure is. And I recognise some of this. Is this one of the corridors in the pyramid?" Ethan replied. "Look, there's a red light. There it is again. He's following the lights. They must be really powerful."

The children looked on as the subject of the video wound their way downwards, into the depths of the structure, drawn in by the throbbing light.

Ethan felt uncomfortable at the lights and the sound of the man's walking and breathing, audible through the tiny speakers of the laptop, over and above the forest sounds around them. "This is freaky, man!"

"Shhh!" Verity was intent on watching as closely as she could, her astute eyes darting about the screen in search of any clue. Suddenly, the man came to an abrupt halt. The blinding red of a light in front of him was almost too much for the viewers in the clearing. As the red light dimmed, though, they could make something else out. The man's flashlight, in the video, shone in front of him.

"That's that statue thing!" exclaimed Ethan, excitedly. "The curse thingamabob!"

"Yes. Yes, it is," was all his sister could add.

The children peered at the screen in shocked awe as the person, whose experiences they had hijacked, crumpled to the ground. The camera pointed up at the ceiling, barely visible in the murky depths of the pyramid, briefly lit by pulses of red light. It was as if the veins of the pyramid were pumping blood, coursing and cursing through the tunnels. *It's like all the blood of the sacrificed Maya!* Ethan's heart was rapidly pumping his own blood in a wave of nervous excitement.

"*Dios mio!*" was all Leo could manage.

"It's that cursed artefact! I swear it is!" Ethan blurted, his mind fizzing with ideas and hastily-formed theories. "It looks like that's what made the guy collapse."

"Hang on," said Verity, with *that* voice, as if she knew better. "We don't know half the details here. Someone could have been standing behind him and clonked him on the head. There are loads of things that could have happened. And. Like..." she struggled to weave her tangled thoughts into a sentence, "How could the red light have been seen from the top of the pyramid down to that room. If you shone a light in the middle of the pyramid, there's no way someone could see it from outside; it wouldn't bounce off the walls all the way out to the top. At least, I don't think it would."

Ethan turned to face his sister, her head oddly close to his, reflecting computer light in the forest darkness so that she appeared as a ghost in the moonlight. "Look," he said, "that artefact was the curse that did the Maya in, right?"

"Well..."

"...And if it's got that kind of power, then lighting up a couple of corridors is nothing too special. I bet Dad was onto this and wanted to tell the world, but Ernesto wanted to shut him up. He didn't want this dark secret to get out because it would ruin all the work they were doing. Or maybe..."

Ethan proceeded to rattle through some exciting theories like a Gatling gun firing off rounds into the surrounding night. Verity appeared to be only half-listening, her mind wandering off into deep thought.

"What do you reckon, then?" Ethan asked, hopefully, sounding out his theories.

"Er...maybe? First thing first, we need to find Dad."

Ethan realised that, in all the commotion and confusion, he hadn't *really* considered the plight of his father. *He could be... he could be dead!* His heart missed a beat. No, it felt like it had been frozen in time, momentarily devoid of life. He gasped after what seemed like an eternity, and it reluctantly skipped back into its regular rhythm.

"My God, Verity, we're in serious trouble. Serious, serious trouble. Dad could be...could be..."

"No," Verity cut in, thankfully sure of herself. "If Ernesto had wanted to kill him, he would have killed him. He could easily have done it. No, they kidnapped him. And that jeep can't drive on forever. It wouldn't have enough fuel. I bet it's gone somewhere not *too* far away. Well, I hope that's the case. Otherwise, we're pretty much done for." She stood up and added, "We're no longer holidaymakers, we're truthseekers."

It was as if this wasn't just a turning point in their trip abroad, but a defining point of their lives. Ethan raised an eyebrow, a common feature of his facial expressions.

Leo chipped in, after listening patiently. "Why we no walk up the path; the jeep track?"

Ethan and Verity sat there for a while, thinking.

We have no choice.

Ethan grimaced. "What else can we do? Let's go."

13

Verity

"The moon is a ghostly galleon tossed upon cloudy seas," said Verity wistfully, staring up at the moon as it fought to free itself from its cloudy embrace. The world around them was the stage, with its actors giving their real-life performances. The clouds were in charge of the lighting and they had a fairly random idea of what these particular child actors wanted, flicking the moon on and off at will.

"Ghostly galleons? Eh?" questioned Ethan, bewildered.

"Oh, it's just a poem that we learnt at school. You must have done *The Highwayman* too?"

"Not in my class."

"It's beautiful. And sad. And if the moon wasn't out, we'd be in serious navigational trouble."

Leo chipped in. "I don't know about poems – English ones – but I know the Maya used to think the moon was a woman, a goddess. She was about crops and growth and water. When it rained, and that was good for crops, it was her. But, you know, different Maya people believed different things in different places."

The three of them had been walking for a good half an hour. Well, it wasn't *good*; it was full of anxiety, and nervous hypotheses and predictions about exactly what was going on. This lunar talk was a welcome distraction.

Quite what Ernesto had in mind was a mystery. What is it that their father had that he wanted? What did he know? How could a simple archaeologist, their own father, be involved in something so dangerous? Was he seriously hurt? All these questions and more had been fizzing about the twins' minds like New Year's Eve fireworks but without all the fun of the party.

Unlike her brother, who had had a few tearful moments, Verity had not shown too much emotion, being wrapped up in what was going on and what they should do about it. She was a practical girl, even in this worst of times. It was her own way of coping.

The track that split the trees into two armies of darkness was roughshod, uneven under foot and only dimly lit by the moon that came and went: a lighthouse in the sea fog. A month or so of jeep traffic in all weathers had formed two ruts in the earth where the heavy tyres had carved their journeys.

Verity stumbled on one of the now hardened ruts, the moon hidden momentarily, and fell to the side with a heavy thud.

Leo flashed on his torch. "Are you okay?"

Suddenly, from back towards the ancient Maya city, the sound of an engine penetrated the thick night air.

"Leo, turn it off!" Verity quickly urged.

As Leo switched off his torch, the children quickly scrambled blindly behind the verge, hiding in some undergrowth. It didn't take long for the headlights of the oncoming vehicle to come into view, twin searchlights fumbling their way through the darkness. Soon enough, the truck reached them.

Verity's heart skipped as the battered vehicle, laden with pallets and worn-looking wooden crates, half covered by a grey-green tarpaulin, came to a halt just next to the children. Its stereo system was playing some Hispanic music, a cacophonous jumble of sound in the otherwise undisturbed silence of the forest.

The driver opened the door, satellite phone in his hand, remonstrating loudly. He walked to the other side of the track, intent on his conversation.

"Now's our chance!" Verity whispered sharply. "Follow me."

"What?" Leo and Ethan both replied.

"We need to get on that truck. And quickly."

The boys looked at each other with eyebrows raised but Verity was already moving. The three crept as quietly as they could, though any noise was thankfully drowned out by the stereo and the loud conversation going on but ten metres away. The tarpaulin was only loosely attached as seemingly most of the crates were empty, ready to be filled at wherever the destination was, no doubt.

Being in the dark and trying to be silent made getting into the trailer a bit tricky for the three wannabe stowaways. Luckily, the driver continued his conversation uninterrupted. He seemed to be having an argument that required his total attention. The aluminium base of the flatbed was cold and dusty and was not in any way comfortable, particularly when, after five minutes, the driver returned to the cab and continued his drive. They bumped around in the dark, hitting each other and banging against the sides, until they worked out that it was most comfortable when they curled into a tightly-knit ball of limbs and bodies, becoming as one.

After a good ten-minute drive, not as long as Verity was anticipating, the four-wheel drive came to a stop. Some dim artificial light seeped in through the rips and tears of the old tarpaulin. The children waited with bated breath as the driver left the cab and walked off.

They heard a door slam somewhere.

"What shall we do?" Leo asked, whispering.

"It's pretty dark out there, just one light coming from over there." Vee pointed vaguely, "We need to get out and find out what's going on and where we are."

Carefully, the children alighted from the truck, crawling out from under the tarpaulin as quietly as their tired bodies could manage. With furtive looks about, they could make out the arrangement of a small compound of wooden huts – six in total – some with lights on, others dark and only murkily apparent. The whole place was lit up (other than from the windows of certain huts) by a single light from a pole running off a diesel generator. Wires from the generator snaked out to each hut, providing energy like the sun's rays to the solar system.

The trio crouched behind the back of the truck, surveying their surroundings and considering their options.

"I think the driver went in there," suggested Ethan, pointing at the nearest hut. "Which means we probably want to look on the other side."

There were two huts shrouded in darkness on the opposite side of the compound. A rough dusty yard, where the truck was parked, bridged the gap between four huts on one side and the two in darkness on the other. Between the improvised taxi from which they had recently emerged, and the two huts, was a second vehicle: a mud-covered jeep behind which sat an equally filthy trailer. This provided the perfect cover and the children slipped like silken shadows towards it. After some deep breathing and nudging each other in the ribs, they crouched low and scuttled over to the first of the two huts, beetles going about their clandestine business unseen by the rest of the world.

They crept around the back of the first building, which had a small, thinly paned glass window through which to peer. Verity grabbed her torch out of her rucksack and flicked it on, pointing the beam into the hut. There were boxes of supplies, crates and objects hidden under canvas sheets and tarpaulins, but nothing particularly untoward, and certainly no Dad.

"There's nothing much in here. Best go look in the next one," she said.

The three scurried along the back of the hut to the next glorified shack. The window was in the same place, and Verity turned on her torch again to scout out the room.

"Holy cow!" she blurted, a little too loud.

"What? Is it Dad?" asked Ethan, excited.

"Yes. Yes, it is."

At which point the other two children turned on their torches and squeezed next to Verity to look through the small window into the otherwise dark depths of the building.

And there he was. Tied to a chair that was itself strapped to a pole in the middle of the room. Dusty and dirty, face bloodied and bruised, their father sat, bound and gagged with his head hanging limply.

Ethan tapped on the window, quietly at first, but when he elicited no response, his tappings became more urgent, mirroring his heart beat. Eventually, and groggily, their father stirred. His head swung slowly from side to side as if trying to shake off a bad memory whilst stuck in a vat of thick glue. After a tense minute, his head swung to look towards the window. His unexpected response was to immediately look away, face wrapped in a wrinkled blanket of pain.

"Turn your torches off," Verity whispered sharply, "we're blinding him."

Verity kept hers on but covered part of it with her hand, pointing it through the window and at the floor, to give some light to the room. Her father turned to look at the window, though Verity could not tell whether he could see them properly and they certainly couldn't have a chat as he was gagged and on the other side of a window.

"We must get in there," she said, "but I'm not sure how much of a good idea it is."

"I'm game," said Ethan. He was always a risk taker. Whether it be in a board game, or in life, he was a risk taker. Indeed, in the board game *The Game of Life*, he took risks. And he never bought the house or car insurance in it. Verity was sometimes worried he would grow up into a gambler. Of course, in the game, Verity always bought insurance, and always followed the path of getting a university education first before getting a job. She hoped real life would follow her ideals in *The Game of Life*. Who knows, maybe she would follow her father into something like archaeology; although, if this was how dangerous it was, maybe not.

Whispers in the night, the children stole around to the front and slipped through the unlocked door and into the hut. Leo stationed himself by the front window as a lookout.

"Dad!" the twins rejoiced as they hugged him. Ethan pulled down the gag and his dad looked at him and then Verity with heavy, dazed eyes. Blood was caked on one side of his head and cheek.

"Ethan...Vee...Wha...what are you doing...here?" he managed.

Verity put her hand reassuringly on his arm, tears welling up in her eyes. "Dad, we saw what happened to you. We jumped in a trailer and got here to find you."

"Bu...But..."

"Look, Dad, what's going on? Why did Ernesto do that?" Verity asked, desperate for answers.

"Not...sure...I think...think..."

"Think what?"

"You have to break...get...curse...thing..."

"What?" Verity was confused.

Her father was struggling to make much sense. "End of...end of the world. Maya prophecy... They want...the end of the world. Inscription. But...don't trust..."

And then his head fell limply to the side.

"This can't be from the hit over the head," Verity stated, matter-of-factly. "He must have been drugged or something."

There was a sound from the other side of the compound as a door opened.

"Oh no!" Leo whispered, shocked. "Someone is coming."

All three turned and made for the little window that they had been looking through.

"Quick! *Rápido!*" Leo blurted. Two men were talking to each other as they left the hut, walking slowly towards their father's makeshift prison.

Ethan unlatched the arm of the window mechanism and hoisted himself up as Leo held it at arm's length. He tumbled out. Next, Leo managed to bundle out.

There's not going to be enough time.

Quickly closing the window, Verity turned around and, with the men and their torches only some ten metres away, she noticed her father's gag around his neck. She scrabbled to his side and yanked the dirty cloth up his neck and placed it over his mouth. It felt odd, no, awful, doing this, like she was making life harder for her dad, like she was helping to keep him captive.

"We'll get you out, Dad, I promise," she whispered, before scanning the hut. She could hear gruff voices from outside. Escape for her was no longer an option. She had to hide. There were some pallets of goodness-knows-what stacked behind the pole and her dad's chair.

The hut door opened to the sound of chattering Spanish just as Verity negotiated the tarpaulins and pallets to crouch down, hidden like a spy.

Some laughs. Some more talk amongst themselves. And then the sound of a face being slapped. Hard enough that it woke her father, it appeared.

"Mister Hume," said one of the voices in a thick Spanish accent. "We have video ready. You need be clean. We need you speaking in video. Have this water. Need your head...clean. You need speak clean."

What was going on? What video? What were they doing? What could *she* do?

Nothing.

Nothing but listen.

14

Ethan

A herd of wildebeest thundered through Ethan's chest, over the sternum, and stampeded through the ribs. The sound filled his head. He wanted to run. To run and run and run. And run some more. As fast as his legs would carry him, matching the pounding hooves of his heart.

But he didn't.

He remembered once, in a science lesson, his teacher telling him something about animals, when faced with danger, either fighting, freezing, or fleeing. He didn't fancy fighting, and was resisting the urge to flee, meaning his only sensible option was to freeze. Safety in stillness. Despite the internal turmoil in Ethan's body, his exterior of a wide-eyed statue meant that the young boy was unable to do anything but listen to what was happening back inside the hut.

He felt a gentle tap on his shoulder and jumped out of his skin. It was only Leo. Nonetheless, he removed his heart from his mouth.

"I think Vee hide, no? We go to see if anyone else here. We might need get out quick. I can drive jeep," he whispered.

"What? You? Jeep? Drive?"

"Yes, I know how. But we need the keys. Also other jeep here. Need to stop it driving."

Together, the two boys left Verity to whatever uncertain future awaited her, and left the twins' father to his imprisonment. They crept through the undergrowth and back to the yard of the compound. There were lights on in only two huts – what was now Daniel, Ethan's father's hut, and the hut from where the two men came. Perhaps there were more men in there?

Ethan, who had now snapped out of his frightened state, was running on the fuel of adrenaline. He beckoned Leo to follow him and moved like a black panther in a midnight hunt to the cabin. He peered through the window from a few metres back, not wanting to press his face up against the thin glass in case there was anyone inside. To his very great relief, there was no one.

And right there, sitting on the table, perhaps more valuable to them now than a great Maya treasure hoard, were a set of keys for the jeep. Ethan turned to Leo and nodded his excitement that the keys were indeed inside. Leo, in turn, pointed at himself and then the hut to indicate that he was going to go in and get them. Ethan looked back to his father's shack in the hope that the men would not choose this particular moment to return.

They didn't.

Instead, all Ethan could make out was loud talking in what might have been broken English. They were talking to Dad. And it didn't sound like they were talking about the weather, or the football results, either. There was an air of menace to the tones of their voices.

Leo soon returned to Ethan's side with the keys and a plastic bag of assorted food. Just as importantly, though, he had a pair of radios.

Indicating his rucksack, Leo said quietly, "And satellite phone." He then pointed at the food. "For the journey."

"What journey?"

***

Letting down two of the tyres to the flatbed truck had been a lot harder than they had anticipated. The rubber was thick, and Ethan's penknife struggled. The hiss of escaping air was dangerously loud but they managed to remove the potential for pursuit without being heard.

Now, the boys sat in the cabin of the other jeep. Everything was unfamiliar to Ethan: sitting in a jeep, in the dark, with the steering wheel on the other side, in the middle of a Guatemalan forest in a makeshift prison compound, with a Spanish-speaking boy as a chauffeur. Well, almost everything.

During his last summer holidays, he had spent a number of days staying at his friend's house; more accurately, his farmhouse. As a special treat, Ethan had been allowed to have a go at driving their Land Rover. He'd ridden in their tractor too. The John Deere was too big and far too expensive to be allowed to drive on his own. But he remembered his solo expedition in the car, across muddy fields, bumping up and over ruts and once, through a hedge-row. In reality, his journey was actually fairly short and involved not being able to properly reach the pedals, stalling three times, and staggering in bunny hops to the other side of the field at which point he failed to stop and gently came to a gentle halt in a brambly thicket.

Ethan didn't like doing things that he felt he should be good at but actually wasn't. It frustrated him. He often felt that sense of indestructible confidence that some young boys do. But when the realities of his own ability was eventually damaged (as it was with driving a Land Rover badly), Ethan had a tendency to fall apart a little.

He had stormed away from the jeep in frustrated tears at not being able to work out how to change gear effectively, even though he could barely reach those pedals. What had he been expecting? To be an instant rally driving champion?

Leo, on the other hand, had had more practice. He had told Ethan, very briefly, that his uncle owned a farm himself and had a jeep that he had played around on, with guidance. Although Leo also struggled to reach the pedals securely, he perched his backside in such a way on the seat that he could just about control the brake pedal, the clutch to change the gears, and the accelerator.

"It's knowing where each gear is on the stick that is difficult," he whispered to Ethan as he made sure the gear stick was in neutral before starting the engine. "Are you sure this is good idea? I think no choice."

"Leaving Vee here? No. No, I'm not. But it may give Dad more of a chance, and it will mean these men don't have a way to get around, and they can't contact the camp, either."

Leo put his hand on the keys and took a deep breath. It seemed like an age before he let it out again. Time stopped. Heartbeats halted. Blood froze, unmoving. Hairs stood on end. Minds were thoughtless.

Leo turned the key.

Cheeka-cheeka-cheeka-chee...

All sensations returned, not least heart-thumping anguish at the engine wheezing into showing temporary signs of life...before dying.

"C'mon, Leo!" Ethan implored, nerves torn apart, like letters in his father's paper shredder.

Cheeka-cheeka-cheeka-cheeka-chee...

"Dios mio!" the Guatemalan boy spat through gritted teeth. He hit the wheel and muttered something in Spanish.

Cheeka-cheeka-cheeka-vroooooooom.

The wheezing became a grumbling growl that soon became a roar as Leo over-revved the engine to jerk the jeep forward. The jeep was still facing the hut in which his father, his sister and the two "prison guards" were situated. Its twin beams lit the ground and hut like stage-lights in a theatre, preparing for the drama that would undoubtedly unfold.

Without warning, the engine stalled. The stage went black.

"Noooo!" Ethan called out, now not so worried about being quiet, just as the door to the hut ahead opened. Two men stepped out, quizzical looks on their faces, not being able to fathom exactly what was going on.

Leo banged the gear stick back into neutral and turned the key again. The coughing engine spluttered back into life at the second asking.

"Eh!" was all one of the onlooking men could cry, arms outstretched. *"Qué diablos está pasando?"* shouted the other, shading his eyes as the two glaring bulbs burned into life once more.

"We steal your car, *señor!*" Leo shouted, a crazed, maniacal look on his face, bright eyes wide and mouth almost laughing. There was more to Leo than perhaps he had first thought, Ethan realised.

The jeep, engine revved high, lurched forward and bounded round, jerking in a tight circle under the guidance of Leo's skills, engine whining. It almost hit the two men as they stood there, remonstrating in angry Spanish, arms shaking and waving.

"Whoah, Leo! Mind out, mate!"

But Leo had other things on his mind, like trying to find second gear. The wipers started screeching across the dry windscreen as he knelt forward, peering into the black footwell. After a couple of seconds of scrabbling in the darkness whilst still trying to keep his eyes on the dimly lit yard, Leo sat up straight. His legs pistoned as he worked the clutch and his right hand thrust the gearstick backward. The high-pitched whine turned to a purr and Leo patted the dashboard affectionately. Meanwhile, just in time. Ethan, instincts taking over, grabbed the wheel as Leo's attention was taken up on the steering column, and swung the jeep to the right as a tree suddenly appeared ahead of them.

"Thanks!" Leo shouted, returning both hands to the wheel. The jeep, engine roaring once again, still in only second gear but safely moving, motored towards the compound exit and the forest track. The two men sprinted after it, shouting in an angry mix of Mayan-Spanish. "We make good team!" Leo smiled to Ethan as they made their way down the track, still in second gear, bumping up and down the rough surface, the trailer bouncing wildly behind them, eventually disappearing into the darkness of the Guatemalan forest.

In the thick jungle either side of the track, mammals, both nocturnal and those rudely awoken, looked on, bemused. Insects fluttered and buzzed, some circling to the moon and being caught by hungry bats, others flitting from branch to branch in the forest night. Snakes slithered and frogs croaked. Grubs grubbed and ants tunnelled. Much of the forest slept, in the particular ways animals of all varieties sleep. Still others used the night to forage or seize their foraging prey. The watched and the watchers. Death (for nature is red in tooth and claw) stood at every forest window, and concerned every forest animal, big or small, scaly or furred.

And after just a minute, around that piece of track, all were again oblivious to the troubled world of humans, for many had troubles of their own, whether they knew it or not.

Survival has always been a challenge for man and beast, and this quiet night was no different. As a spider spins its web to catch its unknowing quarry, exactly what web of deceit and danger lay ahead for the boys was, as yet, a mystery.

15

Verity

Motes of dust swirled in the dim, yellow light of the crude prison. This, and the naked, dirty bulb that swung gently in the night's breeze, was all that Verity could see beyond the stacked pallets and grime-covered tarp. What she could hear, on the other hand, was plentiful.

Both voices, thick with Guatemalan Spanish, were rough and demanding. In her mind's eye, Verity could see their equally rough hands holding her father's face as they forced water into his mouth. Spluttering sounds followed the command and suddenly another *slap* echoed around the filthy, wooden walls.

"Mister Hume. We not ask again. Drink!"

Verity had no desire to watch what was happening but imagining the scene to match what she could hear was driving her crazy. She shuffled as silently as possible to her right, to where the tarpaulin was tattered and ripped, to where she could at least glimpse what was happening. As she moved, she felt a tug at her shoulder and almost screamed. Something, someone had hold of her!

She turned her head so fast that she felt something in her neck pull; a flash of pain seemed to echo all the way down her spine. Her eyes closed in relief: her bag had caught on a protruding nail that had tried to hold her in place as she moved forward. Panic and terror subsided into grief. Tears welled in her eyes. How had she managed to get into this mess? And more importantly, how was she going to get out of it?

"Ahah. No worry Mister Hume," the other, slightly friendlier of the two voices roused Verity from her state of shock. "It not drugged," the voice continued.

Verity tilted her head down to the right and saw a burly, bearded man take a swig from a large bottle of water, beaded with condensation. Her mouth felt immediately dry and she longed for the cooling, refreshing feeling of a cold drink. She shook her head faintly; this wasn't the time to be worrying about herself – Dad had to be her focus. *What did they want from him?*

Mud-covered work boots stomped forwards and she saw gloved hands snatch the bottle of water. Once more the container was forced to Daniel's lips. This time she saw him willingly take a sip, then a gulp. Verity saw his stubbled throat working to swallow the clearly much-needed liquid, but his chest jerked forward and with a mixture of pity and horror she had to watch as her father coughed and spluttered. Regurgitated water and - her eyes widened - what looked like *blood* spurted from her father's mouth. A roar, filled with equal parts anger and disgust, thundered around the small cabin. The gloved hand threw the bottle of water to the floor. Sparkling diamond droplets splashed over boots, dirt floor and wooden walls. The water, immediately collecting, ran tear-tracks through the months of collected dirt before being hastily swallowed by the gaps in the floorboards. All this Verity saw with a clarity of a stunned mind: seeing every detail but being unable, or unwilling, to accept the reality of it.

She barely held in a gasp as the gloved hand swung back, clearly preparing to deliver yet another punishing blow. Before it could, however, she saw a second hand grip the first at the wrist.

"*No más!*" the kinder voice rang out, but this time with a steely edge. Two sets of boots were suddenly pointed at each other, almost toe to toe. Vee's eyes traced up from the well-worn boots, over faded green khakis studded with pockets, up further past a military-looking jacket crisscrossed with straps and buckles, and took in the pulsing veins and clenched jaw of the gloved guard. She saw eyes sparking with anger, a small smile playing at the corners of a cruel mouth – a smile that promised only violence and pain. A dark chuckle seemed to drip from between cigarette-yellowed teeth. Two gloved hands came together like a baseball and a mitt – leather smacking against leather. The tension was palpable, the air thick with jungle heat and long-brewed rage. Perhaps this was something that Verity did not want to see after all. Although, she thought to herself, at least this violence was not to be directed at her father. Not yet.

A metallic choking sound broke the deafening silence of the hut. In that moment, the gathered storm dissipated, the electricity vanishing. It was the sound of an engine spluttering, once, twice and then awakening with a reluctant mechanical moan.

The two men had begun to throw words rather than punches at each other, though with equal force and rapidity. Whilst she understood none of the language, it was clear to Verity that this was something that neither of them expected and the boots were soon moving towards the door, which was then wrenched open.

"Noooo!" a voice cried out in the renewed stillness of the night as the engine decided to return to slumber. *Ethan?* Verity jumped from her hiding place without thinking. Luckily, the boots and their inhabitants were now striding

95

swiftly towards the unmoving jeep and the two small shadows that occupied the front seats.

Before they could reach the vehicle, it was forced back into a wakeful state, its throaty bellow louder than whatever it was that the two men were yelling.

The jeep leapt in jerking movements around towards the men who, in turn, leapt out of its path. Whoever it was at the wheel seemed to gain control over the beast and steered it safely back onto the rough jungle road. The jeep picked up speed and shot off, out of the compound, into the jungle.

Verity watched as the two men ran after it. If she was right, and she hoped she was, Ethan and Leo had just escaped. They would get help. They would come back with Leo's dad, with Cruzar. It would all be okay. The adrenaline which had been coursing through her body seemed to suddenly evaporate, leaving behind only aches, pains and a deep exhaustion. Okay, so things would be fine, but she could not remain standing in the doorway of her father's temporary cell; the two guards would return soon. She couldn't be there when they did.

With leaden legs and one final, painful look at her father still tied to the chair, Verity plodded to the first of the huts that they had peered into. She tried the door. Mercifully, it creaked open and without hesitation, she stepped in and closed it behind her. Using her final reserves of energy, she quickly dragged crates, shifted pallets of cans and gathered a few of the cleaner sheets to create a hidden nest: a secret bed for the night. Once finished, she collapsed in her concealed hideaway and fell into a sleep filled with dreams of temples, tortures and terror.

16

Ethan

The Maya ate a lot of sweet corn. Maize made almost everything from porridge and breads to cakes and tortillas.

That was all good and well, but what Ethan really wanted now was a burger. A cheeseburger. And fries. And a Coke.

Which was all the more surprising because it was about eight in the morning.

The boys had driven successfully back to the camp in the late evening of the previous night, making sure that they parked a little distance out, in what was the middle of the Maya city that the team were so excitedly working on. Walking to the camp by torchlight, they were keen to find Leo's father and Cruzar to relay everything they had experienced. Ernesto was up to something. He had kidnapped Daniel. He had him chained up like a prisoner in a remote, isolated camp. And Verity was stuck there.

Having located Leo's father and rattled off all of the details like a bag of microwave popcorn in full flow, they had been taken to see Cruzar in his tent. Repeating their stories to Cruzar, they were reassured by his huge concern and kindness. He had immediately radioed the police from the nearest town, who promised to be there the next morning, as early as they could.

Ethan had slept fitfully. On the one hand, he was tired with their day's activities, but on the other hand, he was deeply worried about his father. And even more so about his sister. She annoyed him (a lot), but she was his sister. She was Verity. And, he guessed, he probably did love her for it.

Ethan had been dreaming of a fast food burger as he woke to the sound of someone chatting outside his tent. Cruzar had positioned someone to guard the boys' tents in case Ernesto or any of his own men returned to camp. Considering the warm environs of his sleeping bag, he concluded that nothing untoward had happened.

Swallowing his burger-induced saliva, Ethan reached over and grabbed his water bottle, swigging thirstily from it. *What does today have in store for me? Will I get to go and find Dad?*

Breakfast was as unappetising as ever, but he wolfed it down with wild abandon as his hunger overcame his desire for a full cooked English breakfast (his food imagination had realigned itself to the right time of day).

People, scientists and others around the camp, were staring at them, some of them whispering. News had undoubtedly got out as to what was going on, Ethan assured himself. He talked with Leo over breakfast, theorising and postulating. Could it be this? What about that? They had come to no conclusions. Cruzar had said it must be something to do with the inscription they had uncovered. As he spoke to them about it, Ethan remembered, his voice had lowered and the normally enthusiastic and energetic South American rhythm had slowed to a sombre beat.

"The tablet and the glyphs upon them could change a lot. Could change...everything," His eyes were firmly upon Ethan's as he spoke. They glinted gold in the sunlight.

"Not only does the ancient text link the statue to the end of the Maya, but also to the end of the world."

Ethan's mind reeled but quickly began piecing together parts of a puzzle he was already familiar with. He had remembered watching a movie about the supposed end of the world in 2012 – apparently coming from the Maya calendar and prophecy -

"My father say that most professors think that prophecy rubbish," explained Leo, eating some bread. "Many think that prophecy was not for end of world, but for new beginning. Like a...a...birthday...no...cel-"

"Like a celebration?"

"Yes, Ethan. But, you know Hollywood. They make money from movie and this idea of end of world."

"So they have actually found an inscription here that talks about the end of the world? Dad mentioned something about a prophecy. Wow, so this inscription could mean something crazy happens soon!"

Ethan's mind started spinning again, cogs turning excitedly and whirring into action. This was it – proof that something was coming. Something that Maya had known about all along. Then he remembered his father, tied up to a chair, and felt guilty about his excitement and the smile that had crept onto his face.

"Yes, Cruzar and *papá* said there is evidence here that the end of the world will happen in two years! Or, at least, that's what the Maya here thought. The other famous inscription was wrong – or different - and this one is now super-important! This will be big, big news. It will be on all news channels."

"Yeah. Just imagine how freaked out people will be!" said Ethan, adventurous thrill rising again.

Just then, some commotion erupted and people looked to the entrance to the camp from the woods, towards where the children had first come to the site after their helicopter ride. Their arrival seemed such a long time ago, now.

Out of the forest and into the clearing emerged two policemen. The man in front wore what appeared to be an officer's uniform and a more formal cap, compared to the baseball style of the man behind. Together with his brown-lensed aviator sunglasses, the leader of the pair carried himself with a sense of bravado and importance. He walked through the clearing to the main central laboratory area, part of which also doubled as the eating area. As the boys looked on, Cruzar came out of his own tent and walked to meet them.

The police officer shook Cruzar's outstretched hand warmly, and they spoke in hushed voices for a while. Cruzar was pointing here and there, explaining what, no doubt, were the experiences of the children.

After several minutes, both the policemen sauntered towards the two boys, both of whom stood as the men approached. The officer nodded his head upwards in acknowledgement of the boys and Ethan's heart surprisingly skipped a beat. He hadn't realised that seeing these men had put him slightly on edge. The police in a foreign country seemed to provoke a different response in him than police from back home. He wasn't quite sure what to make of it.

The man asked something in Guatemalan Spanish, to which Leo replied. The two spoke at length with Leo, who paused for a few seconds to explain that the man did not speak any English so that he, Leo, would have to translate afterwards. Ethan's gaze was transfixed by the man's dark moustache as he spoke.

At that moment, Ethan felt foreign. His mind absently considered the scene around him. Everything that he had begun to feel comfortable was quickly stripped back so that the world he was in was strange and awkward. Perhaps it was the fact that his family, too, had been stripped away from him. The home that he had been building these past few days had quickly become that of a stranger. On top of that, his ability to communicate independently was non-existent. He was relying on the English skills of a Guatemalan boy no older than he – skills that had been picked up from watching television no less! There were even the differences in simple things, like the very different-looking policemen. Though he had no reason to fear them, they were not the figures that he usually associated with law and order. He felt thoroughly out of his depth, and his father wasn't there for him. Ethan had *no one* there for him. Suddenly, with a tidal wave of nausea overcoming him, he felt tiny and alone, helpless and dependent.

Leo and the policeman talked for a while and then the moustachioed man turned to Ethan.

"Okay *muchacho*, all good. We find *padre*," he said gruffly and then turned to go and speak to Cruzar again. Even though the whole experience had put him on edge, and these men were far from the stereotypical British "bobby-on-the-beat", Ethan felt an overwhelming sense of relief that the forces of law had now intervened. Whatever Ernesto and his henchmen were up to, good would prevail. After all, it always did in the movies he watched.

Leo explained that the police were going to go to the compound and find Ernesto and bring back their father. They weren't to worry as the police were onto it. In the meantime, they were to stay safely in the camp. They weren't to leave.

Leo's father, who had been over the moon to find Leo safe the night before, came over to the two of them.

He knelt down on his haunches, to get at the same level as the boys, who were still sitting at the table in the middle of the camp. His bearded face was probably more unkempt than it would have been, what with being out in the forest for weeks, longer than the Humes. His tanned skin was weathered and wrinkled at the eyes, with crow's feet that moved as he talked.

"Boys," he started, "you must, must stay in camp. We don't want any funny business, no? Any trying to be heroes, no? It is dangerous now. We don't know what Ernesto is trying to do, but he is dangerous. You stay here, where it is safe all the time."

"But what about you, Alejandro? Are you safe?" Ethan replied.

Faltering a little, Leo's father regained his composure. "Yes, yes, of course. There is no danger for us. Anyway, the police are here. All will be well."

After a little small talk, Alejandro explained what project they were dealing with that day. "We are working on the new inscription we have found. The one that talks of the mask. It looks like it talks about a curse, that there is some kind of prophecy. This is rare about Maya inscriptions. They don't usually talk about the future, no? But this one does, and it looks like it says something about a big change, about the end of an era in two years' time. This is very exciting. It is a huge find – perhaps the biggest in archaeology in recent times. We are excited."

"Yes, Alejandro is right." Cruzar had come over and joined in, his soft voice assured. "This is an incredible time. Your father, Ethan, he must have known something about it. Ernesto, I think, is trying to get money out of kidnapping him because he knows so much about this. We think he is trying to get the British government to pay a ransom for him. He is very important to our work here. We desperately need him back at camp to do this work."

Cruzar laid his hand reassuringly on Ethan's shoulder, in a fatherly way. "It'll be fine. You'll be safe here and we'll get your *padre* back to you soon."

"Thanks, Ed." Ethan felt his fears somewhat allayed, and the welling tears appeared to be sucked back into his tear ducts.

The problem for the boys was that they had to remain in the camp for the whole day. In fact, they were to remain there until the return of Daniel, and this meant, for Ethan at any rate, anxiety mixed with time. Of course, when you've got anxiety and nothing else to entertain your mind, you get an often-elaborate set of imagined scenarios of what might or might not happen. Ethan imagined the worst-case scenario and then an even worse-case scenario again and again. He tried to dismiss these thoughts from his overactive mind but to no avail. When you are physically constrained to a particular place, it is only the mind that can wander. And wander (and wonder) it did.

Ethan imagined his father dead, and this then reminded him of the passing of his mother, a victim of cancer. Her cancer had spread to her liver and then her bones, after which it was all too late. Everything had been too late: too late to find it in the first place; too late to catch it from spreading; too late to spend fun and active times with her during those last months; too late to get home from school that day to where she spent her final hours, to say goodbye and that he loved her.

Too late. Too little and too late.

I can't lose Dad. I can't. I won't let it happen. I WON'T!

Being confined to the camp, off to the side of the central field laboratory and under another open tent, was frustrating. And with only his frayed emotions to keep him company (other than Leo and the gruff-looking policeman), Ethan was struggling to remain level-headed.

Leo located a chess game in the camp and convinced Ethan that he wanted to play. Ethan could barely remember the rules having been taught them by his mother some years back, but reluctantly agreed. After all, what else did he have to do?

They whiled away an hour or two, with Ethan getting to know Leo a little better, almost-enjoying (through the nerves and emotional turmoil) their small-talk together. He learnt about Leo's family, about how his own mother had died, also from cancer. About how his father had tried to do everything to cure her and keep her alive, from expensive treatment in America – the best he could afford - to natural and alternative medicines back in Guatemala. All was in vain.

Ethan could feel his pain, and together, because of their shared experiences (and despite the obvious language barriers), they bonded.

Ethan lost every chess game, mind. And, normally, this would have hugely annoyed him; but now, with more important things to worry about, his game-losing played second fiddle to what was going on around him. He was concerned, now, with feeling, re-experiencing, what had happened so seemingly recently, and what was etched in his mind and across his heart.

17

Verity

Verity awoke to the sounds of daylight. Those being, in a compound in a Guatemalan forest, the sounds of insects and birds and life. Verity, however, thought little of this, having greater concerns, namely her father, food, water and the toilet. Food and water were quickly sorted out, with water and snacks in her bag. Snacks went only so far, though, and she would soon need a little more sustenance.

The toilet was the next challenge. Looking through the hut window, she could see the two guards under the shade of a make-shift porch attached to a similar shelter across the yard, busily eating their way through breakfast. She took the opportunity to crawl through the small window at the back of the hut, as the boys had done the night before in her father's improvised prison.

After a few minutes, only her final, but toughest, challenge remained: her father.

She was not furnished with much time to think about this problem, though, because, soon enough, she heard the sound of voices and scuffed footsteps scudding across the dusty yard between the huts. Scuttling behind her father's cell with sadly scant enough time to have seen him or tried to get him out of there, Verity crouched down under the back window to work out what the men were planning. She had just enough time to prise the window open before the men wrenched open the door.

"Mister Hume," said one of the men in his heavy accent, "we have food. It breakfast. See, we good to you!"

"I need water."

"Yes, yes. Water, food, wash. We clean you up in our room then we take you to next door to make video, no?"

"Yes, Daniel," interjected the other man, "we tell you about that now. You come with us."

The two men, judging by the noises from within the hut, manhandled Verity's father out of his erstwhile prison and walked him forcefully across the yard. Verity looked on, distraught, from behind the corner of the cabin.

A few long minutes later, the sound of an engine chugged into her soundscape. From behind her hut, Verity peered out into the yard.

What she saw stabbed her in the chest.

A jeep had pulled up and reversed back to right next to the hut that she was hiding behind. Stepping out of the passenger side of the jeep was Ernesto, smoke puffing from his cigar-filled mouth.

Slamming the door, he hooked each thumb into a fold in his khaki cargo waistcoat (which bulged over his pistol in its holster, slung so that it sat below his left armpit), repositioned his hat on his head and wandered off to the first hut where the two guards were. Verity could see a knife in its own little leather scabbard attached to his belt. He was a dangerous man; a man who had hurt her father; a man who still *might* hurt her father; and a man who had something coming to him. Quite what, though, she was unsure.

Not long after, she could hear the men in the distance, arguing and talking loudly.

Verity tiptoed closer to the rear of the four-wheel-drive vehicle.

Just as she was about to reach the jeep, a fly buzzed into her mouth invoking an involuntary fit of spitting and gentle slaps of her lips as she tried to extricate the insect. She quickly realised that this wouldn't be a huge help in keeping her hidden.

She dropped to the dirt, hands on the dusty ground behind the jeep, but after a nervy minute she concluded that she hadn't been detected.

Unusually for Verity, she had no idea what she should be doing. She seemed powerless, a moth in a tornado. Winds of indecision blew in her mind as she tried to seize onto a plan she thought might work. Scraps of ideas drifted this way and that but there was nothing solid to grab, no plan to follow. Panic began to spread across her thoughts like oil across water. There was safety behind the huts, so she crept back to her relative haven.

Seconds ticked by, buzzing with flying insects, chirruping to birdsong. Minutes turned into half an hour before sounds echoed about the compound. Her father was being led back across the yard. Verity stole a look and her heart ached at seeing her father, a prisoner in a foreign land. He had been cleaned up and looked somewhat more presentable, having been lent a white shirt and cargo shorts.

The three men escorted Daniel to the last cabin in the row and Verity scampered behind them to take a familiar position below the window. However, much to her disappointment, she could hear only murmurs and the odd word. She daren't look through the window for fear of being seen. It was darker on the inside than on the outside and so she would have struggled to make sense of the interior whilst those inside would have had a clear view of the nosey intruder staring in. That much she knew.

After a frustrating five minutes, she felt she had no choice but to edge her way around the hut's wooden slatted walls to the front corner. The door was opened out onto the compound yard and she was able, peering perilously from cover, to get a much better sense of what was going on inside.

Her father's voice was fairly clear and he was speaking as though not to the men there. He must have been speaking to the video: he was being recorded.

Verity just needed to find out what he was saying. Her father's voice drifted to her as if in a dream, cutting through her worries and calming her nerves. His soft, deep tones instantly comforted her.

Listen! Pay attention!

This was no time to be emotional. She had a job to do, and that job was to work out what the devil Ernesto was up to. If she didn't understand what was going on, she would be in a weaker place to do anything about it. As her father himself had always told her: knowledge is power; but the secret was knowing how to use it.

"...and this inscription is...is the greatest find...the greatest find in recent years. It will put Guatemala back on the archaeological map. Together with the mask, we finally have an idea as to why the Maya disappeared. The mystery is finally over...The details are...incredible..."

There was something stilted about the way he was saying everything, as if he were reading. Vee knew that something was amiss. This was not the excited voice of her father that she knew - the one that had animatedly read her bedtime stories or even, when she was old enough to understand, eagerly recounted the events of the latest archaeology conference that he had attended. He sounded distracted, uncomfortable, not passionate and enthusiastic like he would normally have been about something as significant as this.

"It....it...." Daniel's voice faltered, petering out to a silence that was broken only by the hum of the insect world around them that was entirely unconcerned with the human drama unfolding within the confines of the hut.

The silence from within the hut became too heavy for Vee to bear. Just as she edged ever so slightly towards the sand-worn doorway, the rough voice of Ernesto rumbled out into the already stifling heat of the day.

"Do not play games, Daniel." The gravelly voice was level and severe - full of confidence and power. "You know we have your children...." The sentence hung in the humid air like the noose of a hangman's rope.

What is he talking about? Verity's mind began racing. *I'm here, he doesn't have me. He's lying to Dad.* The thoughts, although empowering, changed nothing about the situation. *He's lying to make Dad say these things! What is this all about?*

"Again," the voice of Ernesto commanded. "This time, no stopping. This time, you sound convincing."

The message had clearly impacted on her father as this time, when he began to speak – using exactly the same words, she noted - there was more conviction behind them. He sounded more like Dad. But when she listened closely, there was a waver in it, an underlying hesitancy that once she heard, she couldn't ignore. Dad was lying. But to what end? Was anything real about the site, the dig, the temple, or was it all half-truths and misdirection?

18

Ethan

There would have been a time, and a very recent time at that, that Ethan would have wanted to rush out from the camp and search out his father. Indeed, it was what he had wanted to do only that very morning – to run out of the dig site, grabbing only a few belongings, and charge to his father's rescue. He wanted to be a knight in shining armour, but instead of a maiden in distress, it was his otherwise strong and able father who needed saving. He couldn't quite understand how his father, someone for whom Ethan had so much respect, and someone whom Ethan thought was in so many ways perfect, could be both prisoner and powerless, victim and helpless.

On the other hand, there was his sister – out there, somewhere, doing her best to right the wrongs of this injustice. *She* was the knight in shining armour.

But what was Ethan in all this? Some kind of passive bystander, sitting around playing chess?

Rather than fleeing the camp, though, in the hope of successfully liberating his father, putting it to the bad guys and leaving them tied up for the police to find, Ethan thought about what his sister would do now.

And that was something he never would have considered before Guatemala.

It's amazing what the heat does to your thinking...

It was now around lunchtime and, given that there was only so much chess that Ethan could handle, he was at a loss for what to do.

Looking about, he laid eyes on the policeman who now seemed to be guarding the boys. As he looked into the dark eyes of the guard, and those dark eyes looked back, Ethan felt uncomfortable. He broke the gaze, quickly glancing down at the man's gun in his holster, and turned back to Leo.

"Why do we need a guard? Don't they trust us?"

Leo raised his right eyebrow, as he often did, and replied, "I don't think he's here to stop us, but to protect us. You know, Ernesto and his men."

"Doesn't feel that way, though."

Ethan turned his head further away from the onlooking policeman and continued to speak in a hushed voice. "Are we just going to stay here all day?"

"I guess so, Ethan."

"It just feels wrong. Like we should be trying to get Dad back."

"Leave it to the police. They help us. Maybe we go see the inscription?" Leo suggested, trying to take Ethan's mind off the situation. "We can see what all fusses is about. I guess all TV news will be about here sooner or later. They might even try to start End of the World theme park, no?"

"Yeah, people love that kind of stuff. *I* love that kind of stuff. You could have an awesome action movie made here about the end of the world. Imagine running about these ruins with guns and shooting and all that!"

"I no need to imagine, Ethan. We saw it!"

Ethan sighed. "I suppose we did. I guess I'm not such a fan when it's my own dad getting pistol-whipped."

Ethan returned to what he had been doing, which was drawing in his notebook, doodling aimlessly,

111

connecting triangles to semi-circles, squiggles to straight lines, and colouring in alternative segments pencil-grey.

After whiling away a good fifteen minutes, he looked up and caught Leo's attention, taking him away from the football magazine he was reading.

"Leo," he whispered. "I've got an idea."

19

Verity

Verity had sat, crouched, unmoving, for what felt like hours as she listened to her father talk about the rewriting of history that would occur as a result of the finds at the Maya temple. Truths that she recognised – the size, location and layout of the temple – were blended seamlessly with statements that seemed at odds with Dad's normal approach to his work: evidence, double-checked, led the way, not wild stories and fantasies.

"The inscriptions," Daniel continued, "speak of an ancient curse that laid waste to the Mayan population. A curse that will be revisited on the world, according to our calculations, in less than two years!"

Verity's eyes narrowed and she raised her eyebrows. Although the voice was clearly her father, what it was saying was much more like the nonsense that came out of her brother's mouth.

"As fantastical as this sounds, we have a number of reasons to believe this. After having completed a variety of surveys, including the latest innovations that geophysics have to offer, we have discovered the largest mass graves that Mesoamerica has ever seen. Primarily however, we have seen the effects of the curse first-hand."

Verity's mind was whirling. First-hand experience? That video? The flashing lights! That must be it. The guard who had been rendered unconscious, it was because of the curse?

Before she had time to think about the ramifications of what Dad was claiming, she became aware of a deep mechanical thrum that had joined the staccato clicks and incessant buzz that was the endless insectile soundtrack of the Guatemalan jungle.

A four-wheel drive was approaching. She couldn't stay where she was: the occupants would see her immediately. In now well-practised movements, Vee swiftly tiptoed away from the doorway, hugging the rough wooden slats of the hut. She hadn't done this much sneaking around, she thought, since the marathon games of hide and seek she and Ethan used to play with Mum all those years ago. The thought stopped her in her tracks. The consequences of losing this "game", however, quickly got her moving again.

A dirty jeep with an equally filthy trailer pulled into the yard. A thought began to coalesce in Verity's mind, a memory, an inkling, but dissipated like smoke before it was able to take form, as a pair of boots emerged from the vehicle. The driver placed his hands on his back and pushed his chest forward, clearly enjoying being out of the restrictive cab. He removed his brown aviators and his officer's cap, and mopped his brow with a handkerchief. He straightened his blue uniform and looked around him.

Verity almost leapt from her cover. He was a policeman! She could tell him everything and this whole ordeal would soon be over. Before she could, there was sudden movement and noise from her father's jail cell.

"Ah Gustavo!" a deep voice erupted, "I expected you sooner." Ernesto emerged into the daylight.

The man strode immediately towards him, to the hut in which Daniel was sequestered and behind which Verity

114

was currently hiding. She watched as Ernesto clapped a hand onto Gustavo's back, shook his hand vigorously, and astonishingly led him straight to Daniel. Verity's head dropped. There was no hope to be had here. This police officer was clearly somehow involved in whatever was going on and if he was, who else could be trusted? Fear sparked through her veins once more, though she was unsure who she was more afraid for, her father or herself.

"You have the artefact?" Ernesto questioned the new arrival, gesticulating to the trailer attached to the jeep. "We have the video."

Although the conversation in the hut continued, it washed over Verity unheard. The artefact. It was here. Questions and possibilities raced through Verity's mind. The object that her father was claiming to have wiped out a civilisation and represented a threat to humanity was being carted round like nothing more than an old vase or box of manuscripts? What were they going to do with it? Was it really all that they claimed it to be? She had to see it for herself.

With a confidence that had previously been reserved for maths, science and, in fact, most academic subjects, Verity skirted the camp in short bursts of speed and stealth that would have astounded her PE teacher. Finding herself now positioned roughly fifty metres behind the jeep, Vee surveyed her surroundings and considered her next move. Ernesto had not bothered to park the vehicle, leaving it in the centre of the work yard. Fortunately, the trailer and jeep stood directly between her and the hut where the four men were; there was no other cover, but it was enough.

Abandoning stealth, Verity sped across the open yard, her eyes fixed firmly on the back wheels of the jeep, her feet somehow managing to skirt around or simply leap over the pits and tracks in the hard-packed earth. She twisted her body and her back pushed hard up against the mud-covered tyre of the back of the trailer, her feet in line so that even her legs would be invisible to anyone approaching from the front. Her heart slammed inside her chest, her breathing was ragged and sweat began to drip from her brow, but a smile spread across her face.

The trailer was about two metres long and one metre wide. It had two bars that rose from the sides that seemed to provide either a rack to carry additional goods or longer items than the trailer could hold or a tent-pole type construction over which a tarp could be spread; perhaps it was both. As Vee took in the details, her suspicions were confirmed: a canvas cover was loosely secured on the first of the two bars. Vee peered over the sides and saw a single crate, held in place with a network of ropes. The image of a deadly spider sitting at the centre of its web crawled into her mind and wouldn't leave. Vee's curiosity defeated any misgivings her fertile imagination provided, and, in one smooth motion, she swung herself up, over and into the trailer.

The crate at the centre of criss-crossing ropes was made from plain, sandy-coloured slats of wood. The gaps between the planks should have been enough to allow light through, giving Vee a chance to see the artefact within, but when she put her eyes to the cracks there was nothing but darkness: a black so deep it could have hidden anything. Vee drew away and inspected the lid of the box, as much with her hands as with her eyes. Her fingers tested the edges, searching for a latch or release that would grant her vision of what lay hidden within. Nothing. She felt small dots of cold metal at each corner: nails. Vee let out a deep breath, resting her forehead against the crate in frustration. She had come so close! No, she wouldn't give up. Her fingers worried at a nail; it was not firmly embedded. The lid would, at some point, need to be removed after all. First one, then another, she managed to tease the nails out of the wood. She squeezed her fingers into a gap and began to force the top away from the rest of the box. She managed to grip the whole of the lid and pulled with as much effort as she dared use.

Bang! Vee almost toppled backwards as the lid finally broke free. Panic flooded her body. She hadn't made that noise; it was the slamming of a door!

Flight or fight, flock or freeze. The animal inside her weighed up its chances. If she ran, she would be seen. Although the trailer had provided her cover before, a metre of movement to one side and a glance across would be all it would take for any of the men to spot her and she could not outrun a full-grown man. Fighting was equally as impossible. Without even a chance for conscious thought, her body froze.

"Thank you for your...co-operation," Ernesto's voice rang out, a sinister pleasure within its tone. "They will love this at El Instituto Guatemalteco de Arqueología." The sound of footsteps seemed to crescendo as they approached Vee's hiding place. The ice flowing through her veins, holding her locked in place, melted as quickly as it had taken hold. Vee placed the lid back onto the crate, pushing the nails back in as hard as she could, feeling the metal bite into her fingertips. With her tracks as covered as she could manage, she slipped around the crate, moving to the front of the trailer. With surprisingly calm, unwavering hands, she grabbed the folds of the grease-flecked canvas that she had noticed previously. With a twisting motion, she curled herself up, wrapping the thick material around her like a protective cocoon. Despite the thick folds around her, Vee clearly heard the click of a door handle and then felt the gentle rocking as Ernesto settled himself into the cab, followed by the harsh vibrations of a car door slamming.

Seemingly inches from her head, an engine coughed into life. The metal beneath her vibrated in sympathetic rhythm to the drumming of the motor. Once more she was on the move. Where would she end up this time? Would her camouflage keep her safe? These questions, amongst hundreds of others, ricocheted achingly around her mind as her body too was thrown around painfully while the trailer was pulled inevitably forward to its next destination.

20

Ethan

Getting away from the policeman on guard had been somewhat easier and less exciting than Ethan had been anticipating. They had, over the space of an hour, collected water bottles and a little food, storing it in their rucksacks. And then, at the right time (and the right time being when the policeman went to relieve himself), they snuck out of the field laboratory and into the forest.

It was that easy. Wait for a toilet break and hey presto, away and into the woods.

Storms were definitely not far off in the early afternoon sky. There was a humidity in the air, a heavy moisture that made for a sticky discomfort. The sky overhead, through the breaks in the canopy, was leaden and looked as thick as the atmosphere felt: bulging sacks of grey rumbling but not yet shedding.

The ground was still dry and crunchy, sticks and leaf litter snapping and crackling underfoot. Leo was following Ethan, who knew roughly where he was going, in terms of getting to the main site, but exactly where the inscription was situated was, as of yet, an unknown.

Suddenly, Ethan and Leo were assaulted. Not by anyone pursuing them, but by the raucous sound of the jungle; by guttural and quite frightening noises coming from all around them. If the boys were alive in this same jungle some hundreds of millions of years previously, in the era of dinosaurs, then, they could imagine, *this* is what the forest would have sounded like. There was nothing that Ethan had ever heard that sounded more like the resonating and rough throatiness of dinosaurs (as he imagined them) than what he was now hearing.

It was here, there and everywhere, but at the same time, nowhere. Ethan could not pinpoint where exactly the sounds were coming from.

"Howler monkeys," said Leo confidently. "They must have moved, because I didn't think we had many near the site."

"I've heard them in the distance since we've been here, but nothing like this. They must be warning each other we are here, or something. That is one crazy bunch of sound."

Ethan looked above, into the canopy overhead. There! There was one! A black monkey jumped from one branch to another, moving to where it joined the trunk. It turned and looked towards Ethan and pursed its large mouth into a gaping tunnel of noise.

"BWWOOOOAAAAARRR...BWW...BWWW...BWWW OOOOOOOAAAAAARRRRR!"

Ethan flinched at the deep scream that bridged the gap between low-flying jet and menacing tyrannosaur. Into his line of sight, all of a sudden, monkeys jumped and soared, branches bent and whipped, leaves rustled and shook. The forest was alive, truly alive, and the noise was tremendous.

Ethan couldn't help but stand motionless – part scared, part dumbstruck in wonder - a foreign onlooker into this strange otherworld of mammalian sound. Distant cousins they may have been, but these primates felt thoroughly alien to his all too human ears.

"Come, Ethan, we go. It's raining soon."

Ethan snapped his attention away from the theatre playing out in front of him and moved off up the incline in the forest.

After five more minutes of tramping, the two boys reached a ridge that overlooked the pyramid from the side. Panting, they took a minute to take in the brooding view. Framed by the darkening skies, the pyramid seemed to take on a persona of its own, staunch in its stubborn rejection of the oncoming storm. Its grey bricks more sombre under the foreboding clouds, blocking the sunlight that would normally glance off their sides. There would be nothing nature could throw at this building now that it hadn't already endured over the centuries.

Nature's strength, though, doesn't just lie in her power to beat and pound, to buffet and assault with her tempestuous ways. No, nature's power is not in her battles, but in her wars. And those wars are fought on the ground and her armies consist of seeds: seeds sprout and saplings shoot forth roots. Roots take hold, slowly sucking in the moisture that the storms supply, and they expand. Expansion of living matter eventually overcomes even the most solid of rocks as the tiniest splinter becomes a crack and the crack becomes a crevice. The rock splits in twain, and so falls the foundation of even the most solid of manmade buildings.

Nature is only momentarily kept at bay by one of her most ingenious of creations – mankind. But where mankind plays truant, nature reasserts her will, and there is nothing that can stop her. Because everything is nature. Even, strangely enough, mankind.

Ethan stood there, transfixed. How long would this great edifice hold back the forces of flora and fauna? Would this monument of human endeavour be simply a speck of sand in the desert of time? Would Ethan's own life be even more fleeting? Or would he leave a legacy on this world for others to find? Would he, in some way, live on past the memories of those who knew him, or of those who would come to know his legacy, or would his existence pass with those fleeting memories? Were those sacrifices bled into the stonework of the pyramid by long-dead Maya all in vain? Were those Maya now looking down from somewhere on Ethan as he considered their own existences?

Maybe those Maya were now somehow the howler monkeys, or the trees, beetles or bats. Ethan wondered whether he would ever know the answers to these questions, or whether they would elude him like a leaf in the wind, never finding a place to settle, eternally swirling through time and space.

Down below, several archaeologists tinkered and cleaned, dug and scraped, revitalising the memories, the existence, of these long-forgotten people.

21

Verity

Verity was aching, sunburned, thirsty and increasingly anxious. She had spent what seemed like days hidden in the back of the jeep trailer as it swept along through the jungle on the meandering rivers of hard-packed earth.

To alleviate the boredom, and with no immediate fear of being caught, she had extricated herself from the folds of the tarp and pushed it down to create a makeshift seat, onto which she slumped to watch the magnificent Guatemalan countryside flow by.

For years Verity had wanted to join her father on his expeditions to foreign, exotic lands and when he had suggested that they join him on a trip to South America, she could not believe her luck. Verity being Verity, she immediately began reading everything she could about Guatemala: its customs, its history, its people and its rich flora and fauna. Now, with pride, she recognised the colossal, towering, spiked trunks of kapok trees, so thick that they would put the columns at the Parthenon to shame. Acres of naturally growing avocado trees moved steadily past: an ocean of green broken only by the vibrant yellows of Dickinson's lady's slipper and the eye-catching whiteness of summer coralroot orchids.

Once she was unravelled from the musty tarp, the smells of the jungle were also striking. The peaty smell of warm, wet earth was one she was familiar with by now but it was one she welcomed after too long under the sheet. For a while, they travelled beside an azure-blue river which, upon reaching a cluster of rocks, became a frothing, foamy white. The spray was carried by the wind and Verity felt it fleck her skin like thousands of miniscule raindrops.

After several hours, however, the beauty of this untouched landscape was marred by her discomfort; the sun was relentless and with no water left, the heat was taking its toll. For a while she had sought shelter from the burning rays under the thick canvas of the tarpaulin but the material served only to magnify the stifling temperature and suffocating claustrophobia had threatened to overcome her.

Now she lay as comfortably as she could, her head covered by the tarp – she remembered Dad's lectures about avoiding sunstroke by at least wearing a wide-brimmed hat (not cool, but safe). She had dozed fitfully but a dull ache along her spine and a pain behind her eyes were doing their best to keep her from any meaningful rest.

Verity's head jolted forward as the jeep slowed abruptly and unexpectedly. The braying of a clearly irritated donkey filled the air, quickly joined by irate voices spitting angry Spanish at each other. Whatever the hubbub was, it provided her with opportunity to hide herself away once more, though this time she ensured that there was enough of a gap for her to see what was happening.

As the jeep edged forward, Verity caught a glimpse of scattered baskets and cases, spilling an assortment of fruit and vegetables on the roadside. A large wooden wheel too lay on the grass verge beside which stood an assortment of angry people, a distressed donkey and a one-wheeled cart to whom the other wheel presumably belonged. Young children began to appear from ramshackle housing further along the road. A crowd was beginning to form. Wherever she was, Verity was re-joining "civilization".

The noise of the kerfuffle dimmed as the jeep moved forward, quickly gaining speed. Verity braced herself for another barrage of knocks and scrapes, but it did not come; the trailer's tires ran smoothly along whatever surface was beneath them.

Through her tiny window onto the new world around her, Verity could see that the epic trunks of ancient trees had been replaced by spindly man-made wooden poles, the lush canopies exchanged for a tangle of wires that ran from shaft to shaft – power and telephone connections.

As the jeep slowed once again, and the din of its engine fell away, Verity experienced an entirely new soundscape. Though she could not understand the words, she recognised the calls of street vendors peddling their wares, the squawk of fowl and the lowing of cattle, the drumming of hundreds of feet. Was this a marketplace?

The air was redolent with a complexity of smells. Dust swirled endlessly in and around the trailer, so much so that she could not suppress several bouts of coughing. There was enough of a racket around her that she was not concerned about alerting anyone to her presence. In and amongst the dust, however, were tantalizing wafts of Guatemalan incense (Verity knew that Pom and Copal were both traditional scents but was not familiar enough with either of them to tell them apart). The tang of bizarre citrus fruits – *was it rambutan or mamey?* again, she couldn't be sure - cut through the dusty air, making her salivate at the thought of fresh fruits. Her stomach rumbled at the reminder of how long ago she last ate.

The jeep made a series of short, sharp turns and remained at a steady, low speed. This, decided Verity, must mean that they were closing in on their destination. She had another decision to make: try to remain hidden in the trailer and hope that she wasn't discovered, or hop out now and follow the vehicle to wherever it was headed – Ernesto had mentioned El Instituto Guatemalteco de Arqueología, surely that was to be the final stop of this journey. Both had significant risks but she was tired of reacting to things that happened to her; Verity wanted to take some control. Her decision made, she manoeuvred herself to the rear of the trailer and crouched, like a predatory cat ready to strike. She spotted a junction ahead where traffic was thick and the jeep would have to slow to a crawl. This was it. A large, colourful bus was slowly navigating its way across the T-junction and the jeep braked, pulling in behind it.

22

Ethan

It was a clandestine operation that required careful consideration. No one could know that they were there or it would be further internment in the camp, prisoners to the policeman who was supposed to be looking after them both. The boys had crept down the ridge and moved behind the pyramid, passing the opening out of which they had escaped previously. Moving up the hillside so that they were following the rise of the pyramid, the boys circumnavigated the building to arrive on its other side.

"The inscription must be in one of the ruins on this side, where we just saw some archaeologists," reasoned Ethan.

"Do you know? Is it for sure there?"

"Well, it's an educated guess." *Oh no, I'm sounding like Vee.* "I can't wait to see it. A *curse*! That's totally awesome."

"Is the end of the world awesome, too?" Leo quipped.

Ethan let out a grin. "Good point, Leo, good point."

"Eh, eh, shhhhh!" Leo, just ahead of Ethan and fighting through some of the undergrowth with a decent stick he'd picked up along the way, waved his hand in warning.

They both peered out from behind some undergrowth next to a large tree. From the bottom of the pyramid there was a wide and flat area that helped form the road away from the site (that the children had wearily walked along the previous evening). For the first time, Ethan got a proper sense of the surroundings.

"Look," he whispered, and pointed down the flat channel, "that must have been a main road through this city. The pyramid is at one end, and the other buildings must be scattered amongst the trees and in the forest either side, following the road. They've just not been cleared, yet."

"Yes, that is right. My *papa* told me that they have at least twelve buildings that they know about."

"I'm thinking the inscription is over there, by those people."

There were two archaeologists on their haunches, packing up some tools, some thirty metres in front of them, to the side of the jeep track that ran down the middle of the old Maya central thoroughfare.

"That's Pedro and Nina. Best no talk to them. We must be secret," said Leo. The pair ducked back behind the tree when the two adults had finished putting their tools in boxes and stuck them under a makeshift shelter. The two then sauntered towards where the boys were, walking by to cross in front of the pyramid. They both looked up at the ancient building as if still deeply impressed by its striking features. Engaged, they stopped a while and chatted, pointing at features and discussing them animatedly. This might well be the single greatest highlight of their working lives, and they were not about to waste the time they could spend with these ruins involved in idle chat about football or weather or shopping. Conversations, it appeared to the children, always seemed to revolve around the city and the secrets it was begrudgingly giving over.

Everything else paled into insignificance.

The same could be said for the two boys, who were hellbent on nothing else but to see the inscription that was causing such a fuss, with all its claims about the end of the world, and its supposed verification of the curse that was to have ended the Maya civilisation.

After the archaeologists had left the scene, either for the day or for an extended break back at camp, the boys looked around to make sure they were alone. There was a team inside the pyramid, they were sure, as one of the archaeologists had waved at someone above them some minutes before.

Luckily, the inscriptions were not inside the temple but placed outside, *like*, thought Ethan, *a warning to all those who might want to enter and disturb the dormant curse*. The boys scampered over to where the adults had been toiling away.

The location that they had been working at was what seemed to be an old building of sorts (crested with foliage, walls covered in assorted greenery) with a couple of impressively large stone monuments outside. These two big, grey, stone slabs stood up and stretched tall, imposing themselves above the boys as if guarding the entrance to the building. They reminded Ethan of the stones that built up Stonehenge back in England.

The boys took immediate interest in the one to the right that seemed to have garnered a lot more attention; it was cleaner, as if it had been worked on with scrapers and brushes and whatever other tools that the archaeologists had been using. The sides were worn, worked on over time by rain and nature. All the way down the inner part of the front of the stone stelae were inscriptions – tiny pictures carved into the stone – organised into quadrants. The style of the miniature carvings that adorned the stone guardian were curved in nature, depicting what looked to the untrained eye like writhing beasts here and there, heads similar to the jade mask, hands and arms, symbols and shapes... Occasionally, within shapes, Ethan noticed what looked like eyes so that the shapes took on new identities the closer he inspected them. There was not a single sharp, angular line, everything being curved or soft cornered, oval or circular.

It was nothing like he had ever seen, especially since Ethan was not one for poring over monuments or artefacts in museums. But this held his attention in a way that other artefacts had never before done. Well, nothing except for the jade mask which had a habit of appearing, unbidden in both his waking thoughts and his dreams. Occasionally, he could not help but imagine the cruel ivory barbs growing from within him – a deadly disease that corrupted and then burst from its host. He shook his head. Perhaps it was the context: the danger, his father kidnapped, the jungle, the foreign country and climate. Everything in his field of vision was so utterly foreign that he probably could have inspected a tree trunk and been captivated. Maybe allowing himself to be captivated gave him temporary release from the reality of being separated from those he loved and relied on.

The problem with looking at a monument full of such inscriptions is that, even though the words were little pictures in essence, it was still a foreign language. Ethan had absolutely no idea what any of it meant. *A dragony head thing looks at a circle on top of an oval with two teeth whilst a big hand holds a stone-thing.*

He might as well have been reading Ancient Greek for all the sense he could gather from it.

This made for something of an anticlimax. The excitement and attention he had initially given the monument dissipated into confusion; ideas of conspiracy and the end of the known world being proven by this monument were quickly quashed.

"I have no idea what any of this means. Why couldn't they have written this in English?" asked Ethan jokingly.

"Or Spanish... It's pretty cool though, eh? Look at these pictures. It's like these Maya are talking to us now. They are coming alive again."

"Unfortunately, I'm kind of deaf to them. They're speaking but I'm just hearing gibberish."

"It's why my father learns all this stuff. He is learning the language of history so he can talk across time," said Leo, fingers gently following the curves of the inscriptions.

"Wow, Leo. Deep. Reminds me of what my dad said on the plane here: history tells us where we came from. Science tells us where we are going. Politics tells us how we get there. Not sure what it means, but it sounds pretty cool."

"Well, if this says we are going to have a, what do you call it, a 'doomsday' next year, then history, science and politics will all be silent, no?"

Ethan started feeling the stone carvings himself and felt his eyes close. Though their written meanings were impossible to unravel, the smooth stone glyphs beneath him still spoke to him. He recognised the curve of snake, its forked tongue protruding malevolently. His fingers read on finding rows of skulls and then, to his discomfort, the raised barbs of curved teeth. He opened his eyes and eyes of sorrow, pain and despair stared back at him. The same eyes as the mask. With sudden revulsion, Ethan took a step back.

"Hmmm. Do you think it's real? This whole prophecy thing? I mean, this gives me the creeps but the last one in 2012 didn't amount to anything."

Leo gave an ambivalent expression with his upturned mouth. "I dunno. The last one was not correct. The inscriptions no really say that, it was all... what's the word?"

"Hype?"

"Maybe, yes. All people making money out of these things. Making movies, writing books, interviews, news. Always, people make money out of anything and everything. But the people here are good people. My *papa* is good man, Your *papa*. All working with Ed Cruzar to find truth about Maya. This is science. This is history."

Ethan dropped his hand as he thought about his father. "Well, they're not all good. There's Ernesto."

"*Manzana podrida...*"

"Eh?"

"You know, apple. No good apple," Leo tried to explain.

"Yup. He's one bad, rotten, decaying, stinking apple all right."

Ethan turned to survey his surroundings in more detail. There was so much here yet to be properly uncovered. Where people had evidently cut away at the undergrowth to reveal and flatten the central thoroughfare, there was open access and viewing. But to the sides, things were wilder. And where stone buildings and monuments poked their heads and bodies out, the forest sought to contain them, to muffle them, to hide them. It was as if the forest didn't want people to discover this lost city. It was its secret that it was reluctant to give up.

The flat ground that spread out from the base of the hill upon which nestled the pyramid was mottled with the greys and greens of humanity and nature. Ethan's eyes sucked it all in.

132

"This place will be awesome when they get it cleared up and open to the public," said Ethan, in awe of everything around him.

"Yes, it reminds me of Tikal. That's a famous Maya city with the Temple of Ah Cacao, which means big jaguar. And then there is the famous pyramid there. This will be just as amazing, I'm sure."

Ethan's imagination overlaid his surroundings with what he supposed the city would have looked like in its heyday. A bustling place full of people and life developed in his mind's eye, an ancient city full of vitality and culture.

"Come on, Ethan, let's take a look." Leo brought him quickly back to reality.

The two boys wandered off amongst the ruins of the lost city, climbing walls and stones, jumping over fallen logs and rocks, having a sword fight here, navigating boiling lava there. For a moment, all of Ethan's worries were forgotten and he was able to be a child again. Freedom of imaginative thought and action led the two boys the length and breadth of the ancient city.

However, thoughts of his father were never far away, and his child's play was eventually curtailed by these returning feelings of danger and worry. The boys had a camp to get back to, and a father to save.

And then it all ended with a bang. Or, more accurately, a shout.

"*Dios mío*! Leo, Ethan! *Qué estás haciendo*?"

Leo's father had found them. Reality beckoned.

23

Verity

As the jeep braked sharply to avoid the juddering bus, the sudden shift in tempo took Verity by surprise and almost knocked her off balance. But, with her decision made, she swung herself over the rear of the trailer. Even though the jeep had seemed to be travelling at walking speed, she had to literally hit the ground running to avoid a rough tumble to the dusty road. She ran, crouching along behind the trailer until both the jeep and the bus had passed through the T-junction, at which point she smoothly joined the flow of pedestrian traffic on the bustling pavement.

Verity's immediate concern was keeping track of and pace with the jeep. Although she had been uncomfortable in the trailer, she now realised it had provided her with relative safety - trying to jog along through the streams of busy Guatemalans, she suddenly realised how precarious her situation was. She had no idea where she was and little clue as to where the jeep was going – she could get lost very easily. With no money, no phone, no one that knew where she was, getting lost would be disastrous. She was immediately reminded of when she had once been separated from her family back at home in England.

***

One bank holiday, the twins had been taken to a theme park on the outskirts of London. Though some of the rides had interested her, the exotic animals in the small but charming zoo, with its well-designed habitats - tiny bubbles of lands from far away - had captured her attention in a way that *The Cork-screw* and *Spinning Death* never could.

They had eaten their picnic lunch and Mum, always the one to enforce the boring but sensible rules, insisted that they wait at least half an hour before going on another stomach-churning rollercoaster – much to Ethan's disgust. And so it was that they found themselves surrounded by the thick, virescent vegetation of *The Tropical Dome* – an enthralling, mysterious swathe of rainforest seemingly teleported from the other side of the globe, kept alive only by the science of the glass construction and the maze of pipework that issued forth a continuous warm mist that formed droplets on Mum's glasses. This was Verity's first, but, she now reflected, far from her last experience of humid jungle.

Before even seeing any of the animals, Verity had felt a sense of love in her surroundings. Indeed, even back then, she had understood the moral quandary that zoos represented. They had once been places where children and adults alike would gawk at pitiful creatures locked in squalid cages for the visitors' viewing pleasure. Over many decades, zoos had become far more concerned with conservation and breeding programmes – respecting animals and their precarious position in such a ruthless, human-centred world. From the care and attention given to every enclosure, Verity could tell that this place had clearly been designed with the animals' interests at heart.

Within minutes of entering that alien biome – as it had been those years ago - Verity had been absorbed by the other-worldliness of her surroundings and the creatures that shared them. With a bravery forged by her insatiable curiosity, she let get of her mother's hand and was swept away by the sights around her. Was that a crocodile? No, it was too small. *Caiman crocodilus* – the sign read. Ah, a caiman: a South American relative of the crocodile. She watched it with awe as it undulated through the water – a living dinosaur! Over a warped, wooden bridge, whose handrails were hidden under a tenebrous mass of thick, twisting vines, the caiman's lake became home to a multitude of animals from floating terrapins with their stripy green skin and red ears to a small herd (was that the collective noun?) of capybara – the dog-sized rodents – of which some were relaxing in the shallows of the lake whilst others were flopped down on the banks of this shared watering hole. A number of much smaller capybara were tripping over themselves as they played together further up the grassy slopes. A number of larger, adult animals stood either side of the preoccupied infants: their parents, Verity presumed.

Parents!

With that singular thought, Verity had been returned to the real world. Where were Mum and Dad? Where was Ethan? Where was *she*? The strange and splendid world around her quickly forgotten, she scanned the now vast-seeming jungle environment. The unusual sights and sounds which had enticed her away now appeared to mock her as she fought to remain calm. The proud and protective capybara parents were now reminders to her of what she was: a child needing that very same protection. *I'll find them. They'll find me.* She kept the thought firmly lodged in her head as she began to push through a tide of people that up until then, she had barely noticed.

She rushed back over the bridge; the gnarled planks wanted her to trip and the vines either side reached towards her, snagging at her jumper. Although this was very much in her imagination, thin fibres of anxiety began snaking their way through her. She could feel them tighten around her heart, her lungs. *I'll find them. They'll find me.* The conviction behind those thoughts was beginning to drain. The roots of fear were taking hold, and with them, a sense of panic blossomed.

Looking back now, Verity couldn't help but smile: a little embarrassed at the state she had been in after having been separated from her parents for only, what, five minutes at most? She remembered colliding with a pair of legs, flinching as a hand reached down and touched her shoulder before she realised that she knew those legs and had felt the touch of that hand a thousand times or more in the past. Her mum had sunk to her knees and given her the kind of hug only a mum can, uttering soothing words that Verity couldn't remember but whose meaning was still remarkably clear: I've got you. You are safe. I won't let anything hurt you.

The smile that had crept over Verity's face at the memory faded quickly. Her mother would never again be there to protect her, to shield her, to save her. And her Dad? Well, he was counting on her to be there for him!

As she continued to maintain pace with the truck, Verity marvelled at how her life had shifted: years on from that event, she had escaped from a very real rainforest full of very real dangers, but it was here, surrounded by people, cars, shops, civilisation, that she felt those same tendrils of fear take hold. It was her time to be the rescuer, not the rescued. She needed to be strong.

***

If she had had the breath to, Verity would have sighed with relief as the steady to-ing and fro-ing of not only cars, trucks and larger vehicles but the seemingly oblivious pedestrians – who casually stepped into the way of oncoming traffic – ensured that the jeep couldn't move much faster than jogging pace. The blare of angry horns did little to persuade the citizens that the road belonged to the four-wheeled creatures, not the two-legged variety.

Just as her legs raced onwards, so too did Verity's mind. Ernesto had the artefact and a video of David Hume claiming it to be a powerful, mystical object that was somehow responsible for the collapse of an entire civilisation. Both the item and the video were now being transported, as she remembered Ernesto saying, to El Instituto Guatemalteco de Arqueología. But to what end? What was Ernesto hoping to achieve? The answer, Verity supposed, was money. Perhaps, she thought to herself, she would find out soon as the jeep had slowed to a stop, indicated to the left and made very slow progress first across the left-hand lane of traffic and then even slower through the never-ending river of criss-crossing walkers.

Verity looked at the building that the truck was heading towards. The building was adjoined by a plain car park of sorts which, she presumed, was where the truck would stop. Although the compound (for it was no simple car park, surrounded as it was by a chain-link fence topped with barbed wire) was unimpressive, though vaguely menacing, the building itself was grand and ornate.

A flight of at least twenty stone steps rose from the pavement. The steps were worn and weather-beaten but clean and cared for; the building was old but was clearly maintained well. The front of the building itself was an orangey terracotta colour accented with gleaming white, smooth stone which bordered the windows and doorways. Four impressive columns, made from the same shining white stone, stood at the top of the steps. Verity watched as people walked between them, leaving the blazing sun behind and entering the cool, deep shadow of the building's foyer.

Although the architecture was very different, the building had an air, an atmosphere that demanded respect; it reminded her of museums and embassies she had seen in London. This comparison was strengthened when Verity saw the deeply engraved lettering that made it clear to whoever looked, that the building was old and important.

El Instituto Guatemalteco de Arqueología

Verity, and the precious cargo nestled in the back of the trailer had reached their destination.

24

Ethan

Being told off in such a severe way by several adults is never pleasant. It's particularly disconcerting when most of it is done in a foreign language. The boys had been shouted at by Alejandro (Leo's father) as well as Cruzar. The latter had been particularly irate, saying that the two children had risked their lives with the dangerous Ernesto at large, that there was no knowing what the unpredictable man could and would do.

Scolded, the pair were sitting dejectedly at the mess tables in the middle of the camp, where they had previously been playing chess. They had been made to feel pretty small. And for what? For walking to the lost city and having a look at some ancient ruins. What were they supposed to do? Simply sit for days in the same place whilst the police looked for Ethan's father?

It was early evening and Alejandro came to join his son and Ethan before the evening meal.

"I'm sorry for shouting earlier, boys. You had us so worried. We are doing everything we can to find your father. The police are helping and they have sent people to search all around here. Ed will not let you come to harm, but you need to help us, too. You need to stay here, where it is safe."

"Why would Ernesto want to get *us*? Why would he even want to hurt my dad? What use could he get from doing that? He's just an archaeologist. Nobody has a go at archaeologists!" Ethan could feel the anger rising, tightening his throat and causing his teeth to grind together as he spoke.

"I just don't know. I am guessing he wants ransom as he might see Daniel as a British citizen who the government will pay good money to get back. I wouldn't worry, if anything happens to your father, then Ernesto has no way of getting money. I am surprised that this has happened in Guatemala; this kind of thing can happen in other South American countries, but rarely Guatemala," Alejandra explained, and he put a hand on Ethan's shoulder in reassurance.

"Well, I think it sucks. This all sucks. This country sucks. This stupid city sucks. The Maya suck. Howler monkeys suck. Ernesto sucks. The pyramid sucks! THIS CAMP SUCKS!" Ethan's rage morphed into anguish and inner turmoil. Nothing inside him could hold back the tsunami of emotion that swept out, accompanied by an inundation of tears. Leo moved round the table and sat next to him, giving him a friendly hug whilst his father patted Ethan on the back in concern.

After what seemed an age, Ethan managed to calm himself down. Soon, no one in the camp was looking at him in anxious alarm. The three took on their evening meal in the darkness that had quickly enfolded the campsite.

Collecting their meals from the camp kitchen (a table set up with gas cooking stoves topped with pots and pans of steaming food), they returned to their seats with plates full of *pepian* vegetable stew served with rice and tortillas. Contrary to Ethan's predictions, it tasted good. The main dish was followed by some rambutan fruit with its red, leathery skin covered in soft green spines. It really was a very alien fruit to Ethan's eyes. He wondered whether a cherry or an apple would look so alien to a Guatemalan. He decided not. Rambutans were *definitely* weird fruits. Objectively and without doubt *weird*.

He had certainly tried more fruit here than he ever had before – fresh mangoes, papaya, and something the locals called *jocote*. This was the outcome of a boy who normally ate sweets by the bucket-load having no access to any sweets whatsoever, and still needing to eat. Ethan was in danger of leaving Guatemala a little healthier than when he arrived.

Although, as it stood, Ethan wasn't sure that he would get to leave at all.

25

Verity

Verity stood in the mighty shadow of the home of Guatemalan archaeology, considering her options. As well as needing time to plan her next move, the shade the building provided was a welcome relief from the afternoon sunshine. As she stood there, a man holding an expensive looking briefcase knocked into her as he walked past. He turned and, with a concerned look on his face, began to talk to her in rapid Guatemalan. Verity had known full-well that she was not fluent in the language but her lack of understanding and reluctance to open her mouth and even try to communicate was a startling disappointment. She shrugged wordlessly at the man and gave him a thumbs up. He looked uncertain about her response but, clearly in a hurry, smiled at her and continued on his way.

Minutes ago, the barriers to the compound attached to the museum had opened, allowing the truck and its precious cargo to enter before promptly being closed by two stern-looking security guards. The truck had pulled up next to a large door that looked to Verity like it must roll up into the building. This, she had assumed, must be where the large artefacts were brought into and taken out of the institute.

Verity had visited just one of the many institutes of archaeology back in London with her father. It had been an exciting mix of museum, library, college and research centre. She had been thrilled that, as well as being able to enjoy the museum part of the building (which had been full of intriguing objects from all over the United Kingdom's chequered past), she had been allowed to watch students and historical researchers – like her father – at work in a section that was strictly off limits to members of the public.

Assuming that this institute worked in a similar way, and having watched a number of people and small groups enter and exit the building, Verity began to pull together a plan.

This building and the relic that it now contained were Verity's only link to her father and her brother, wherever they were now. And, like a struggling swimmer hugging a life-ring, she was desperate not to lose this lifeline to her family. Wherever she was going to go, she would always try and get back to the institute. In fact, she thought, perhaps this could form her base of operations for however long she was going to be in this town.

The thought of getting help, of talking to the police rose in her mind. But with her faith in trusted adults shaken by Ernesto's betrayal, Verity felt like the only person she knew she could trust was herself. Her experience of just moments ago had also beaten down her confidence in trying to tell anyone what was going on. She was, for the time being at least, on her own.

Getting into the institute became Verity's primary objective; one, she soon realised, that shouldn't be too tough. She observed the building from across the street for a while after the truck had disappeared.

Watching the security gate and the patrolling men guarding it helped Verity to confirm her initial suspicions: getting in that way was going to be too risky. The glass doors of the main entrance, however, were continually opening and closing, welcoming and disgorging plenty of individuals but also, more usefully, no shortage of families. She was right: members of the public could certainly go in. Her only problem was that the museum was probably not free and her pockets were empty of quetzales or even centavos (the Guatemalan equivalent of her native pounds and pence). Verity however, had a plan – she'd seen it done on the TV. She wouldn't need money; all she needed was confidence. This sort of confidence was not something that she was used to having. Verity was firmly out of her comfort zone.

She waited for a lull in the traffic before scurrying across the road. She brushed herself off, took a deep breath and began climbing the stone steps. *I am meant to be here. I am with my family.* Verity kept the thought firmly in her mind as she reached the top and stepped between the intimidating stone columns. She stole a glance of her reflection in the glass doors before they automatically swooshed open to allow her entrance: not looking too shabby, especially considering all that she had been through and just how long she'd been wearing the same clothes!

She stepped into the foyer, feeling the cool breeze of the air-conditioning on her sweat-beaded forehead. A smile was plastered on her face: *I am meant to be here. I am with my family. I am happy!* She added emotion to the tourist character she was now playing (acting was not her forte and she had never volunteered for any school plays, preferring to do the lighting if she had to be involved). Verity took one nonchalant look around the entrance hall, ignored the large desk that stood directly in front of her and half-ran towards the turnstile that marked the entrance to the museum. Predictably, one of the assistants on the desk called out to her before she made it through.

"*Discúlpeme señorita.*" The middle-aged man was not angry but clearly was not just about to let Verity through. Verity looked quickly at the man but turned her gaze back to the museum, pretending to search the visitors for someone in particular.

"Dad!" Verity called out, waving to a man laden with bags, holding hands with a toddler. "Wait for me!"

The father turned to look at her, obviously curious as to what the shouting was about. He saw Verity waving, and, as she had hoped, waved back albeit with a slightly bemused expression. Verity pushed at the turnstile as if expecting it to just open. She turned to look at the assistant and gestured with her head towards the waving man.

"My dad: he has already paid. He bought a family ticket. He told me to just come through and meet him and Tim," she reeled off as quickly and confidently as she could. She didn't know if the assistant could understand her or not, but in some ways, it didn't matter to her. *I am meant to be here. I am with my family.* The assistant looked at her for what seemed like an eternity, placed his hand under the desk and a light turned green on the turnstile. She waved a brief thanks to the assistant before rushing straight over and then past the father and toddler. She did not look back. Children who were meant to be there, children who were with their families, did not look back.

As the adrenaline, the hormone that for millions of years had asked the survival question of fight-or-flight, began to leave her system, Verity began to feel another age-old biological demand: the need for food. Before solving that though, she thought to herself, she needed to find somewhere that would allow her access in and out of this building at whatever time she needed. *Has to be on the ground floor,* her logical brain was back in control over the lizard brain that was clamouring for food.

In other circumstances, Verity would have been fascinated by the history that unfolded around her. Hundreds of Maya artefacts filled shelves and cabinets, all adding their own voice to the chorus that sang of an ancient civilisation as full of life and all its wonders as that in which she lived now. In her current situation, however, she was deaf to the song that echoed wordlessly throughout the museum. Verity wandered around the halls, surveying the windows – the most sensible and obvious way that she may find a sneaky way in and out. She very quickly realised that she was too high up – *makes sense*, she thought, *had to climb up those steps to get in!* Her next job, therefore, was to find her way downstairs.

She quickly made her way to a pair of lifts. When the doors hummed smoothly open, she stepped in and pushed the button marked PB. She had no idea what it stood for but it was to the left of the button with a number "1" on it so she assumed that would be one floor lower. The lift did not move. The button was not illuminated. She pressed again and the noticed that, on the LCD display, the words "*Ingrese clave*" flashed twice before disappearing. Verity's Spanish was not great but she thought the word *clave* meant *key*. A key or password or something was needed to get to the ground floor: it wasn't going to be quite as simple as Verity had hoped.

A different call of nature began to sound louder to Verity and she began to follow the signs to the toilets. She reached the top of a flight of stairs and smiled. At the bottom was a small hall-space with three doorways, two potted plants and two benches separated by a metal bin. Two of the doorways clearly led to toilets: the universal symbols of a male and female stick figures stood unmistakeably on the wooden doors. The other was marked with the word "*Privado*"; it didn't take a gifted linguist to guess that this

147

might mean *private*. The handle on that door was accompanied by a metal panel about fifteen centimetres high on which eight buttons, in two rows of four, sat: another password required. First things first though – Verity pushed on the wooden door onto which the stick figure in a dress was emblazoned – thank goodness for the unspoken language of symbols.

The door swung easily and silently on its hinges, allowing Verity access to what was clearly one of the older sections of the museum. Although the room was clean and bright, the two sinks were set into a wooden counter that had seen better days. In places, paint was peeling off in large, green flakes and the whole surface was bowed as if the weight of the porcelain sinks over goodness-knew how many years of service was beginning to be too much. Verity looked around – the stall doors and walls were in very much the same state, as were the window casements and sashes; at least everything matched, Verity thought with a smile. Her smile widened as she peeked out of the open window: it looked out into a narrow alley-way that, by the appearance of the mountains of cardboard and dunes of street detritus, wasn't used particularly often. Not only that, but the window was set low enough in the wall that even an eleven-year-old could haul herself up and through should she wish. This was no time to rely on theory, though. Verity pushed the window up as high as it could go and hoisted herself up onto and then out of the bathroom window. She delicately dropped herself feet first onto the alley-way ground. Even were the sounds of her exit not muffled by the carpet of ruined boxes, the noises of the roads and all of their users were as oppressive as the baking heat: she would not be heard.

Verity looked side-to-side, checking that she wasn't being watched. When she was satisfied that she was unobserved, she gripped the window ledge and pulled herself up, her feet scrabbling at the terracotta brickwork for any purchase they might find. Verity realised with sudden dread that she had not even considered the possibility of somebody else entering the bathroom, nor of being watched by the unblinking eye of a CCTV camera. *Too late for that,* she thought as she heaved herself through the open window back into the cool, tiled room. With her feet back on the floor, Verity once again took stock of the room she was in. Nobody else was in there and the walls and ceiling were free from any kind of surveillance devices: Thank heavens!

Verity brushed herself off and a smile crept onto her face: she had found her way in and out. Now Verity tackled the question of how she would ensure that this "entrance" was always going to be available to her. Luckily there was no modern lock on the aged wooden frame. The only way to secure the window was a simple metal catch that bent easily when Verity applied a little pressure. She bent the catch first up and then down, weakening the metal until it finally sheared in two. Somebody could come in and fix the window, she supposed, but judging from the general state of the bathroom, it was unlikely. Verity closed the window: the less need there was for someone to go anywhere near it, the higher the chance there was for it to be left in its broken state.

Verity left the bathroom and took a seat on one of the two benches. Hunger gnawed at her but she had one final task to accomplish before heading off to find some food. She positioned herself so that she could easily see the private door and, more importantly, the security panel next to it. She had to wait only a few minutes before a woman carrying a box full of paper and folders – it was so much like the kind of mess her dad used to bring home it made her blink – approached the door. So as not to have to put the box down, the lady simply shifted her weight against the cardboard so that the box was wedged between her and the wall. She clumsily entered the key code of the panel, with one hand steadying her cargo. Verity was able to see clearly the buttons she pressed: A-2-B-3. Not the hardest code to crack nor to remember. This, Verity reasoned, was mostly likely why such a simple code had been selected. The woman pulled open the door and before it swung shut behind her, it revealed a corridor lined with various office spaces – somewhere in there would surely be a more comfortable place than the street where Verity could sleep for the night. As the lady had only just gone through, Verity decided that she would leave it till later to find a suitable place to hunker down for the night; for now, she was hungry and she had a town to explore.

26

Ethan

Mosquitos buzzed with sonic irritation around Ethan's ears. There was something distinctly annoying about that sound, as Ethan had discovered since arriving in Guatemala. He had never really experienced mosquitos much back in his home country, but here, you couldn't ignore them.

After the early evening meal, and the remonstration from the adults, Leo and Ethan had played a few games of cards, though there was little by way of fun that the pair could extract from the time spent. Ethan dealt the last hand and the two played in almost silence.

He kept being washed over by waves of nausea and anguish, thinking he might never see his father again. And this then sparked torrents of bitter-sweet memories, like when his parents had taken them to Alton Towers, the popular theme park, a few summers ago. Verity had refused to go on any of the rides for fear of her life. Ethan had wanted to go on them all, naturally. But the most pleasing aspect of the experience was gloating to his sister about how utterly amazing the rides were, the rides that she did not go on. But he especially cherished the memories of those rides he did with his dad, as Mum and Verity looked up from below.

Of course, this then spurred on memories of his mum, who had then just been diagnosed with her aggressive cancer.

It was all almost too much.

Death. Why did people have to die? Ethan had done a lot of thinking after the death of his mother and had talked things through with Verity. One thing they often dwelled upon was the idea that, if they were to create a universe, it wouldn't have pain and death. There would be no need. Everyone would be happy and live forever. It would be an eternal sort of heaven, they considered. In the discussions, *he* had suggested that the pain and suffering people felt could be useful for some reason, that perhaps it served a purpose. He spent much time thinking what the purpose could be. It made him feel so much better to think that his mother's death wasn't in vain, didn't just happen for no reason. *Ah, but Ethan, it's dangerous to believe things just because they feel good,* he remembered Vee saying. But it took the pain away, the pain of his loss, to think she was somewhere now, somewhere happy and fulfilling, and that her passing away meant something. What was wrong with thinking that, no matter whether it was ultimately true or not?

"Goodnight, Ethan. I'm tired. I go to bed," said Leo, breaking the silence that had developed, unnoticed. He stood up, touched Ethan on the arm compassionately, and took his plates to wash them up, before retreating to his tent.

Ethan sat there, staring into the middle distance for a while longer, before realising that being anxious and depressed was somehow just as tiring as playing several football matches, as if his brain had been chronically exercised, non-stop, for over a day now, sapping all of his energy into some happiness black hole.

152

He trudged back to his tent in the vague hope that a night's sleep would give him the energy to take on the next day with some kind of renewed vigour.

Around him, the forest chirruped and rustled with neither happiness, nor sadness, and certainly oblivious to Ethan's emotional torment.

In the nearby undergrowth, an ocelot pounced on a pocket mouse, with the mouse serving as a much-needed meal for the hungry wild cat.

27

Verity

Verity once again let herself down into the grimy alleyway. She didn't want to be seen going through the main entrance alone again: questions might be asked. She ensured that her body language spoke of confidence and familiarity when she turned out of the gloom and onto one of the main thoroughfares. She had a brief look around to mark firmly in her head where she needed to return to, before heading off in search of food.

In order to find her way back, Verity decided that she would use obvious landmarks, the first of which was a grand archway – unmissable due to its vibrant yellow hue. During her pursuit of the jeep and trailer, Verity had had little chance to appreciate the town in which she had found herself. Now, strolling along, following nothing but her own whim, she was struck by the colour and the energy of the place. She marvelled at the archway with its neat white trim as she passed beneath, but the smaller buildings, the shops and houses, were equally as remarkable. She passed a row of buildings on her right, each one a different colour, shades of red, blue, yellow and orange. Verity was of course accustomed to and oddly comforted by the solemn, stoic architecture of British towns and cities. These buildings, though, projected a joy, a vigour that perhaps came alongside or was bolstered by the reliably beautiful weather that Guatemala enjoyed.

The sun was noticeably lower and an orange glow began to fill the sky. The heat that earlier in the day had been oppressive was now a pleasant warmth on her back as she wondered the streets. The late afternoon sunshine seemed to make the colourful paintwork on the buildings glow, making the vibrant facades even more resplendent. The people on the street, as if in response to the welcoming rays of the sun, had also taken on a more leisurely air. She saw couples and families heading in the same direction – towards an open square that was filled with covered stalls. The walls of the courtyard were dotted with small cafes and bars, some little more than collections of tables outside of tiny, open kitchens.

As Verity approached the square, she was hit by a barrage of sounds and smells, the latter of which made her suddenly salivate. The aroma of charcoal grills and cooking meat was unmistakeable but other scents were much more mysterious. An odd clapping sound echoed around the marketplace, adding a percussive beat to the music of countless conversations. Upon nearing one of the food stalls, the origin of the claps became apparent; two women were sat on short stools behind a large flat stove-top. The women were taking small balls of white dough and flattening them out in their hands. They swapped the dough from one hand to the other, their hands meeting very briefly – each time this swap occurred, the dough became thinner and thinner. Verity watched fascinated as one of the women carefully ensured the roundness of the dough by patting its edges and then continued to "clap" it from one hand to the other. When satisfied with the shape, she placed what Verity now realised was an uncooked tortilla onto the hot iron of the griddle. It took only a minute before the baker skilfully but effortlessly used a pair of wooden sticks to lightly flip the tortilla in order to cook the other side. The skill with which this operation was completed was highlighted by the fluency, for as soon as the tortilla was flipped into a woven basket, the process immediately began again.

Although Verity could have watched this process for hours, spellbound by the rapidity of movement and delicious fragrance of freshly cooked bread, it was not going to quieten the growl of her hungry stomach. She plunged her hands into her pocket and began to walk further into the market. A frown creased her brow as her fingers reminded her of the emptiness of her pockets, a tricky obstacle that may ensure the continued emptiness of her tummy. With no money, this was not going to be a typical trip to the shops.

Verity turned a corner and was almost knocked off her feet as a small crowd of children of about her age ran happily across the walkway. She watched them go, flowing around the oncoming foot-traffic, splitting into twos and threes, squeezing between stalls, tables, chairs – anything and everything in their way - before fluidly reconverging into one continually shifting whole once again. There was something compelling about not only the group's movement, its freedom within such a confined, busy space, but with the children's seeming indifference to the world around them.

As Verity followed their progress she saw three of the children colliding with a man serving plates of steaming grilled meat to a middle-aged couple who were sat at a flimsy looking table. Unsurprisingly, the food, the table, and the couple all went flying. What was surprising to Verity, however, was the fact that this collision had occurred at all. Up until then the children had navigated the pathways with a carefree fluidity that spoke of childhood confidence and assumed invincibility – how did they end up in this mess? The answer became apparent as Verity shifted her focus to the children who had avoided the incident. With everyone's attention on the food and people spilled over the marketplace floor, something else was taking place. Whilst the harassed-looking server – who, judging from his hat and grease-stained apron, also appeared to be the chef – shouted and gestured angrily at the now sheepish-looking trio of children, the remainder of the gang were carefully removing skewers laden with more of the delicious smelling meat (likely to be chicken – the most common of Guatemalan meat, Verity's mind automatically reasoned) from a charcoal barbeque. A distraction! *That's* what this was all about. Upon understanding the shenanigans that were occurring, Verity's initial response was to shout a warning, but before she could, as if the children knew that the ruse was about to be unravelled, they bolted. The children with the meat and the trio who were still being admonished by the large, red-faced proprietor ran. Without looking back, the youthful band of thieves disappeared into the crowd, the howls of outrage coming from the chef unheard or simply ignored.

Verity, like the "restaurant" owner, was angered by the casual theft that had taken place; that was, until she remembered that this was the very act she was here to perform. Her anger was immediately replaced with guilt. She hadn't even stolen any food yet, but the wrongness of what she was going to do suddenly hit her. An invisible struggle began in her brain: stealing was definitely wrong but would any moral person let a child starve? She remembered a question her father had posed to her before: would she steal to feed her own family if they were going to die? At the time, Verity had answered yes without hesitation. Now, faced with the reality of the situation, she realised the grip that the notions of right and wrong had on her. Going against her own moral compass already weighed heavy on her, though it was a weight she was going to have to bear if she wanted food. Well, she thought, if she was going to break her own code of conduct as well as the law, at least she knew how to do it now.

Verity resisted an inexplicable urge to follow the troublesome mob of children with whom she now felt some sort of connection – they were, after all, here with the same objective. Instead, she ambled along the pathway, taking in the scene around her. The small street food vendors were interspersed with fresh goods stalls. Verity recognised some of the myriad fruits on one stall but so many were a mystery. One stall in particular seemed very popular; the queue of customers almost blocked the flow of pedestrian traffic. Satisfied patrons were leaving the stall with tubs of fresh fruit but also ice creams and milkshakes. When she got closer, Verity recognised the odd-looking *mamey sapote* fruit – they'd had plenty back at camp. Its skin was like the fuzz of a peach but rougher and brown and the flesh beneath (the only bit that is eaten) was a vibrant salmon pink. Verity watched the workers on the stall as they cut the fruit in half and cut out the large seed – much like the process of preparing an avocado. The flesh had a delicious creamy texture and a sweet taste – perfect, she realised, for making into ice cream or milkshake. The thought of cooling, sweet ice cream was almost more than she could bear. She dragged herself away from the stand. Ice cream would be delicious but not enough to sustain her; plus, there was no way she'd be able to sneak away a tub.

Whilst it was her logic and reasoning that tore her away from the *mamey sapote* stand, it was Verity's nose that led her to her target. In amongst the tangled mix of foreign scents, the aroma of freshly baked bread was immediately familiar to her and she quickly located the source. Open baskets of baked goods were stacked high on several wooden tables behind which a man and a woman, powdered all over with flour, were efficiently moving around trays of a variety of bread rolls, loaves and pastries. One of the bakers would stop periodically to serve a customer, but other than that, their focus was on their baking. It shouldn't be too difficult, Verity considered, to snatch a roll or two.

Although she had reconciled herself to the fact that she was going to steal, Verity felt incapable of causing more distress (to herself as much as anyone else) by creating some sort of scene in the style of the earlier ruckus. Instead, she decided to wait in the hopes that something, anything, would happen that would give her an opportunity to take something, anything, without anyone noticing.

Luckily, Verity did not need to wait long. As the man replaced an empty basked with one full of worm-shaped *gusano* – a sweet bread that Verity had enjoyed for a number of breakfasts – the baskets below gave way, spilling a variety of breads over the table and floor. The female baker immediately turned to help her partner clear up the mess, a look of irritation on her face. The man, however, gesticulated worriedly behind the tables and the two of them returned quickly to the large ovens, presumably to avoid ruining their latest batch in addition to what was now scattered across the floor. She realised that she would not have long, so Verity seized the moment to grab two large rolls from the table and then a delicious looking pastry with jam oozing from one end. In the style of the pack of children, she immediately strode away, refusing to look back, quickly melting into the stream of shoppers. Once enclosed on all sides by the ever-moving throng of customers, she felt a wave of relief wash over her. She was now just one amongst many – the anonymity seemed to enable her to shrug off her guilt for the moment at least. She took a bite of one of the seed-covered rolls – it was warm, soft, and the seeds on top added a nutty flavour. It may have had something to do with the fact she hadn't eaten for a long time, but she decided it was one of the best things she had ever eaten.

Absentmindedly, Verity meandered through the market square, periodically tearing off chunks of bread and popping them in her mouth. She couldn't seem to concentrate on any one thing, she was too tired, so, like her legs, she let her mind wander. Before she knew it, she had arrived back at the entrance. With no desire to compromise her ideals any more than she already had, she decided to head back to her temporary home.

Verity used the walk back to the museum to reflect on the previous twenty-four hours. Only this morning, she had been with her father before being inadvertently whisked here, wherever here was. In thinking through the day's events, she felt her stomach tighten, not through fear or desperation but regret. At the time, each thing she had done had felt right, felt necessary, but the gravity of her actions, like a black hole of morality, was inescapable. She was doing what she needed to get by and yet the reality was that she had broken the law – and not just once. She had gained entrance to the museum without paying, vandalised property, stolen food, and was about to break and enter back into the museum. Had someone predicted that she would commit any of these crimes, she would have been horrified, but in one day, she had committed them all.

She remembered a few people claiming back at home that immigrants came to England and broke the laws. That notion had never sat right with her. Just because these people were new to the country did not mean that the basic principles of morality were new to them. Rights and wrongs, laws and morality, had never been as real as they were to her now. These ideas that used to seem so black and white, were now a much murkier grey. Her stomach, previously satisfyingly full, now felt like it was full of hot lead. Verity's eyes were glued to the pavement, her brow furrowed, as she passed under the archway, its jaunty yellow paintwork now hidden in the dusk.

***

Finding her way back to the institute was not too much of a challenge for Verity and she arrived back with no trouble. Upon nearing the museum, though, Verity's curiosity was piqued. The flow of traffic on the streets had died away with the sunlight but the compound of the museum was busier than ever. The rolling door to the museum, beside which the truck had stopped when it had first arrived, was now open and on the concrete docking bay there was a podium. A line of trucks, all sprouting antennae and various domes and dishes, circled the podium. In between the vehicles and platform, a crowd of people milled around. Boom mics swayed and camera lenses flashed in the harsh white of spotlights that flooded the area from the corners of the yard. Surely, this was no coincidence: it had to have something to do with the newly arrived treasure.

Verity was barely aware of the few cars that sped by as she crossed the road to join a growing crowd of onlookers that had gathered outside the security gates. The gates were now manned by four guards who, though they did not look belligerent, made it clear from their body language alone that this was a private event and that nobody was going to be admitted to whatever was happening. Although they were not allowed in, the crowd were definitely being encouraged to remain where they were. Large television

161

screens had been set up facing the street – they currently showed a live stream of the empty podium but a timer in the corner was counting down. Whatever was going to happen would begin in less than five minutes.

Verity stopped watching the clock in the corner of the screen and peered through the chain-link fence trying to get a clearer picture of what was actually happening – the empty podium was providing neither riveting viewing nor any enlightening information. She was jostled around by the impatient crowd as more people swelled its ranks, which made focusing on anything tricky. This, combined with the morass of television vans, generators and technicians, made it impossible for Verity to glimpse anything that gave her any further clue as to what was soon to take place.

A flurry of movement on the huge displays caught her attention. Two men were positioning a set of lights at the base of a table to the side of the podium, which Verity had failed to notice. Something was set atop the table but was hidden under a black cloth. If Verity's suspicions were correct, she had seen what was hidden underneath before.

Suddenly her breath caught in her throat as she watched Ernesto stride onto the stage. She had not seen or thought much about him since he had been her inadvertent driver this morning. What he had been doing, she had no idea, but he had clearly had enough time to make himself look more presentable – his tribal chest tattoo was hidden beneath a khaki shirt and safari vest; surprisingly, rather than being hidden under his dusty hat, his hair was slicked back and the large knife that had been strapped to his thigh was nowhere to be seen. A bulge under each side of his vest was the only thing that suggested to Verity that he had not removed *all* of his weaponry. Though he was dressed more formally, an air of menace still hung around him. The technicians finished with their lighting rig and looked towards Ernesto for approval before scurrying around him and off stage.

Verity watched Ernesto on screen as he surveyed the pack of reporters before him. He angrily gesticulated at the screen; Verity shuddered as if he was communicating directly to her. Two of the vans shook as their engines came to life. As they drove carefully to the back of the compound, the crowd on the streets were given full view of the concrete docking bay and the podium, which now stood in a pool of light. Verity watched as cameras swivelled to pan across the crowd; lights too were turned, illuminating the street on which she stood. Verity felt suddenly vulnerable. She could now see Ernesto in the flesh, standing strong and firm on the platform, his arms crossed and his jaw set. He seemed to be staring right at her.

Verity pushed herself back through the forest of legs. Although the smell of kicked-up dust and sweat soon became overwhelming, Verity was once again enveloped by the safety of anonymity. Even were he to suspect her presence (which he had no reason to, Verity assured herself) there was no way that Ernesto would be able to spot her in this throng.

Once she had her fear under control, she shuffled, pushed and finally barged her way towards the front where she could once again see the TV screens. As the timer ran down to zero, the whole screen was taken up with the image of a Maya calendar. Verity identified it immediately as she had been fascinated by the fact that, despite it being developed thousands of miles away and thousands of years ago, the Maya calendar had certain things in common with the modern calendar – in both, for example, there were 365 days in one year. Unlike the Gregorian calendar that was adopted in Europe, which on paper looks like a grid of rectangles, the Maya Calendar was represented with a set of concentric circles, smaller circles set within larger ones. Verity remembered that as well as the year with 365 days, there was a shorter year which lasted 260 days. Oddly, these years ran at the same time, which (even having studied it a while) was very confusing to Verity. She smiled as she remembered Ethan loudly voicing his concern that keeping track of birthdays must have been really tricky.

On the screen, the circles within circles began to spin. A voice began to speak but, unsurprisingly, everything was in Spanish. Thankfully, subtitles sprang up underneath the ever-whirring calendar.

To the Maya, just as it is to us today, the calendar is crucial. Their calendar tracked seasons, the movement of the moon and the time for religious ceremonies. It predicted the best times for battles, marriages and planting crops. It protected them, they believed, from the trickery of the gods and evil-spirits. They believed that once their calendar came to an end, the world died and then was reborn. In one way at least, the Maya were right: their world did indeed come to an end. Something extinguished the bright flames of a flourishing civilization. A new discovery sheds light on what killed the Mayans and, what may in fact threaten the world in which we live.

Verity frowned at the phrasing. Some of the things the voice was saying were verifiable fact; some of it, however, she was not sure about. It all sounded too...dramatic.

The voice stopped and the calendar was replaced with footage from a camera, footage that Verity had seen before. A gloomy tunnel lit up by a torch held by a hand and arm that often flashed past the camera.

Verity's stomach clenched, knowing what was about to happen. The screen filled with a vibrant, blood-red light. The screens pulsed a deep red followed by bottomless darkness. This was the video from the security guard's body-cam. The flashing of the light grew quicker and quicker until it suddenly stopped. The footage was frozen. A probing finger of white light stretched forward through the vastness of the sanguine red light. Captured in the fragile beam, glaring with an inhuman intensity, was the artefact – the "cursed" mask.

Once more, the image on the displays changed abruptly. The podium and the concrete platform filled the screens - only this time the docking bay was lined with people. A sharply-dressed, middle-aged man with a dazzling smile and perfectly styled hair stood behind the rostrum. To his left, a wizened man in a tweed jacket leant on a cane and peered through a pair of spectacles balanced on the end of his nose. Verity decided that if she looked up "professor" in the dictionary, this man's picture would be staring back at her – talk about a walking stereotype! On the other side of the lectern stood Ernesto. He looked grim, imperturbable, but Verity got the sense, from the way he very occasionally shifted his weight, that he felt slightly uncomfortable.

"*Buenas tardes,*" the pristinely turned out man began. *Good evening.* The words popped up on the large screens making Verity wonder if perhaps this was being televised not just in Guatemala but maybe in America too, maybe even worldwide!

"*Se ha hecho un descrubimiento.*"

A discovery has been made. Verity read. The voice of the presenter was, to Verity, simply background noise as she stared at the text as it appeared on screen.

A discovery has been made. A discovery of immense importance. The civilisation of the Maya people spanned many countries and thousands of years. The Maya constructed the first fully developed written language as well

165

*as the monolithic temples and cities of thousands of people –
the skeletons of which are all that we have left today. Why?
Where did they go? What happened to one of the largest
Mesoamerican societies that ever existed?*

In a word, this:

Was there an audible intake of breath or had Verity
imagined it? The presenter gestured to his side, to the table
upon which sat the veiled object. The image on screen grew
larger as the camera zoomed in. The black cloth filled her
vision until it was swiftly and smoothly removed, revealing
the vicious teeth, howling mouth and haunting eyes of the
jade mask.

*This mask can do, and has done, unimaginable
things. It was found alongside one of the largest intact sets
of Mayan writings yet discovered. After the extraordinary
and terrifying event that you have all now witnessed, a
carefully selected team of specialists were flown from around
the world to examine the mask, the writings, and the historic,
mysterious site in which they were found.*

The scene on the televisions smoothly segued from
the menacing mask to the man that Verity had left tied to a
chair, at the mercy of the men behind this murky plot:

Daniel Hume
World-renowned archaeologist and scholar.

His name and title appeared in a banner under his
image, just like on normal news. At that moment, it felt like
someone had their fist around Verity's heart and was
squeezing harder and harder. The pain at having to leave
him, the helplessness of her situation and the anger at
seeing how these people were using her father churned
inside her like roiling magma at the heart of a volcano.
Unlike the unrepentant, unstoppable power of what lies
beneath the earth's crust, Verity knew that she could

control her emotions and, in order to put things right, to survive, she needed to prioritise rational thought over emotional action.

The image of her father had begun to move and speak; the text that accompanied the video was now in Spanish and Verity was able to concentrate on the sound of her dad's voice. Although by the time she was able to concentrate fully, she had missed some, the final words from Daniel stuck with her – they were words that she had heard before.

"It will put Guatemala back on the archaeological map. Together with the mask, we finally have an idea as to why the Maya disappeared."

A stunned silence had fallen over the crowd. Surely people wouldn't just accept the notion that this mask had a powerful, evil magic that could kill hundreds of thousands of people; surely someone in the congregated mass would challenge this notion. But the silence went unbroken. Verity imagined the thoughts growing rampantly like insidious vines throughout the minds of the gathered journalists and attendees: Could its power still be active? Could this mask hurt them? Could it somehow make them money? Could they somehow use it for their own will?

Finally, the stillness of the night was fractured as the presenter took to centre stage. His mellifluous voice seemed to have a magic of its own, warming the air, giving people permission to stir, to breathe again. He began as if he had read Verity's mind:

I am certain that people across the world will have many questions. It is my pleasure to announce that tomorrow, on my show "Buenas Noticias" with me, Vinicio Cerezo, we will have a live special where I will be joined by lead researcher and eminent archaeologist Daniel Hume, who will at least begin to help us understand this ground-

breaking discovery and the power it wields. Be sure to join us here on Canal Dos, the home of world exclusives, tomorrow at 10:00am.

The camera panned over the people on stage as Cerezo shook hands with those lined up on either side of him. He did not spend much time with the elderly gentleman; perhaps, Verity wondered, the professorial figure was little more than stage dressing to give the proceedings the appropriate gravity. When the presenter arrived at Ernesto, he clapped him on the shoulder and whispered in his ear – it was clear who had the real power and authority here.

Nothing more happened on the platform and, as the TV monitors faded to black, so too did the excitement of those gathered on the street outside. Like now-empty clouds after a storm, individuals and small groups drifted away till nothing was left. Only rubbish strewn across the ground gave any indication that mere moments ago the place had been a flurry of activity. Verity was left to ponder the revelations of the brief but dramatic conference. It was clearly only a taste of things to come, meant only to whet the appetite of a now hungry public and, most significantly, ensure that viewing figures for Vinicio and *Channel Two* were at an all-time high. For Verity, most important, however, was the fact that Dad would be here in the morning. Perhaps that would provide her another opportunity to at least speak to him, to sort out all this nonsense and get everything back to normal. This mask may or may not have obliterated an entire civilisation, but to her and her family, it was both a blessing and a curse: an artefact that had ripped her family apart but hopefully, finally, would bring them back together once more.

***

Verity's legs carried her back to the alleyway and she was too weary and absorbed in her own thoughts to even check if anyone was watching her movements. Whether it was because of the excitement and tension of the press conference or just the culmination of all of the events of the day, Verity was exhausted. Where before she had carefully picked her way over the treacherous terrain of discarded cardboard, plastic sheeting and mounds of other detritus, now, in the darkness of the night and with her leaden body, she scuffed, slipped and tripped her way towards the museum window. By the time that she arrived, she was adorned with smears of grime and more than a few fresh bruises painted her shins a painful pink. Verity was simply too tired to care.

Despite her fatigue, when Verity reached up to the window sill, her heart hammered in her chest and sweat slicked her palms. If the window had been fixed, if she didn't have the strength to pull herself up, she would be forced to spend the night in the alleyway and who knows if she would be able to gain entrance to the institute the next morning. The only connection to her father and Ethan would be severed.

With a shake of her head, Verity banished the thoughts from her mind; torturing yourself with thoughts of things that may never occur was a pointless, counterproductive act. Instead, she put her hands against the peeling frame of the window, applied pressure, and pushed upwards. The sound of old metal scraping against metal seemed to fill the entire world, as if the casement itself were letting out a scream, trying to draw attention to the crime being committed.

Verity froze.

She waited. She watched.

A sudden motion and thud drew her attention from further down the alley. Two glittering, opal eyes surveyed her from the darkness before a plaintive meow revealed the owner's identity. Verity released a breath she hadn't even realised she was holding. The shabby cat took one look at Verity before lithely springing through the now open window. *Well, at least I won't be the only one trespassing this evening*, Verity thought with a wry smile before hoisting herself up and through the window.

Verity moved quickly and lightly through the silence of the institute. The cat, whose illegal wanderings had been stymied by the closed toilet door, glided alongside her, almost invisible in the low light. It paused at her feet as Verity input the code on the security panel, and flowed its way round the half-opened door; in her sleepy state, Verity marvelled at cats' ability to become almost liquid.

It was Verity's turn to follow as she found herself in a maze of office space, having carefully closed the door behind her. The cat wove in and out, over and under, various cubicles; some were filled with hi-tech looking equipment whilst others were piled high with papers and books. Verity drifted down the central corridor, watching the cat's progress and all the time keeping an eye out for somewhere to crash out. When the cat did not appear out of one alcove, Verity poked her head around the sides of the partitioning screen. The space was being used as storage: the single bench was piled high with trays of brushes and trowels whilst the floor was awash with sheeting, both plastic and canvas. This would do, as long as she was awake promptly, the thought moved sluggishly through her mind as she flopped onto a pile of rough, hessian material. She used her final scraps of energy to position herself under the table and loosely cover herself with more of the same coarse fabric before her eyes closed and she fell into a deep, dreamless sleep.

28

Ethan

Muffled sounds drifted into earshot.

Ethan's mum gave him a kiss on the cheek.

"Have a good day at school, darling. And don't annoy your sister!"

"Oh, really?" he pleaded.

"No. She's the only one you have. Treasure her." And she smiled at him. That warm, loving smile that lit up her face. Ethan's mum was one of those people who smiled with both her mouth and her eyes, glittering, as they did, with loving happiness.

Crackling and rustling. Foreign voices.

"Anyway, here are your packed lunches. Tell Vee I love her and to have a good day. You need to follow her lead and brush your teeth, too. Now!"

And with that, his mum grabbed her car keys from the kitchen sideboard and strode out to the front door.

"I'm late for work. I'll see you after school. Don't forget it's football practice tonight. Love you. Bye!"

"Bye Mum!" he replied through a mouthful of toast.

Ziiiiiiiiiip.

Ethan leant against the sideboard and thought about the day ahead. *Oh great... double science...* He harrumphed to himself in his head. *Why can't it be P.E.?*

Dad had already left, with Verity and Ethan old enough to make their own way to school (well, if you could include getting a lift with Jason and his mother from up the road in the definition). *Well, I suppose I'd better do my teeth. You win, Mum.* And with that, Ethan thumped upstairs to join his sister, who was already keenly flossing her pristine teeth.

"Hola! Morning Mister sleep!"

Ethan's mind jolted from one dimension to another; visions of his mother quickly disintegrated and were replaced by blurry oranges of early-morning light fighting through tent fabric.

Rubbing sleep from his eyes, Ethan's vision started to better represent reality, with Leo's face poking through the tent door, sporting a friendly smile that brought an involuntary return smile from Ethan.

And then he remembered what was going on in his life and that reality quickly shrouded him in a gloomy mist that forced his smile to ebb away.

"Hey, Leo. Another day for you and me in paradise, I guess."

Ethan had often considered and even researched the meanings of dreams. Verity had scoffed a little but, he had noticed, joined in with his Googling that some people believed dreams to be prophetic – to tell of their futures. Others believe them to be the result of our brains processing our experiences, subconsciously pulling them apart and storing the useful and not-so useful in different memories. Whilst taken with the idea of being able to predict upcoming events, none of his dreams had as of yet come true. This dream could, of course, never become a reality so perhaps it was his subconscious mind trying to cope with the last few days. Although his smile had faded, the ghostly feelings of loss lingered. Ethan closed his eyes and exhaled deeply.

He had lost Mum. Whatever happened, he would not lose Dad and Verity. Without thinking, he clenched his fists and his lips pursed. He may have lost countless games of chess to Leo, but this game was not over, and he was not going to be beaten.

After a brief, invigorating field shower, breakfast of omelette, cheese and plantain slices (they looked a bit like fried banana slices and were pretty tasty) greeted the boys at the centre of the camp. The pair joined Cruzar and Alejandro to eat their fill.

"Morning Ed, Alejandro," said Ethan eying up the two men as he sat down with his plate and cutlery. These men weren't his enemies but they were in the way. He knew they were just looking out for him but a tickling irritation began in his mind – *we are sat here eating a healthy breakfast whilst goodness-only-knows what's going on with Vee and Dad.* Ethan knew that renewed interest in the curse and his dad's kidnapping would result in a stern reminder that he was to stay out of it so he adopted a care-free, cool-as-a-cucumber approach – a logical approach, a *Verity approach.*

The table and breakfast-goers were dappled by morning sunlight as it broke through the canopy overhead. The day was warm and the wet weather from the previous evening had passed, leaving a fresh feeling to the atmosphere around them. The slight breeze on the air helped Ethan's own emotional atmosphere remain cool and fresh too. This calm would end soon, Ethan guessed – surveying the sky – it would turn into a warm humidity that would get them sweating again. The heat was not far away.

"It look like rain has passed. It rained much in night time," Alejandro said in his best English.

"I didn't really hear it. I slept through it," Ethan replied, briefly recollecting the various vivid dreams that had flitted through his sleep. "Actually, I think I remember dreaming about the rain, so maybe I heard it after all. I had lots of dreams last night."

"I bet you did," said Cruzar. "It's not easy for you. However, I am hoping we have good news today. I think we will. The police are working hard."

"Do we have to stay in the camp again? Can't we get out into the ruins?" Ethan asked hopefully.

"Maybe," said Cruzar. "We shall see."

Breakfast passed rather uneventfully, interrupted by small talk about this and that, pyramids and temples, digging and brushing. Ethan knew that he needed to sound casual, almost disinterested but when the conversation turned towards the importance of a few of the artefacts, he took his chance.

"So, Ed, you think this curse thing is real?" Ethan asked; Leo's eyes widened in expectant excitement while Ethan nonchalantly took a final fork-full of omelette.

"Well, it's hard to say. What I can say is that there is a lot of mystery about the Maya, and this is definitely part of the…the…jigsaw. It looks like we have discovered some kind of prophecy on the stone outside the temple. And this is *very* exciting. If you put this together with the jade statue, we have some really exciting news for the world. It will make this place come alive with interest and news stations. Believe me. Guatemala will be on the map."

"It was crazy enough before 2012 with all of those other prophecies," added Alejandro.

"But they were phoney, right?" asked Ethan.

"*Phoney?*"

"Yeah, made up – not real."

"Yes," said Cruzar, looking at Ethan with piercing eyes. "We don't want to have the world make that mistake again. It makes us look like, what is the word… Yes, amateurs. This," and Cruzar gesticulated out towards the forest and the ruins beyond, "this is real. Good archaeology from some of the best in the business. Your father is one of the best, and he has seen it with his own eyes."

"I still don't get what this has to do with Ernesto," said Ethan, brow furrowed, probing the adults to see what connections he could find.

"I am sure it will all become known when the police catch Ernesto. Very soon, I am sure. Then you can be together with him once again." Cruzar smiled comfortingly at the young boy, sitting there in isolation in the middle of the camp – an outsider out of his depth.

Ethan sat for a moment, thinking about his father being this great archaeologist. He knew his dad was good, after all, most children think their parents are great. Ethan remembered his dad talking about his own parents and their flaws and saying that it's only when you become an adult yourself that you see your parents on a level playing field. Ethan returned to thinking highly of his father. Ethan thought the world of his father (of both his parents), but it was all the more pleasing to hear someone else in the field talk so highly of him.

"Is he really that good?"

"Oh yes," said Cruzar, with Alejandro nodding across the table, "that is why we got him from all the way over in England. It is why we allowed you two here, as well. He wouldn't agree to come without you. He is really important to us. The world will pay big attention to what he says."

Ethan couldn't resist his own warm smile. He suddenly had newfound respect and admiration for his father.

"Now, I have work to do. You stay around here today. I will let you go, with someone to look over you, down to the city ruins later. But for now, you stay here." Standing up with his dirty plates, Cruzar walked over to the washing up area.

Alejandro spoke to Leo in hushed tones, Ethan unable to understand anything (other than hearing his name being mentioned on occasion). He waited until the pair had finished and then motioned to his friend towards washing their breakfast plates.

Side by side in domestic boredom, rinsing their plates in as little water as could be spared, the two boys talked about what the morning had in store for them.

"I was hoping someone would know something by now," Ethan stated, mouth downturned with frustration.

"Don't worry, my friend, your father will be fine. I know it. You must have faith," and Leo grinned at Ethan hopefully.

"Faith in what? The police? This jungle? My poor sister, out there? The Mayan gods? All the gods my father has ever worked on in all his ancient digs?"

"Okay, Ethan, I get it. Have hope, then."

Ethan dumped his plate to the side of the communal washing up bowl and trudged back to the tent to get ready for the day ahead, whatever it might bring.

29

Verity

A soft poke to the side of the head roused Verity from her much-needed rest. Without opening her eyes, she could tell that morning had arrived: the Guatemalan sunshine painted the world hidden beneath her eyelids a golden yellow. A poke came again, only this time it was accompanied by a slight scratch. This time, more awake, Verity reacted with alarm and sat upright, her eyes snapping open. Her movement was met with equal alarm and four legs skittered backwards over the hardwood floor. Her partner in crime, the somewhat scruffy cat, eyed her suspiciously then sat down and began to clean its paws, quickly satisfied that she posed no threat. Verity shook her head, half in amusement and half in despair: scared by nothing more than a feral cat. *This is going to be the death of me!* Verity ran her hands through her hair then stretched and yawned.

Now fully awake, Verity took in her surroundings in the early morning light. Her "bedroom" space was cluttered and dirty but not unwelcoming. It was, as she had supposed that night, a storage area for the old-fashioned but still essential gear for any archaeological dig. Perhaps it was these accoutrements that made her feel at home. As she got to her feet, wincing at the all too familiar pain of a night spent in a make-shift bed, she picked up a brush with wide, soft bristles and smiled. She vividly remembered the games that she and Ethan had played with her father in their sandpit as children. Dad would bury items and it was their job to excavate them, not like excitable children at the beach with buckets and spades, but like budding archaeologists with fine brushes and tiny trowels. On one particular Easter, he had hidden hollow chocolate eggs under the sand but with his uncontrolled enthusiasm, Ethan had managed to crush most of them. Memories from a time long since gone, a happier, simpler time.

A glance at her watch told Verity that it was time to get moving: 7:30am – who knew what time the building's staff would arrive, especially with such an important event beginning in a matter of hours.

Although the museum section of the institute would still be shut, she was surely less likely to be discovered there than if she stayed in what could clearly become a busy office environment, Verity reasoned. Under the watchful eye of her feline companion, she tried to remove any trace of her stay – the last thing she needed was anyone on the lookout for anything suspicious.

Once back in the museum, Verity visited the bathroom to try and tidy herself up: a dirty child on her own was certain to raise eyebrows at least. There was little she could do with her somewhat wild hair without giving it a good wash but putting it into a simple plait would make her look much more presentable straight away. Her fingers danced through her tangled locks, completing a routine with a rhythm and grace that came from years of repetition. The morning, which had already provided her with a glimpse of the past, seemed determined to remind her of the life she once lived. She closed her eyes, and, though it was her own hands that continued their work, she could almost feel the soft pressure of her mother's fingers complete the braid she had always requested as a younger child. Without thought, she flicked one of a few worn hair bands from around her wrist (how she had managed to keep them, she wasn't sure) into place, securing the fraying ends of the plait. She could almost hear her mother tutting at the state her hair was in but it was the best she was going to manage.

With the use of handfuls of paper towels, she scrubbed at her face and arms until her skin was pink and rosy, unlike the sink which she had been using, which was now smeared and streaked with drying, muddy rivulets. The white porcelain was now a river delta: on the outer edges, brown tributaries snaked steep, downhill pathways before combining force with brothers and sisters to form broader, meandering rivers of sludge which came to a sluggish end in an opaque marsh at the bottom of the basin. After a few minutes, and plenty more sheets of paper, the landscape of waterways had been wiped clean and the only evidence of her time there was scrunched in a ball at the bottom of a bin.

With little else to do for the moment, Verity began to wander the halls of the museum. For a while at least, she was able to lose herself in the rich history, the thousands of half-told stories that the accumulated ornaments, objects and relics waited to share.

The story of the Maya people, according to a large plaque beside a glass cabinet containing tiny shards of pottery, seemed to begin in earnest at around 2600BC. Verity thought back to her time at the younger end of junior school; while the Maya were developing farming techniques and forming long-term settlements, at least some of the inhabitants of Britain were creating the iconic Stonehenge. Verity took a closer look at the small remains held gently on wooden stands and could just about make out a human shape amongst the earthenware objects, its edges smoothed by thousands of years as well as, most likely, at least a few human hands.

Verity floated from exhibit to exhibit, adrift on the currents of time that moved her through hundreds and then thousands of years of history. She watched as small settlements turned into villages and, after over two thousand years, the first of the incredible Maya cities formed – first El Mirador and then Tikal in the northern highlands of Guatemala. Huge stelae, columns of intricately carved stone covered in the images of long-dead kings and absent gods, guided Verity on her travel through a time in which they had been pivotal, central monuments. Verity learned that it was often from these pillars of rock that historians had gathered much of the information that she now so readily absorbed – the great events of the past, inscribed, conserved forever on these pitted, worn surfaces.

Pausing briefly, Verity thought of Ethan. It was he who had first put the notion of museums being not just a collection of things, but of time itself in her head. Gaining entrance to a museum was like being slipped the keys to a time machine, he had said. She smiled at the pleasure he had taken at running through a motor museum in the south of England. The huge building had been filled with row upon row of cars, all set out in chronological order. More than a few eyebrows were raised as he zoomed up and down the aisles, shouting out dates as he raced past various exhibits. He had lurched to a halt in front of Verity, who was holding the hand of their mother, and, in between gasping breaths, excitedly told them that he had managed to go back over 80 years in less than 30 seconds.

Dad had joined them then, and Ethan, inspired by his own temporal expeditions, had asked him if he thought time travel would ever be possible. Verity watched her father's expression fluctuate as he grinned (he always did when his children's curiosity led to a question of this nature) and began to explain. He had said that if time travellers existed, they would be here, now, amongst them. It did not matter how far in the future, did not matter how many years away it seemed from them, the years were irrelevant. The effect of the creation of a time machine would impact (would have already impacted) across the entirety of time in an instant. His final summation had caused in Ethan an odd mixture of excitement and disappointment – either time travel was possible and there were already people from the future around them or it was impossible. Ethan had waited a moment, lips pursed; his eyes told the story of the furious thinking occurring behind them, and then he rushed off looking this way and that: his search for people from the world of tomorrow had begun.

She remembered furrowing her brow at Ethan's behaviour and his science-fiction questioning, but now she smiled and felt something shift inside her. Goosebumps broke on her skin and she swallowed hard to suppress a wave of emotion that had surfaced with the memory. With Ethan's ideas in her head, Verity decided to continue her own passage through the annals of time that were held carefully within the stone walls of the institute.

Verity learned of the rise of the city of Teotihuacan and its conquering of Tikal under the leadership of the warlord Siyaj K'ak' (or in English, as Ethan would have been thrilled to know, Fire is Born). Recovered murals from the city told the tale of its peak in the 5th century. A recreation of the architecture of the city, dominated by deep reds, jade greens and shining gold astounded Verity in its angular intricacies. Verity felt a strange disappointment upon learning of Teotihuacan's fall, approximately one hundred years after its zenith. She was fascinated that the original theory (which drew a picture of a city beleaguered by invaders who slowly ground the inhabitants down) had been replaced by the idea that the Maya were victims of their own success. The cities grew too big, the populations too vast to feed. Drought, malnutrition and lack of resources were perhaps responsible for the eventual collapse. Verity couldn't help but feel that there was a lesson to be learned. The Maya drained their homes, their soil, their world of value until it could no longer support them – could this be the fate that modern society soon faced. Was this what faced her world, now?

Verity's escape to the past ended abruptly as she entered a circular room whose walls were adorned with stone tablets. Some were covered with hundreds of glyphs whilst others depicted bizarre and other-worldly scenes from the Maya past or perhaps imagination. It was not these slabs, however, that brought her back to the present with a jolt. In the centre of the room, there were two chairs. At the sides, cameras were gazing with lidded eyes as microphones craned over, ready to capture every sound, every word.

Verity had found the place that she hadn't even been looking for. This is where the interview was going to be. This would be where Dad would be. This was the place that she needed to be.

30

Ethan

One of the scientists working at the site was accompanying the boys to the ruins. She was a stern woman by the name of Maria, who had also been invited to work on the dig. She was from a university in Chile and told the boys in faltering English (for Ethan's benefit) what she was doing there as an expert on Mesoamerican cultures. Being slightly overweight, she was puffing a little by the time they all got past the pyramid and to the temple they were looking at the previous day. Sweat ran down her olive-skinned cheeks. She decided to take her thick grey hair out of its ponytail and tie it up even tighter, getting every last strand out of her face.

"I work on these buildings," Maria said, sitting atop a stray boulder near the temple. A few teams were toiling in the growing late morning heat, moving about here and there, or resolutely staying put and intricately going about some very focused work. "My job is to find out what each building is. What it was built for. I have been looking into this temple and what they use each room for." Her accent was thick and Ethan had to concentrate in order to decipher what she was saying.

A cool breeze picked up and ran over Ethan's neck, evaporating his sweat and cooling him a little. Evolution at work. He remembered Verity lecturing him on why humans sweat and how evaporation is a cooling process and how dogs hang their tongues out to cool their hairy bodies and...and...

Ethan realised, at that moment, how often he acted as a captive audience for his sister's lectures. He couldn't quite work out if this meant she would make a really good teacher or a really boring one. He came down on the side of boredom.

A mosquito irritatingly buzzed in Ethan's ear.

"Man, why do these things exist? Their only purpose is to be irritating and to cause pain by drinking our blood!" Ethan exclaimed.

"Some might say the same about you. About us. We just annoy other animals by stealing their land and homes, and then we eat them!" Maria replied with a wry smile.

"Point taken. You sound like my sister. In any case, we don't make irritating buzzing sounds in people's ears," Ethan replied.

"Have you heard the music of young people these days?" She laughed at her own wit.

Leo piped up. "I wonder how cows and goats feel about us milking them!"

"Okay, clever-clogs, you've all got me. I guess I'll just have to let these stupid insects milk me for all my blood. Oh what joy. I'm glad I'm of service to nature."

The three took a look inside the temple, with Maria being guide, getting herself worked up and excited over explaining the work they were doing. She was even pleased to answer the seemingly endless questions about human sacrifice for the Maya and death in the ancient world, about battles and weapons, war and famine.

After about an hour of looking about various buildings, Ethan asked if they could have a break to play for a bit.

"Well, you are children," Maria observed. After agreeing, she set the boundaries of where they could go and how long they had, before getting some books out of her rucksack to do some background reading.

The two boys eventually settled for a game of hide and seek, or Maya and Conquistadors, as they renamed it in an attempt to make it at least partially relevant to where they were.

The heat of the morning sunshine was quickly evaporating the damp remnants of the rain from the earth around them. Scant clouds lazily drifted across the sky in a vain attempt to evade the sun. In the heady heights of the upper atmosphere, there simply was no escaping the sun without the help of the Earth's rotation, and, right now, Guatemala was facing the flaming gas ball some ninety million miles away.

Perhaps it was the sacrifices of those Maya, or Aztecs, or whoever, all those years ago that kept the sun in the sky. Or perhaps it was the laws of physics. Either way, the day was hotting up and Ethan fancied getting out of the way of all those photons of light that had travelled such a distance to fall on this clearing in the Guatemalan forest.

The boys came to an agreement on the rules of the game and Leo was selected to be the first conquistador. Ethan was a hapless local Maya, escaping the Imperial desires of the Spanish soldier.

A few minutes after a rule agreement and safety talk from Maria, in her broken English, Ethan darted off into the forest that bordered the ruins, somewhere across from the temple outside which Maria was sitting and reading. As soon as he was within the shady confines of the treeline, there was a sharp decline down which he scrambled. Rapidly and nimbly, he skipped and jumped over half-rotten logs and small bushes as he darted up an incline that formed a small gulley in between, trickling with last night's rain water.

The ground was damper than the clearing, drying more slowly from the rainfall. Luckily, for the purposes of navigating through the forest, the brush and scrub were not dense on the ground beneath the trees. Instead, it was mainly a dirt covering to the undulating ground. Occasionally, he had to dodge spiky leaved saplings. The palette was one of various greens and browns without too much showing from any other colours. There didn't seem to be much in the way of flowers. Perhaps it was the wrong time of year.

As much as Ethan loved sitting indoors and playing endlessly on his console, he was also very much an outdoors child, revelling in running, chasing, kicking things, throwing things and generally getting dirty.

This was right up his alley.

The more he could run about in this otherworldly place, the more he could forget his worries. His only worry now was to escape the evil conquistador that was Leo.

Before long, Ethan realised he had been running without too much thought as to *where* exactly he was running. It was not as if he was playing a wide game with some thirty other children; he was playing a glorified hide and seek game with one other child. And, on reflection, there was no chance of Leo finding him *this far* into the forest!

Indeed, it was after jumping his twentieth log and scrambling over the third gulley that he realised he was quite possibly a little lost. Of course, he couldn't shout out for help as this would give the game away. A game was a game to Ethan, and he would not lose easily. Preferably at all.

He looked up to try and work out where the sun was. The canopy was quite dense here and he wasn't able to... *Aha! There it is! Oh, hang on, where's it supposed to be? How does this help me?*

It didn't help.

Ethan spun on the spot, panic rising an iota. He opted to climb a little embankment of damp scrub. Pushing broad leaves of verdant shrubs out of the way, he broke out of the dense undergrowth to be met with direct sunlight.

And something he wasn't quite expecting.

Instinctively, Ethan ducked back down behind the nearest shrub. There, in front of him, was the track that led from the ruins to the compound they had returned from the night before. To make matters more intriguing, on the other side of the track, a few dozen metres away, was a truck. It looked like the truck from the compound, muddy and with a large dent in the passenger's door. Leaning on the bars attached to the truck's front was definitely one of the men from the compound, that much Ethan was sure. And talking to him?

The police chief.

This was good, surely. The man from the compound helped kidnap his father, and the police chief was onto him.

The men laughed.

The men laughed. That's not what criminals do when confronted by the law. It's not what the law does when it confronts serious crime by serious criminals.

The police chief then clapped the bearded man on the shoulder. The man spoke a few words and took something out of his pocket.

What was it? Money? Yes, and quite a lot from the looks of things.

He unfurled a number of notes from the wad and handed them to the police chief in a handshake.

Ethan sat behind the large-leafed plant in complete disbelief. He was agog. The police chief in front of him should be unhooking his handcuffs and arresting this man so that he could lead Ethan back to his father. The police chief – smiling from cheek to cheek – pushed the notes into his pocket and said a few more words to the man. So, either the bearded compound man was actually a good guy, or the police chief was a seriously bad guy. There was no other way for Ethan to look at the equation.

"*Pttttuuuurrrgghh!*"

Frivolous nature has, on occasion, a funny way of getting involved in serious human situations.

Two flies were chasing each other around Ethan's face in a game of "Who Can Annoy the Human the Most", and one had the misfortune to pop itself into his mouth. Before he could think about controlling himself, Ethan was spluttering and swatting at his face. With a flailing arm, he knocked the broad leaves of the plant behind which he was hiding.

The world seemed to change speed and enter into a period of slow motion.

In reality, Ethan didn't have long to gather himself as the two men across the track turned in shock, spitting out choice words in Spanish. What he *did* have was a good fifteen metres of head start and the spritely legs of a young boy. Whatever these men were up to, it wasn't good. But everything seemed to take an age as all of these realisations hit Ethan and his body reacted. It was as if a slow-motion action sequence from a Hollywood movie was playing out in real life.

When your heart stops; when the sounds of the forest around you evaporate like a puddle in a hot desert; when your body takes over and leaves the mind to catch up, that's when you know you're in trouble.

Ethan was in trouble.

The last thing he saw before he ducked back behind the cover of the forest were the two men turning to run and the police chief unholstering his pistol.

Ethan was facing quite a spot of bother. There were now a few more conquistadores. Except these ones would show no mercy. And they really *did* have a gun.

31

Verity

Verity's excitement and relief at having stumbled upon an opportunity to at least see her father again was quickly evaporated by the flickering heat of anxiety. This room, although cavernous, would be brimming with adults and (her heart seemed to quicken at the thought) Ernesto would undoubtedly be present. Her brain kicked into gear, quelling the emotions that threatened to engulf both the remains of her hope and her ability to act. Maybe the sheer number of people present would work in her favour, like at the market the previous evening. She pursed her lips and frowned. Last night, people had expected to see children there, but this morning she would stand out as the only child present, and trying to hide would raise suspicions. No. Perhaps trying to stay out of sight was not the answer. A plan began to form in Verity's head; it was risky, it relied on her Spanish, a good portion of luck and more heavily, her confidence. It would also quickly unravel if she was seen by Ernesto.

Although part of her wanted more time to consider her options, Verity knew that the window of opportunity to enact her initial plan was already shrinking. You can't weigh up the pros and cons of two plans if one doesn't even work anymore! It was time to put all her eggs in one basket.

Verity raced across hallways and down corridors, retracing her steps through the museum, travelling backwards through time at a pace that would impress even the most skilled of time-travellers gracing the silver screen. She paused only for a moment back at the private doorway to ensure that she was not being watched. She moved through the central corridor until she reached several cubicles that were set up as small office spaces, rather than the storage type areas in which she had slept the previous night.

With efficiency and focus, Verity began to carefully pick through the first of the workspaces. Most of the drawers were locked and the organisers on the desk were filled with pens, highlighters and other sundry stationery. Her face darkened and her jaw clenched. *Relax,* she told herself, *there are plenty more places to check.* The second cubicle contained less than the first; it was clearly home to a fastidious employee who kept their work environment impeccably tidy. The image of Ethan sitting at this desk appeared in her mind and she suppressed a laugh: the only way he could keep an office this neat would be if he were on holiday, and his office cleaner wasn't.

Verity searched through two more cubicles (one festooned with family photos and pictures clearly drawn by children, the other decorated with newspaper cuttings of archaeological digs) but came up empty-handed. Finally, as the space around her changed into a more open-plan setup, she found what she was looking for. Next to what looked like a sign-in sheet (it was similar to the one at her school that the staff used in case of a fire), in a plastic tub, Verity found a lanyard attached to which was a small plastic card with the words *Pase de visitante.* It was almost exactly the same as the one she and Ethan had been issued upon arrival at the dig-site with Dad – a visitor's pass. She quickly put it around her neck and immediately felt a sense of calm begin to spread through her. She was no longer an intruder, she was an invited guest.

As Verity began to make her way back to the museum, a thought sprang into her head. She doubled back, heading to where she had seen the children's drawings. That office clearly belonged to somebody with a family, a family that (she hoped) other workers in the building would be familiar with, though not too familiar! Upon reaching the small but somehow warming desk, Verity scanned the photos. A smile played at her lips. Quite clearly, holding a dripping ice cream, a girl of similar height and age smiled back at her. *So this is who I am going to be today,* Verity told herself, taking one last look at the photo before gathering a clip-board and some pens, and noting down the name that appeared on the name plate attached to the cubicle wall: Cristina Morales.

The number of ifs and buts in her plan seemed to be expanding, making failure seem more and more likely, but she now had an identity, a reason for her to be in the building and a story to tell anyone who stopped her. Staying out of sight wouldn't be possible, but Ana Lucia Morales, the daughter of Cristina, who was visiting her mum's place of work for the day, could, with confidence and poise, walk the halls of *El Instituto Guatemalteco de Arqueología* without worry.

32

Ethan

He ran quickly and nimbly, jumping bushes and skirting trees. Everything was a blur – greens of tree leaves, browns of tree trunks, fleeting blues of the sky as it broke through the canopy. Ethan's mind was a blur, or it was absent. All there was to Ethan, in those moments, was his body reacting automatically and without thought to the environment around him.

After what seemed like an age but was probably only ten or so seconds, the fleet-footed would-be prey looked back towards his predators. With nothing untoward in sight, he stopped to gather himself and orientate to any landmarks. Except in an unknown forest, there were no landmarks, only trees and dips and troughs and earth and scrub. To his right, he heard heavy footsteps of someone running. He caught sight of the man from the compound a good twenty metres away.

Then, to his left, he heard similar sounds. A shout. He had been spotted.

They must have split up!

There was only one way: forward. There was only one speed: top speed.

Going from nought to sixty in record time, Ethan shot forward, darting between a pair of trees. A branch snagged his T-shirt and leaves slapped his face.

More shouts, but he couldn't tell from which direction. The experience was both terrifying and exciting in some weird sense. If he had had time to think about it, Ethan would have recognised the similarities between this moment and playing capture-the-flag as a wide game on a camping trip he had enjoyed with his school. Verity had been there, too, but had opted to stay back at the camp and help with organising the food for that night. Food duty was a definite preference for her over running around in some woods pretending to be in the army. For Ethan, though, nothing could be more fun and apt. That was him in his element. Swiftly dashing through the trees of the New Forest, in Hampshire, avoiding enemies and helping teammates, he had certainly given himself good training for an eventuality he never would have predicted, in a country he had not even then heard of, running away from people with no idea as to why they were chasing him. The rules were different here, but the game was essentially the same.

Don't. Get. Caught.

Ethan was probably at an advantage over the slower men, encumbered by their clothing and older, more fatigued muscles.

He would certainly have outrun them in a straight line. However, Ethan was not running in a straight line, but in a panicked zig zag of sorts. Intent on making it to a large tree up ahead, set apart on a small mound, he didn't notice the policeman spring out of the undergrowth to his left like a velociraptor: arms reaching in front of him, mouth curled into a snarl. The man's arm clattered against Ethan's side as the Guatemalan man careered to the ground, hat flying from his head. Ethan involuntarily let out a gasp of fright as he was sent sideways and into a bush. Twigs and branches pierced his skin.

From on his knees, the policeman called out in Spanish to the other man, who returned a shout from some distance behind Ethan. Muttering to himself urgently, the policeman was scrabbling about in the damp earth, sweeping leaf litter away with his empty hands.

Empty hands.

He's dropped his gun.

Ethan's eyes skimmed and scanned the forest floor before settling on the black pistol a few metres from those searching hands.

This was his chance.

Using the knotted central branch system of the shrub, Ethan hauled himself up to his feet. With eyes on the prize, he leapt over to the gun to pick it up.

He was a split second too late.

The police captain grasped the gun. Luckily, though, he had managed to pick it up by the barrel; this afforded Ethan a vital second. Without thinking, he swung his right leg in his best imitation of one of his favourite fighting games and kicked the gun out of the man's hands. His bushy eyebrows arched in shock and then narrowed in anger. What must have been swear words escaped from his moustachioed mouth as the gun landed a good few body-lengths away.

It was now or never.

Ethan opted for now.

Turning on a sixpence, and with renewed hope fuelled by opportunity, he ran.

A blur appeared from the right like a charging bear, but Ethan sidestepped back in the direction from which the blur was coming, and the other man couldn't readjust in time; he slipped on the leaf litter, skidded down a small embankment, and crumpled into a writhing heap.

With added vigour, Ethan sprinted off into the forest, hoping that he could find his way back to Leo and the ruins.

33

Verity

With a new confidence, Verity, AKA Ana, swung open the door to the main museum. Immediately, she was confronted with her first trial. A man wearing blue overalls was placing a yellow cone onto the floor outside the toilets. He turned to look at her. She forced a smile to her mouth and she waved brightly. Verity could almost see the micro-expressions of surprise bleeding into curiosity run across his face. She was summoning up the courage to speak the sentence she had been rehearsing since her plan had taken shape – "*Hola. Mi madre trabaja aquí*" – when his eyes narrowed, fixing on the laminated card that swung around her neck. His frown vanished, and he waved, smiling.

"*Buenos días, señorita,*" he said, touching his cap, before turning his back on her, picking up a yellow bucket and mop and climbing the stairs that led to the museum hall. Verity watched him go. Her blood was pumping furiously but she did not allow herself any outward reaction. This was just the first of goodness knew how many times that she was going to be spoken to, perhaps even questioned. She was Ana Lucia Morales and Ana would not sigh with relief at the end of every interaction. On the contrary, she would be confident and carefree. Verity straightened her clothes, brushing off the dust that still clung to her, and sprang up the stairs with a levity that only a child who is missing a whole day at school could possibly enjoy.

On her return to the main halls of the museum, Verity found the place buzzing with activity. Several more cleaning staff were clearly ensuring that the building was as prepared as possible to host the day's upcoming event: polishing the glass cabinets, buffing the hardwood floors, and tutting loudly as technicians lugging their heavy equipment left trails of scratch marks and slightly bashed paintwork. Although many of these adults cast a glance in her direction, she had no interaction further than the occasional "*Buenos dias*" or irritated flick of the hand as she accidentally got in the way. All the while, Verity maintained an inquisitive but confident manner; she waved at people, read some of the placards dotted around the artefacts and made some notes on her clipboard. She had seemingly been accepted into the melee of that morning's busy world.

The next question to consider, now that Verity was fairly confident that she was not about to be thrown out on her ear, was what she was going to do about her father. He was going to be there soon; he may even have already arrived, but just seeing him was not going to free them from this web of deceit in which they were currently tangled. She needed to talk to him, alone, away from whoever might still be forcing him to complete this interview. Verity sucked a breath between her teeth. There was really only one person she knew that was pulling the strings: the same person who would bring her life as Ana Lucia, and perhaps even Verity, to a crushing end – Ernesto.

Verity considered the previous night's events. Although Ernesto had been centre stage, he had not played a pivotal part in the media circus. He had in fact looked sheepish and uncomfortable under the scrutiny of hundreds of inquisitive eyes and almost as many staring lenses. Perhaps today he wouldn't even make an appearance. Maybe, with clipboard in hand, she could approach her father as an excited member of the audience seeking an autograph from the world-renowned archaeologist. It might give her a few moments with him and a few moments could be - may be - enough.

Although deep in thought, the heavenly smell of fresh bread was enough to utterly capture Verity's attention. The strong aroma of coffee (a drink that she had no appetite for but which Dad often credited much of his success to) wafted through the air - an invisible trail that beckoned her forward.

The corridor leading to the temporary television studio had been transformed since last night; clearly a lot of people had been working whilst Verity had been hidden away, sleeping in her storage room. The walls were lined with trestle tables upon which sat steaming urns of hot water; shining stainless steel machines from which streams of hot, rich coffee gently ran; serving bowls piled with cereals and trays of fresh fruit nestled on glimmering chips of ice. A breakfast buffet fit for a king! And indeed, there was the king of this particular court: the presenter from the previous evening, selecting choice morsels from a bowl of vibrantly coloured fruit salad. The man, Vinicio Cerezo (if Verity had remembered that correctly – it had sounded familiar for some reason), was smiling brightly at those around him, clearly enjoying the energy of the morning. A woman rushed up to him holding a variety of delicate brushes and paper tissues. She brushed crumbs off his salmon shirt and then offered him the paper, rolling her eyes. The man grinned, wiped his hands on some and then tucked several sheets into his collar. His stylist, Verity presumed, clicked open a circular compact and gently flicked at its contents with a soft brush. Still smiling, the man moved his hand in the international gesture of "wait a minute" and looked directly at Verity.

Suddenly aware that she had been, and still was, staring directly at him, Verity dropped her gaze. Unsure what else to do, reminding herself that she needed to belong, she looked back in his direction and held out her clipboard. What was she doing? Part of her wanted to turn and run – a big part - but she was in control. She refused to allow the seeds of fear to sprout and take root. Ethan would be proud.

Vinicio's smile broadened when he saw Verity's outstretched hands gripping the clipboard and pen. Luckily, he was not close enough to see her white knuckles and shaking arms. He put his bowl down on the table and all but bounced over to her. His enthusiasm was contagious and Verity felt an authentic smile bloom on her face.

"*Buenos dias senor. Mi madre trabaja aquí,*" Verity blurted out when he stood before her.

"*Excelente,*" Senor Cerezo responded brightly. "*¿Cómo te llamas?*"

"*Me llamo Ana Lucia Morales,*" she said, silently thanking her junior school teachers for their commitment to teaching them at least a little Spanish.

"*Hola, Ana Lucia Morales,*" he said, taking the clipboard from her hands. Yes! She felt her shoulders rise and her smile widen. Although it was earlier than she had anticipated having to put it into action, her plan clearly worked; not only was she an official visitor, she was now an autograph collector.

Verity found the clipboard being passed back to her and she mentally slipped back into character. Hugging the board tightly, she squealed and bounced up and down on her tiptoes. Several members of the crew had turned to watch the scene play out and now smiled at the endearing girl who was clearly over the moon at having met a celebrity. Verity knew that she had taken a risk at drawing attention to herself like that, but in doing so, she had made herself known to the crew around her and had cemented her place in a world in which she did not belong.

"*Sírvete,*" Cerezo said, gesturing at the tables laden with food and drink. Verity had no idea what the words meant but his actions spoke an international language: help yourself! The presenter ruffled her hair and beamed down at her. "*Disfruta tu día señorita.*"

"*Gracias senor. Muchas gracias.*" Verity was not entirely sure what he had said but comprehension was unnecessary. He was already strolling away. He retrieved his bowl of fruit, continued walking through the corridor and disappeared into the circular room that was to be the site of the interview. Verity took in the room for the second time that morning. Unlike her first visit, when it had been calm and still, crammed with cameras with nothing to watch and microphones with nothing to hear, the place was now alive. It couldn't have been more than thirty minutes since she was last here but now she saw row upon row of chairs, most of which were filled with professional-looking men and women who were also enjoying the free breakfast that had been laid on for them.

Although affected by the buzz of excitement in the air, Verity decided to take up Cerezo on his generosity. She piled a plate high with slices of melon, orange segments and two particularly delicious looking pastries. With the clipboard gripped tightly under her arm and her visitor pass deliberately noticeable on her chest, Verity weaved through the bustle of the corridor and adjoining room and took a seat, balancing the plate brimming with breakfast on her lap. She tucked in immediately – her fears and anxieties held at bay, temporarily at least, by the satisfaction that comes only from quieting the growls of a hungry tummy.

34

Ethan

The sunshine was blinding and hit Ethan as if with a physical force, knocking him back a step. Although the forest wasn't so dense that it was dark, the open area by the ruins received the full brunt of the sun. The brilliant rays bounced off the broken buildings and the lush foliage that surrounded them.

He was back. Thank the heavens, thank the stars or the gods, thank his legs or Lady Luck. He was safe, and, by goodness, he had to tell someone about this.

Ahead of him, reading her book, was Maria, unchanged and unfazed by what had been taking place in the forest. Next to her was Leo, hand over his brow, scanning the forest edge, looking for someone. *Looking for me!*

"Leo!" Ethan called, a mixture of panicked excitement and overwhelming relief in his voice. "Geee, am I glad to see you!" With that, he ran over to his friend, jumping blocks of ancient stone and shrubs, fallen logs and roots.

The two embraced as if they had been separated by months and a sense that they may have never seen each other again. By the look on Leo's face, he was hugging with some good deal of confusion. After all, they had only been playing a simple game of Maya and Conquistadors - nobody was supposed to be in real danger.

"Almost...almost...died..." Ethan panted to a wide-eyed Leo. Ethan turned to gesture towards the forest out of which he had run.

Is that? Could it be?

He was certain...no it couldn't be. But it was.

It is.

A shadow had appeared in the darkness of the forest at the edge of the clearing that formed the thoroughfare between the ruins. But as soon as Ethan thought he could make out the police chief, the shadow vanished, swallowed up by the depths of the forest behind. As it did so, something flashed in a ray of sunshine that broke through the canopy. It was the glint of metal; sunshine off weapon; brightness and life bouncing off the threat of death.

"That...that...that was..."

Leo's brow furrowed even further as his surprised eyes looked from Ethan to the forest and back at Ethan again. "What was what? Where you go? I could not find. Got bored. I shout. Loud!"

"We've got to get back to the camp"

"Why? What is problem?" Leo asked.

"I'll tell you later. Maria, can we go back now?"

Their campsite chaperone looked up from her reading, unaware that anything untoward had happened.

"We go back. I have too much work to do. Can't read all day, eh!" she said, pinching her top and pulling it away from her sweaty skin. "Come on, then, boys."

Ethan turned to Leo and grabbed him by the shoulders. "You won't believe what I'm going to tell you."

***

Back at the campsite, sitting at a table drinking bottled water, the boys were deep in conversation. Whispers slipped between them like bats flitting in the darkness.

"Something funky is going on," said Ethan quietly.

"Funky?"

"Weird," he continued by way of explanation. "That policeman tried to kill me. He's not a good guy. He was talking to the man from the compound who helped kidnap my dad. They were friendly. He must be in on it too – whatever *it* is."

"And the policeman said he was going to help get your dad back. Does this mean he not going to do this?"

Ethan thought for a short while. "No. Worse. It could mean that he is helping to kidnap him. Or at least keeping quiet about it. I just don't know who to trust."

Leo's eyes brightened. "You can trust my father."

"But can I? How do you know?"

Leo's eyes narrowed in disdain. "'How do I know?' He's my father! Of course I can trust him! You trust him too!"

"Bad guys have families, too, you know."

"Hey!" Leo shouted, causing the adults still in the camp to pause in what they were doing. Maria looked up from her laptop down at the end of the table. Leo smiled at her to appease the questioning glance, before crossly looking back at Ethan. Through gritted teeth, he said, "You no call *mi padre* a bad man!"

"I'm sorry, Leo. I just don't know what to do and who I can count on. Look, you're the only person in the whole world I can trust and that's weird anyway because I hardly know you. This camp here, this is my world right now. And I know no one. Something dodgy is going on here. It's rotten. It's like this Maya curse is seeping out of that mask and into the camp. I think we're all cursed. This camp, these ruins, these archaeologists, my dad, my sister, me. We're all bleedin' cursed and I just don't know what to do."

"I think we should tell my father. He will help us," Leo suggested.

"Okay. I guess you're right."

Just at that moment, Cruzar walked into the centre of the camp, clearly looking for someone. "Ahaaa. There you are, Ethan."

"Ed?"

Cruzar had a wide smile across his face as if he had a cargo of good news to offload to the nearest port.

"Ethan, Ethan. Wonderful, wonderful news. We know where your father is. The police have found him. They came here just an hour or so ago to tell us. This is great news, no?"

Despite the fog of confusion that was floating around his mind. Ethan couldn't stop the inundation of emotion that gushed forth. Joy and laughing smiles, and Leo hugs, morphed quickly into tears. Huge gulping sobs of tears.

"Ethan," interrupted Cruzar, "if you get your things together, we can get you there as quickly as possible. We need to go in the truck we have here."

"I'll...I'll get my things together. Give me a minute to go to my tent. Then I need to tell you something. It's really important. It's about what just happened." Ethan had resolved to tell Cruzar about what had happened in the forest.

"Okay, Ethan. You can tell me when we get to the jeep."

35

Verity

The magnificence of the room and the history that it contained was overshadowed, defeated by the modern world and its technologies that had colonised it that morning. Verity had sat and munched through her breakfast with glee, ignorant of everything other than her hunger. Having eaten one warm pastry filled with a vanilla custard and a good portion of the cantaloupe melon, however, Verity began to take in her surroundings and the to-ings and fro-ings of all those around her. Large lamps flooded the room with light but it was not the incredible tablets of stone that were illuminated. The focus this morning was not on the verified history that adorned the walls but on one small, knee-high table, flanked on the right by two black leather chairs and another on the left. A conspicuously empty glass stand stood on a black velvet material that covered the top of the table.

Verity watched with interest as three men took up the seats. Various crew members tweaked the angles and brightness of the lights that lit the area whilst small teams of technicians moved small sections of what looked like train-tracks before fixing large cameras upon them. The men in the seats began to chat animatedly. One appeared to tell a joke as the other two fell about laughing. A fourth man appeared beside them, also chuckling, and adjusted several boom mics that Verity hadn't even noticed. He gave the three men small packs that they attached to their belts before clipping what Verity assumed were more mics to their collars. They continued to check sound levels whilst being undecidedly unprofessional (in Verity's opinion) but the atmosphere in the room was undeniably one of excitement and fun.

An approaching buzz, a confusion of raised voices, stole Verity's attention from the stage. Two hassled and weary looking adults were shepherding twenty or so teenagers towards rows of chairs. Each chair had a piece of paper taped to its back, the words *La Escuela de Santa Catalina* printed clearly across them. *Escuela* – that meant school. Another reason for Verity to be there; luck was on her side this morning! For further camouflage, Verity decided to place herself at least near to these children who looked to be only a few years older than herself. She squeezed past several people and clambered inelegantly back towards the chattering teenagers who were clearly more interested in each other than anything else happening in the room. Verity managed to get herself in the same row but a number of adults separated her from the group itself. It would have to do.

The animated, exuberant atmosphere was rapidly replaced with an air of anticipation and austerity when a dozen or more men filed into the room. They all wore similar clothing: forest-green shirts made from a lightweight material, over which some had multi-pocketed jackets. Their boots, shiny and black, were laced up above the ankle and their trousers were covered in suggestively bulging pockets. Similarly, their belts were loaded with poppered pouches, the contents of which Verity could only imagine. Although clean and smartly pressed, this was not attire that belonged on a television set but in the jungle: these were Ernesto's men.

Their appearance heralded the beginning of the morning's main event. As the military looking men spread themselves around the room, a hush fell across the attendees. Even the few remaining voices fell silent as an older man in a white coat, the man from the previous evening, appeared, carrying the mask. Two further security men walked either side of him, making the walk to the stage seem like a solemn procession. Cameras flashed and notes were scribbled but the large room was silent of voices. The man in white carefully placed the mask on the glass stand; its mournful eyes stared at the audience as if pleading for help but the none came. Nobody spoke. Nobody moved. The mask was the master of the room.

After a few minutes, murmurs began to fill the room and the school children soon started to mutter to each other impatiently. It was still quiet enough, however, for Verity to hear the sound of heavy footsteps on the hardwood floor. She glanced behind her and immediately sank low in her chair. Ernesto had entered the room from a dimly lit corridor. He strode purposefully to the first of his men on his right. In his hand, he had several sheets of paper, one of which he handed over to the guard in front of him. He spoke briefly to the guard before turning and looking out across the assembled audience. Verity felt suddenly foolish slumped in her seat and a the woman to her right was shooting her irritated expressions. She couldn't do anything, though. Verity had a nasty suspicion, the paper that he was handing out had something to do with her. If he saw her, she would be trapped here and she dreaded to think what would happen if he got her hands on her. Goodness only knew where Ethan was, but she remembered what Ernesto had said to her father before: We have your children. Ernesto needed her father to believe that to keep Daniel under his command.

She watched as Ernesto continued around the room. He spoke to each of his men and provided each with a sheet of paper that they studied before tucking into one of their many pockets. Each man seemed to scrutinise the crowd in front of them, checking every face. Verity's own face burned, embarrassed by her seemingly childish actions, painfully aware of the precarious situation she had placed herself in. Her back began to ache but still she would not move. She caught glimpses of Ernesto, and as he turned his back to her, she shifted slightly, raising herself up on her seat. She ensured that her trusty clipboard covered as much of her face as possible as she turned her head to see what was happening. It was then that she saw her father.

Daniel walked out onto stage alongside Vinicio Cerezo. Applause built quickly; the sound echoing from the curved walls seemed to fill the building with a thunderous storm which died when an illuminated sign that read "*Silencio, por favor*" flashed red.

What followed, to Verity at least, was bizarre and uncomfortable. She recognised her father clearly but his words were not his own. Daniel was wearing a clean white shirt with their sleeves rolled up, and brown chinos. He looked smart but casual: likeable and believable. His hair had been styled and his glasses were perched jauntily on top of his head. He looked like the expert that Verity knew and loved.

When he spoke, Daniel had an energy, enthusiasm and confidence that gave what he said an authority, a ring of truth. But his words were unlike anything she had heard him say before.

For over half an hour, Cerezo questioned Daniel on the mask. Where had it been found? What had happened to the guard? What tests had been performed on it? What evidence did they have for what had been claimed? Daniel spoke with confidence and by the end of the interview there could be little doubt in the room that everything he said could be believed. In little over thirty minutes, Daniel had convinced a room of journalists and perhaps millions watching that the mask sat in front of them was imbued with a terrible power. A power that for thousands of years had remained dormant but that had spread a virulent curse to the people of the Maya. A curse that, according to the scripture found with it, caused seizures and fainting, weakness and trouble breathing. It caused pain and suffering to those that saw it. But its effects were more widespread and insidious. At first, so the writing told, when spring came and there were no animal births, the Maya made sacrifices to their gods – baskets laden with fruit and mewling livestock before finally turning to human sacrifice. But it was all in vain. And worse, there were no babies, no new generation to continue the royal lines, no new blood to work the fields or to train as soldiers. The mask, which had simply appeared at the top of the temple in which it had been found, was being credited with a curse that ripped apart an entire civilisation.

Verity watched and listened, torn between believing the man who had raised her and doubting the talk of mysterious magic that defied logic. By the end, her brain was buzzing and she barely registered the applause that signalled that it had come to end.

The interview was over. Cerezo was obviously pleased with the way it had gone and leaned forward and shook Daniel's hand with both of his. He got to his feet and various men and women rushed to his side to congratulate him, clapping him on the back and shaking his hand. Daniel remained seated, his eyes staring blankly at his feet.

One of the black-booted men stepped from the edges of the room and tapped Daniel on the back. Daniel slowly turned, as if now drained of all his previous energy and looked in the direction that the soldier (for that was now how Verity thought of them) was pointed. Verity followed his gaze and saw that a table had been erected and a queue was already forming, snaking backwards into the main crowd. Daniel visibly sighed and got to his feet. Verity could not help but notice how sunken her father's face appeared. His hair, though professionally styled for his television appearance, seemed to droop and the grey at his temples looked like it had spread. His eyes, normally so full of vitality, were sombre and dull. If she could get to him, though, she knew the spark would come back.

Daniel sat heavily at the table and was joined moments later by the older, Guatemalan man who had brought on the mask – the man she assumed to be a member of *El Instituto Guatemalteco de Arqueología*. They spoke briefly, gruffly, before the lady at the front of the queue was ushered towards the table by an officious looking assistant. The lady held out a small grey device. She must be one of the invited journalists getting a quote for her own newspaper, radio or TV station.

Despite the presence of the men around the room, Verity knew if she was going to make contact with her father, she was going to have to join that queue. The people on her left had already moved on, either lining up themselves or joining the throng of people swapping notes and discussing the conference. As the woman on her right collected her belongings and got to her feet, Verity fell in step behind her. There was no sign of Ernesto since his first sweep of the room but she surreptitiously looked around her just in case. The female journalist meandered through the mass of people that included the loud teenagers and joined the line of people waiting to get a personal comment from the two historians. Verity followed in her wake and was relieved when a large man chewing on a twist of flaky pastry stood behind her. She was effectively invisible and now all she had to do was wait and keep her cool when it came time to step forward.

Time seemed to slow. The attendant at the front had been ensuring nobody spent too long questioning Daniel and his Guatemalan counterpart but had left his duties when he saw an opportunity to talk to Cerezo. Verity had watched him with disapproval as he sauntered over and awkwardly introduced himself to the host who had looked fairly uninterested. As a result of abandoning his post, the queue moved forward at a dismaying pace. Verity's nerves, which had been frayed since the appearance of Ernesto, were now at breaking point. She shuffled forward a few steps and was horrified to find herself in the direct line of sight of one of the guards. She did not know for sure that they were looking for her but she didn't want to find out. Verity stared down at the board she still held. She could almost feel the eyes of the guard sweeping across the people in the line. Only when she shuffled forwards once more and the bulk of the man behind her hid her from view did she have the courage to look up and check around her.

She was going to make it. Only a few people stood in her way of seeing her father. Excitement bubbled in her stomach. She just had to hope that her father wouldn't react to his daughter's sudden appearance and give the game away. She needed him to play along so that they could talk without any of the "security" feeling the need to intervene. Dad would know what to do, how to fix the situation.

Another reporter left the queue, satisfied with whatever quote he had recorded from her father. She shuffled forward. Only minutes to go. Perhaps less. She summoned up her courage to peek her head out of the queue, to look toward the table behind which her father and the stuffy Guatemalan professor were sitting. She leaned to her left but a camera man blocked her view as he wheeled his equipment away to join the rest of the technicians packing up their gear. She bobbed back in line and began to move to her right.

She stopped in her tracks as a firm hand gripped her shoulder.

36

Ethan

Panicked excitement had not yet abated as Ethan rifled around his tent without the faintest idea of what he was really looking for.

Dad's alive! He's really alive!

Quite what he needed, Ethan wasn't sure. He grabbed his rucksack and threw some spare underwear into it. Toothbrush and toothpaste (always essential, such that Ethan couldn't sleep at night if he knew he hadn't brushed his teeth). Torch. The last of his snacks.

Penknife.

It still felt to Ethan as if something wasn't quite right. He remained in the frame of mind that he couldn't trust anyone, save Leo. A penknife wasn't exactly a hunting knife, and it certainly wasn't a gun (not that he knew the first thing about how to use a gun outside of the world of toys and video games) but it was all he had. It had already got them out of once scrape, perhaps it would come in handy again. He put it in the side pocket of his bag. And, as an afterthought, he retrieved it and put it in his cargo shorts pocket. He threaded a thin jacket through the fastenings on the back of his rucksack and slung it over one of his shoulders.

He was ready. Ready to find his dad. Ready to be reunited.

A broad smile broke across his face as though the sun was breaking through leaden clouds.

Back at the centre of the camp, Cruzar was ready to go, waiting for Ethan with the jeep keys in his hand. Leo was there too, smiling at Ethan.

"Hey Ed, I'm ready. Leo, stay cool, I'm sure we'll be back soon, quicker than you can say 'Jack Robinson'."

Leo looked at Ethan quizzically.

"Don't worry mate, just something Grandad says a lot. Get the chess set ready."

The boys slapped hands, giving a handshake with interlocking thumbs, and pulled themselves towards each other.

"*Aguas, cerote!*" Leo said.

"Laters, mate," Ethan replied.

Cruzar took Ethan down to the ruins near where the truck was parked.

"We'll go in the truck here and we'll change over down the track. Bruno will take you to see your father from there. I have work to do back at the camp," Cruzar explained as they descended a pathway towards the pyramid. "Are you excited, Ethan? This is good, no?"

"Yeah awesome. So, what has happened to my dad?"

"Well, we are not totally sure yet but the police have located Ernesto and have found your father with him. They have Ernesto in...what is the word?"

"Prison, jail, custody..." Ethan offered.

"Yes, yes, yes, this is right. We do not know yet why he did this. We will find out, though. He will, er, pay the price, no?" Cruzar looked at Ethan as he said this.

"I hope so, Ed. Someone needs to pay the price. Someone needs to face justice. What's my dad ever done to deserve this?"

Even saying this, though, Ethan still felt a chill sense of confused anxiety. Things just didn't make sense He knew he had been chased by the police chief, who had tried to *shoot* him. This same person couldn't have found his dad and wanted a happily-ever-after reunion between kidnapped father and son. But *Ed* couldn't be a part of this, so what was going on? Was he being fooled by the police chief?

Ethan mulled over his confusions and internal dilemmas as he scampered down the hillside.

"Ed...I need to tell you something." Ethan proceeded to tell Cruzar about his scrape with danger in the forest, and how the police weren't to be trusted.

Cruzar stopped in his tracks and turned to Ethan before dropping to his knees. "I promise you, I will get to the bottom of this. This is very serious and I am sorry that you got muddled up in this. I think the police chief is not to be trusted, too, but all his men are good men and they will look after you. I will go back to camp and contact the authorities. I promise you, Ethan," and Cruzar gently pinched Ethan's cheek and patted the side of his face, "I will sort this all out. I promise that you will be...what's the word...reunited with your father."

And with that, they continued on their way. Ethan was still unsure of what to think. He had a nagging feeling that something more urgent should be done about him being chased and his life being in danger at the hands of someone in such authority.

The two arrived at the truck after a few minutes of quiet walking, Ethan lost in his thoughts. Cruzar unlocked the driver's door and jumped in, leaning over to unlock the far door. The four-wheel drive was quite aged and without central locking.

"Jump in, *hombre*."

Ethan slung his rucksack into the footwell and stepped up into the rear seats to nettle with his back against the far door. The engine spluttered into life. To Ethan, it felt like a roar. The roar of excitement. Or was it nervousness? The vehicle pulled away, bumping over ruts and channels, furrows and grooves.

As they drove along the rough track, Ethan stared out of the window at the alien landscape that flickered past the passenger windows across the seats from him like an old Victorian zoescope. His class had made their own zoescope with stop-motion animated pictures rotating inside a wheel with slits cut on the outside so that the picture merged into one. This had reignited a fad in his classroom of the children drawing sequenced pictures in the corners of notebooks and flicking the pages so the pictures merged into one continuous moving image. His teacher had told him how odd it was that these things come and go in cycles, because she had done that as a child at school as well. Perhaps it was similar to the cycles of time in the Maya calendar.

Ethan's train of thought then ambled its merry way onto the subject of time. He wondered to himself whether time repeated itself in cycles. Had he, Ethan Hume, already experienced this in a previous cycle of time? Had his father been kidnapped already a thousand times? A million times? An infinite number of times? Or maybe there was another universe and cycle of time where his father hadn't been kidnapped, and Ethan had been kidnapped instead. Perhaps there was another cycle of time where his father had a beard or had lost a leg or was an international sportsman because he had kept up his interest in running as a young man. Or a reality where he had decided not to come out to Guatemala. Perhaps there was another reality where Ethan's mum hadn't died. She hadn't had that chance mutation in her body where cancer took its grip. How he desperately wanted to live in *that* reality.

This romp through the landscape of his imagination lasted until the truck came to a stop, roughly and without grace, at the side of the track. Cruzar turned in his seat to face Ethan.

"We're here and you need to change vehicle," he said, smiling to Ethan.

Picking up his rucksack from the floor of the vehicle, Ethan opened the door and alighted.

"So, what's going on?" he asked Cruzar.

"You need to transfer into another truck because I need to get back to the camp. One of my colleagues, Martin, will take you to where your dad is," Cruzar replied. He indicated a truck that was waiting on the same side of the road and pointing in the same direction. Cruzar walked over to the driver's side of the four-wheel drive and spoke in hushed tones to the driver. "Come on, Ethan, your father is waiting for you! Hop in the back."

Ethan, with an air of slight excitement, walked up to the rear door, opened it, threw in his rucksack again, and jumped in the back. Within seconds, the engine started and the truck moved off. Ethan waved out of the window to Cruzar, who returned his goodbye. Cruzar turned to walk back to his truck and soon disappeared from sight. The young boy could sense the reunion with his father getting ever closer, like the evening inevitably closing in on the late afternoon.

The four-wheel drive lurched from bumpy rut to bumpy rut and Ethan felt the need to fasten his seatbelt. After a few minutes of being thrown around the back seat, Ethan thought it would be wise to introduce himself to this unknown colleague. He leaned over and looked into the rearview mirror at the eyes of the man driving.

It was at this moment that he realised who was driving him. It was at this moment that his heart skipped a beat. It was at this moment that he realised he was in serious trouble.

37

Verity

The hand on her shoulder spun her round. Verity was facing a tall, frowning man, a man whose lined face and strong grip communicated menace. A badge on his khaki green jacket read *Seguridad* but this was no museum attendant checking for tickets; she didn't know how she knew, but Verity could tell that this was a man who had hurt people.

The man looked her up and down and then reached into his pocket. He held a piece of paper up before him. Verity couldn't see what was on it but he nodded to himself grimly and then thrust the paper at her.

"Verity." He spoke the word as if he knew of its origins and was angry at her betrayal of it: truth. She turned the printed paper over to see her father, Ethan and herself smiling and waving back. It was a copy of a photo that her mother had taken on one of their final family holidays – a surprise trip to Malta to visit the ancient walled city of Mdina. The three of them stood before the main city gate holding hands in a way that Ethan would now be horrified to see, let alone do. Verity tried to take a breath but something inside her seemed to crumple and she felt her eyes prickle with tears.

From behind her, she heard chairs scrape across the hardwood floor. She turned to get a momentary glimpse of her father being "guided" towards a smaller entrance, flanked by two men in similar attire to the man whose hand was still digging into her shoulder. She felt fingers press deeper into her flesh and then a rough hand gripped her chin and forced her head back round.

"Do not worry," the man's voice was thick with both the Guatemalan accent and a mixture of malice and amusement. "you will meet family again soon."

What would, in a different context, have been reassuring, filled her with hot dread. There was a mirth in that voice that was polluted, unclean, that somehow promised violence. Or perhaps it was simply the pain in her shoulder that coloured Verity's perception. Perhaps not.

"Do not make scene." The man's cold eyes conveyed as much threat as the words coming from his mouth. His hands turned her and then took secure hold of both her shoulders. They pushed her forward and she took a stumbling step before she righted herself at the sudden pressure applied between her shoulder blades. The man's fingers sent sharp lines of pain down her back and through her arms. He clearly did not want her to draw attention to them as they made their way across the room. *He can't do anything here.* The thought whipped into her mind as she shuffled forwards, watching the teams of museum staff help the television crews coil cables, stack chairs and pack electronic equipment into foam-padded boxes. *I could scream. Somebody would stop him.*

No sooner had the thought formed, than Verity felt a hot breath on her neck. The pungent smell of coffee and cigarettes reached her nostrils as a voice spoke quietly in her ear.

"You do anything, your brother is dead."

Verity's eyes widened and she had to suppress a violent urge to thrash and writhe, to get clear of this man and the horrors he promised. There was no wasted emotion in the words that were spoken. No anger. No room for negotiation. It was a statement of fact, as if he were saying nothing more than two plus two equals four. Verity's legs felt suddenly weak but the strong hands would not let her buckle.

Her mind was a turbulence of emotion with little space for thought, but Verity's legs carried her forward nonetheless. She was urged forward by the man at her back, their pace steady and, to anyone who happened to look, calm. Every breath she took, however, threatened to bring forth the storm of emotion that was raging inside her. A flood of tears were held at bay only by the knowledge that bringing attention to herself would bring far worse to Ethan. Her anger was tempered by the almost tangible menace that clung to the man at her back like a noxious cloud.

They were following in the footsteps of her father, Verity realised as they made their way towards a darkened corridor off to the side of the room. The thought sparked a tiny light of hope that was immediately doused as the promise (or threat) echoed in her head – *You will meet family again soon.*

A few steps down the corridor and Verity was squinting into darkness. Weak light from the room that they had just left played at the floor but failed to penetrate the space ahead of her. The only sound she could hear was their footsteps on the smooth floor and her own heavy breathing and thumping heart. It was like being back in the temple in the jungle. That felt like months ago, but could not have been more than a few days!

Verity's world turned black in an instant. A deep breath sucked a rough cloth into her mouth. Something had been put over her head. Panic erupted and Verity was no longer in control. She threw her arms outwards, upwards, punching, clawing, tearing. Her right hand took hold of the material that covered her head but was almost crushed by a hand much larger and stronger than her own. A low sound at the back of her throat rapidly built in volume and pitch but before it could shatter the silence, pain seemed to course through every nerve in her body. Verity's thrashing came to abrupt end as she hit the floor.

38

Ethan

The last time that Ethan had been in a similarly perilous situation (although in light of its present scenario, it wasn't nearly as dangerous), was when he went on a school residential camping trip and found out that he had been put in the same tent as the school bully, Jake Trent. He realised he would have to spend the next four nights in a three-man tent with someone whom he both feared and despised.

What Ethan was less confident in predicting was that this present situation would turn out nearly as well as his camping trip. In the event of being stuck in a confined space with someone whom he thought was a pretty terrible human, he was forced to get to know Jake somewhat better. The end result was that, through spending time with each other, they discovered what they actually had in common and found the positives in each other's company. By the end of the trip, the two boys had started up an unconventional and unexpected friendship.

There was little chance that a friendship would spring up in this similarly confined space. The driver of the vehicle wasn't Jake Trent.

Things were worse.

Martin appeared to be one of the henchmen from the compound from which Leo and Ethan had escaped. Although Ethan had only managed rushed and panicked glimpses at the two men from the compound, there was no mistaking his rounded, olive-skinned face. Ethan was struggling to put two and two together to make a sensible answer. His mind was racing chaotically towards a dangerous black hole with this man's face at the very centre. He was being sucked in and yet caught glimpses of his father floating in distant space away from this strong and malevolent gravitational pull.

Ethan needed desperately to get out of his destructive orbit.

"Excuse me? Could you please stop the car as I need to relieve myself? Er, please, I'm desperate..." Ethan pleaded with the eyes in the mirror.

"No. I cannot do. Need to get to your father," the man said in faltering, heavily accented English.

"Please can you stop the car? Please stop the car!"

The man turned, while still driving, and looked directly at Ethan with a look of menace.

"No! No, I say!"

Whilst the driver had turned to look at Ethan, he had naturally slowed down the vehicle, his focus taken away from the bumpy track. Ethan, without even thinking about it, took this as his moment to react to his precarious predicament. Grabbing the door handle, he opened the door. He was met with the browns and greens of the track beneath whizzing past the gap between door and vehicle body. Grabbing his rucksack with his free hand, Ethan pushed the door as wide as he could, and with both feet planted on the sill that ran alongside the body of the truck, he thrust himself out into the open and onto the ground below.

Thud.

Oof!

Roll.

Mud. Long grass. Pain.

Ethan was vaguely aware of the truck from which he had jumped scudding to a halt somewhere up the track. It took him a good few seconds to gather his senses. He had bashed his knee on the way down and could feel some pain but adrenaline was able to overcome any immediate obstacle to him getting up onto his feet. He swung his rucksack over both shoulders to make sure it was secure and looked back towards the vehicle.

Holy cow!

Martin was already a lot closer to him than he had bargained for. Even though he wasn't the lithest of people, the man from the compound was covering the distance between Ethan and the truck with considerable ease. Ethan hardly had time to collect himself before he had to spin rapidly around and start running the other way.

Ethan was a big fan of action movies. He loved going to the cinema. He loved streaming movies at home. The more action, the better. However, one quibble he often had with films was the unrealistic way that people, usually women being chased, would trip over far too easily and allow the chaser to gain ground and even catch them. This always seemed to Ethan like a really cheap cliché for films to include. It annoyed him. How often do people really trip over when running? Ethan couldn't remember ever having tripped up whilst running. Not in school sports day running races, not when being chased in a game of tag, not whilst playing wide games on his school camping trip.

After fewer than ten running paces, Ethan's knee gave way and twisted awkwardly and his foot caught on a tuft of long grass sticking up from a small mound.

In other words, Ethan tripped over.

If he would ever have the chance to look back on this moment, especially when watching those movies, Ethan would no doubt hold his head in his hands and admit that, occasionally, people do trip. Occasionally, people are idiots.

Occasionally, Ethan was an idiot.

This was one such occasion.

39

Verity

Black faded to grey and then light somehow found its way once again into Verity's world.

Raising one hand to the back of her head, Verity winced as she found an egg-sized lump protruding from under her hair. Her eyes tightened at the feel of a sticky wetness that matted her hair. *At least I am still alive.*

As the pain subsided, Verity's other senses began to bombard her with messages. The all-too familiar rumbling of an engine and the bumpy swaying told her that she was on the move again. She opened her eyes slowly and looked around, taking in a car that she seen before, though not from this perspective.

The pick-up was the same slightly worn and dented vehicle that Verity had hitched a lift in to the city previously. However, now she was well and truly inside it. The large cabin had a front and rear and she was on the right-hand side of the rear seats whilst her father was slumped over to the left. Her father's hands were tightly secured to the seatbelt with a thick, plastic cable tie, tightened so that it was just about biting into his skin. He looked like a tranquilised seal. Or was he a tranquilised panther?

Verity rather hoped for the latter.

Like her father, Verity was unable to move. She couldn't open the door and jump out of the truck because the seatbelt strap fed through the circle that her arms made, given that her hands were securely fastened together at the wrist. Her ankles too were bound with a sturdy loop of tough plastic.

Things did not look good.

Not a single person outside the vehicle, milling about the roads, going about their daily business, was the slightest bit aware of the plight of these two foreigners, kidnapped and being taken to goodness knew where for goodness knew what outcome.

There was no denying it: Verity was scared. She had done so well to remain out of captivity, to have evaded the clutches of Ernesto and his cronies. She was proud of herself. Well, she *had* been proud of herself. Now she was simply annoyed. Disappointed. All had come to nought.

What were her options? She couldn't jump out. She couldn't even extricate herself from the simple power of a piece of plastic, couldn't even escape from her sitting position. All she could do was wait. Wait and watch. Wait and watch and hope - for an opportunity, a chink in their armour, a hole in their plans.

Right now, though, their plans seemed pretty simple and pretty impossible to chisel a hole in.

The truck dodged its way between the obstacles of the bustling little city: cars and people, animals and stalls. Before long, they were out of the urban landscape and into the countryside. Soon enough they were onto smaller and smaller roads until they diverted off the proper road surface and onto the bump and bounce, the jolt and jerk of the dirt track.

Back, it seemed, to the ruins.

Verity wasn't sure if this was a good or a bad thing, but concluded, or hoped, that this was a better outcome than being taken somewhere completely different and unknown. What would they want with them, now? Dad had said his things, dutifully, it appeared. He had kept his side of the bargain. Did they still need him?

A dagger through the heart, Verity lurched forward in pain. Emotional pain.

What if they don't need him anymore? What then?

Verity gasped involuntarily. Ernesto, in the passenger seat, turned around to look at her. Instantly, she turned away and looked out of her window at the forest as it jumped about, dancing to some unheard music.

He couldn't see her weakness. He couldn't see her being afraid. She had to stay strong and score those small victories.

For the next half an hour, Verity was lost in thought and worry about the very precarious position that she and her father were in, with the dawning realisation that they might have outstayed their welcome, and more importantly, outgrown their usefulness.

The monotony of the drive and the endless maze of her thoughts disappeared in the crackle of a radio. Ernesto answered the Spanish of the incoming call with his own rapid-fire talk. The conversation continued for a few minutes with the definite inclusion of the words "Daniel" and "Hume".

Ernesto's plan was evolving, but Verity just couldn't access it. She was searching for a black cat in an unknown room in the middle of the dark night.

Some mentally torturous time later, the pickup slowly trundled to a stop at the side of the road. The driver tapped Ernesto on the shoulder and pointed up ahead to another truck that was parked further up the road.

Who was it? There was definitely someone in the back, but Verity couldn't make out anything.

Ahead of her own vehicle, on the left-hand side of the road, there appeared to be a sharp decline just shortly beyond the edge of the track. There was no railing or safety barrier here, on a dirt track in the middle of the forest, just a drop beyond some low bushes. Verity could see out to the other side of what must have been a sharp valley or gorge, the bottom of which there was no doubt some kind of river.

Ernesto and the driver exchanged some words before indicating their backseat passengers. The driver nodded whilst Ernesto opened his door and stepped out, but not without a piercing and somewhat menacing stare back at Verity.

You're not going anywhere, it said in no uncertain terms.

40

Ethan

The plastic of the cable tie was painful and bit into his skin causing him to wince with every jolt and bounce of the four-wheel drive. Martin had put the child lock on the rear doors so that Ethan couldn't open them if he had wanted to again. Bundled into the back of the vehicle, Ethan had his hands tied (with the cable tie being looped around the seat belt as well) and was prisoner to the driver. He didn't know where they were going but had recognised the compound as they passed through without stopping. He predicted that they probably were going to meet his father, but that the meeting wouldn't quite be the joyous reunion he had dreamt of.

This holiday wasn't going to plan. How he would love to be in the south of Spain, frolicking in the warm Mediterranean Sea with a bodyboard and a smile on his face whilst his sister no doubt read a book on the beach, looking on at her brother with only feigned interest and little concern.

Instead, he had been forcefully bundled into a truck by an essentially unknown man, kidnapped to be taken goodness knew where to an equally unknown fate. Was this his destiny? Was he on a collision course with disaster with no way of getting his train off the track?

No. I have to do something.

Ethan recognised that he had to derail this train. He thought, brow furrowed in focused concentration.

And then it came.

Of course, you fool! My penknife.

Contorting his body, he reached his hands so that he could gain access to his pocket. Reaching it was easy but actually getting it out of his pocket was more of a challenge. The belt chafed against his wrist and he had to angle his shoulder painfully backwards to allow his linked hands and desperate fingers to find their way into the tight denim to retrieve the knife. He could feel the shiny red plastic but it slipped on his sweaty, fumbling fingers. Again and again he tried but he could not get a grip on the knife. He took a deep breath.

Think. Use logic.

His sister's voice sounded in his head. Yes! That was it - if he couldn't pull the knife out, perhaps he could push it, wedging it up, out and free. He immediately put his plan into action. Verity's smile entered his head and rather than being irritated by it, he was comforted: she would be proud. Little by little, centimetre by centimetre, he was able to work the penknife up and out of his pocket. By the time it was in his hands, his wrists were tattooed in red stripes and his fingers were sore. But he had it.

This was his only hope, he thought. Suddenly, a strange image flitted into his mind. He was a big fan of the *Star Wars* films, and he suddenly heard the words of the moment when Princess Leia bent down to give R2-D2 the plans to the Death Star, famously uttering, "Help me, Obi-Wan Kenobi, you're my only hope."

Help me, penknife, you're my only hope.

He managed to manipulate the penknife into the right position and open the larger blade. He had to be careful because the track wasn't providing the smoothest ride, and so had to slip the blade between skin and plastic cable tie whilst Martin was driving on a flatter piece of track. The penknife was facing backwards towards his body, held awkwardly in his right hand. The process was not nearly as simple as he was hoping, what with the bouncing of the truck and the thickness of the plastic. The blade was sharp, but the angle was difficult and the plastic was putting up a fight. After a number of minutes of sawing with the blade after he had cut a small notch to give him purchase, Ethan managed to cut through the cable tie. It was a minor miracle that he had not cut his own skin in the procedure.

Yes! You beauty!

Putting his penknife back in his pocket, Ethan held the tie in place so that it would appear to the casual onlooker as if he were still perfectly well secured. Yes, his hands were free but there was still nothing he could really do. He had to patient and bide his time.

After a good half an hour of travelling through what would otherwise have been recognised as stunning countryside (the lush green vistas of mountains, hills, forest, flora and fauna were the least of Ethan's worries), the vehicle slowed down and came to a stop. Martin turned the engine off.

"What...what are we doing?" Ethan asked nervously.

"We wait."

And wait they did.

The afternoon sun was high in the sky and beating down on the landscape around them. Insects made an almost deafening noise through the open windows of the car. The world around them, the world of nature, appeared to continue unfazed by the world of Ethan and his family and the danger that they faced. It had been hard enough to remain calm during the journey but the constant movement had at least given Ethan some form of distraction. Sitting in silence, his mind circling through the worst possible scenarios, was unbearable. As the minutes slipped away, so too did his composure. Ethan was definitely starting to panic.

After another quarter of an hour or so, an engine could be heard in the distance, its sound unmistakably alien to the world of birds and insects and leaves rustling in the breeze. Martin had parked on the side of the track, which, up ahead, was bordered on the right-hand side by a sharp ridge, a sheer drop, the bottom of which Ethan couldn't see. Another four-wheel drive trundled along the track in the distance and stopped a few hundred metres from Martin's, on the other side of the ridge that dropped away from the side of the road.

Who was that? Was it...could it be?

There was, of course, every chance that the vehicle ahead contained his father. Perhaps even his sister. He had no idea what had happened to her. Poor Verity, how had she coped being stuck on her own? She was useless at these sorts of things. Good with books. Good with history and geography and science. Rubbish at running around and saving people and generally being athletic. Ethan suddenly wished they had been in each other's shoes, that Vee had been back at camp, working out what was going on, and he had been trying to save his dad from certain doom. Alas, it was not to be. He was here, now, and he had to come up with a plan, and quick. Careful planning wasn't his forte; risky and hasty attempts to be a superhero, without looking too far into the future at the consequences, were more his thing.

Ethan turned around to look through the tiny window in the back of the cabin. Behind him, was the back of the truck – an open flatbed that contained various pieces of equipment and a hodgepodge of odds and ends all strapped down to stop them rolling around. However, one thing did stand out: a rack of three jerry cans. Jerry cans. Fuel.

Fire.

But how could he do anything with the driver still in the vehicle? At least his hands were free, and he was not restricted to remaining in the back, attached to the seat belt as he was. In between the driver's seat and the passenger seat, next to the handbrake, was a packet of cigars and a lighter. Thank goodness that Martin was a smoker! All he needed to do was to get hold of that lighter and for Martin to be away from the truck. Easy...

And that's when Lady Luck looked down upon Ethan, gave a winning smile and a wink. Someone got out of the other four-wheel drive and waved towards Martin, beckoning him out of the car and over to the other vehicle.

Hey! That's Ernesto!

Straight away, Ethan's blood started to boil with intense fury. Emotions bubbled: hatred and anger, vengeance and fear.

Martin looked round and gave Ethan a cursory check, visually making sure that he was secured to the seat belt with the cable tie. Giving a derisory snort, Martin opened his door, got out of his seat, and started to slowly saunter over to his colleague.

There was not one second to lose. Ethan had no idea how much time he would have or whether he would alert anyone to his clandestine activities. He discarded the cable tie and grabbed the lighter, flicking it quickly to check it worked. He thumbed the metal cylinder – a spark followed by flame. A smile lit his face as the flame lit the cabin. He snatched his rucksack and as quietly as possible, opened the left-hand front passenger door that could not be seen from the other side of the road and down the track. He had a plan, though he had no idea whether it would work.

With his insides a maelstrom of chaos and turmoil, Ethan carefully crept to the back of the vehicle. He could reach the jerry cans from where he was standing as they were lined up against the left-hand side of the flatbed. He unscrewed the three caps to the jerry cans. The stench of pungent petrol was strong and made him involuntarily wince.

Perfect.

Ethan grabbed the can nearest the rear and unfastened it from its securing and, given that it was quite heavy, struggled to lay it down so that its petrol poured all over the back of the vehicle. He did his very best not to get any petrol on his skin. After all, he didn't fancy getting burnt. Down on his haunches, Ethan quietly unzipped his rucksack and found the first piece of material he could. Ethan retrieved his spare pair of boxer shorts from the top of his pack. Batman often came to the rescue in times of need. He would fight crime in Gotham city, whether it be dispatching the Joker or Penguin or some other villain. However, never in the wildest imagination of the comic's creators would Batman be employed to save the day by being stuffed into a jerry can and lit.

As well as *Star Wars* and sci-fi films, Ethan was also partial to the action-packed antics of the various superheroes who inhabited the movie and comic world, and his daydreams. In this way, his Batman boxer shorts were probably his favourite pair. And now they were doing a hero's duty. He stuffed them into the middle jerry can opening, making sure that the material touched the petrol within so that the liquid could wick upwards. He was able to drape the end of his underwear over the side of the truck and away from the fumes and petrol within. The next part was tricky because he had to light his boxers so that the material would catch fire; but he didn't want the petrol to catch straightaway, otherwise it would all blow up in his face. He had to be quick but he also had to be sure.

With trembling hands, Ethan thumbed the lighter. Once. Twice. Three times. No luck.

C'mon!

On the fourth time, behind his other cupped hand, a small flame flickered almost imperceptibly in the afternoon sun, like blowing a kiss in a gale.

Yes!

He carefully stood up, and with cupped hand carefully shielding the important flame, he moved his lighter to the side of the truck and towards his waiting boxer shorts. They didn't catch immediately but eventually the singed material started to burn. He stayed just a second or two to make sure it didn't go out and then grabbed his rucksack and bolted into the edge of the forest next to the track.

Once inside the safety of the forest, he started jogging towards the other truck and looked to see if anyone had noticed what he had been up to. The two men appeared to be talking next to the ridge, pointing down and gesticulating as if they were formulating a plan.

And then the back of the truck exploded.

41

Verity

What were they discussing? What part could this ridge play in their plans? What opportunity did this part of the landscape provide? One of the men made a gesture with his hand that looked like a plane taking off and pointed at the truck. A terrible thought came to her...surely, they weren't going to drive over it?

Were they?

Oh my goodness! Are they going to push us off here and make it look like an accident? Are they going to get rid of us?

Verity thought she recognised the man from the other truck as one of the men from the compound, though he was shielded slightly from her view by Ernesto. These were, without any shadow of a doubt, bad guys. Yes, they might have families, children, friends they play cards with, aunts they spend Christmas with. But right now, and to Verity and her own family, these were bad, bad people.

Verity had previously wondered about bad people. She was always taught, or at least society around her assumed, that Hitler was a *bad* person. He was always held up as being the most famous example of a bad person. But during a *Philosophy 4 Children* lesson at school (other than Science, her favourite sessions were the P4C ones), her teacher, who had a love for challenging the pupils' thinking, asked whether Hitler used to wake up in the morning and decided, "I'm going to be a really bad person today."

"Very few people, I reckon," so her teacher had suggested, "wake up and *decide* to be bad. Most people, unless they are proper psychopaths, wake up and think they will do right, that they are good people. Hitler would have woken up and *thought* he was *being good*, that he was doing the *right thing* for his country. The thing is, *our* idea of good and *his* idea of good appear to be very different things."

This had inspired thought in Verity. There were little elements, little nuggets, that this teacher had given to her that stuck with her and this was one of them. Hitler was bad, terrible even, from *our* point of view, but not from *his*.

So, did Ernesto realise *he* was being bad, or were there reasons that he had that justified this behaviour? Did he wake up this morning and knowingly decide to be bad? When the kids in class were being naughty, did they just *decide* to be naughty, or were there more complicated reasons that they were being naughty? Their home life, what they had eaten, their sleep the night before... There were any number of reasons that people behave like they do. Verity knew that she was a very ratty girl when she didn't have enough sleep, and this affected the way that she thought and acted.

And then there was an explosion.

Verity intuitively ducked in her seat. After a second, she looked up and over to where the sound and sudden heat had come from. Already a plume of smoke was drifting off flickering flames that had engulfed the back of the other four-wheel drive parked some way down the track.

"Oh wow!" she exclaimed.

Her father shifted and murmured in his seat but his eyes didn't open.

In front of her, the driver let out his own exclamation. He quickly looked around at Verity and her father to check that they were secure and then got out of the truck. Taking his hat off and throwing it on the ground, he ran towards the other men, who were themselves running towards the inferno that was engulfing the truck.

Suddenly, from the corner of her eye, Verity noticed something in the woods, a hint of movement out of the ordinary.

Who's that? No! Surely not!

Her surprised thoughts were confirmed when her brother Ethan silently erupted from out of the forest. With rucksack bobbing up and down on his back, he sprinted and vaulted, albeit with a bit of a limp, towards her own vehicle.

"Ethan!" she exhaled through gritted teeth, eyebrows raised in excitement and alarm.

Whilst the other adults were rushing to the burning vehicle, gesticulating, shouting and most probably swearing, Ethan was launching himself over tufts of grass and rutted track towards his destination.

Verity suddenly had an idea of what he might be up to and looked towards the steering wheel of the truck. There, dangling from the ignition, was the key to the four-wheel drive on a long, black leather keyring. It wasn't just the key to the truck, it was the key to their escape, the key to a plan she was only just becoming a part of.

Ethan reached the truck and placed his hand through the open window to grasp Verity's. Verity had never in her life felt such an outpouring of emotion towards her brother. Tears instantly welled up in her eyes, ready to gush forth – an unstoppable flow of feelings to match the tears that threatened to fall.

"Ethan!" she mumbled, the words tumbling out in a confused waterfall of relief, love, fear and anxiety.

42

Ethan

Ethan didn't have time to reply, but jumped in through the open driver's door on the other side of the truck.

"Yes! The keys are here!" The sheer joy in his voice was plain to hear. "And it's an automatic! This should be easy. I think."

Ethan had spent several years playing racing games on his console and was most comfortable with the automatic gear change that the games offered. One of his friends had a gaming chair with a gear stick but even always used it in automatic. Automatic gearboxes were a cinch. He just needed to put it into D for drive and he was off. Without even taking his backpack off, Ethan slammed the door shut and twisted the ignition key.

Nothing happened.

He twisted the emission key again.

Nothing happened again.

"What's wrong, Ethan?"

"I don't know. I don't get it."

Ethan glanced up at the clustered adults who were standing near to the burning vehicle, remonstrating. The thickset figure of Verity's driver had turned to look back at the four-wheel drive in which they were sitting. He must have heard the car door being slammed! Ethan watched as the man clapped a hand on Ernesto's shoulder and pointed back towards the children panicking in the four-wheel drive.

"Come on, Ethan!" Verity cried. "They've seen us!"

"Yes! That's it!" It was as if something had hit Ethan like a surprise lightning bolt out of the sky. He bent down and released the catch that enabled him to move the car seat and rammed it forward. It clicked securely into place as close to the steering wheel as it would go.

"I need to put my foot on the brake to start the engine," he said rapidly to himself. "It won't start without my foot on the brake pedal!"

Ethan rammed his left foot down on the brake pedal and twisted the ignition key.

The sound of that engine sputtering into life was probably the most excruciatingly anticipated relief that Ethan had ever had. He jammed his foot so hard down on the accelerator (which he could only just touch) that the wheels spun before gaining traction on the track, firing up damp mud onto the body work of the truck.

"Oh boy. Here goes..." Ethan gripped the steering wheel with both hands, knuckles white with nervous exertion, and directed the large vehicle into the middle of the track. His head only just managed to peer over the top of the wheel.

By now, all three of the men were standing in the centre of the dirt track, a burning four-wheel drive with smoke billowing from its now blackened shell, blocking Ethan's route down the track and out of there.

Ethan squeezed his eyes shut and stepped on the accelerator.

"Wahhhhhhhhhhhhhhhhh!" he yelled as the truck scudded over ruts and grass, mud and weeds. He didn't see first-hand, but roughly saw in one of the wing mirrors that the three men had thrown themselves sideways and to the ground.

"Woo hoo! Yeah! Take that!"

"Awesome, Ethan. You did it!" Verity shouted in excitement and clasped him on the shoulder, half in congratulations, half in relief. "But I think you might want to slow down now. I don't fancy being saved and then dying straight afterwards in a car crash."

Ethan shook his head: she was always so sensible.

43

Verity

Stern clouds of dull, gunmetal grey amassed in the sky like a tidal wave inevitably washing over the land ahead. The clear sky, scattering the sun's rays into hues of brilliant blue, could offer scant resistance to the oncoming and increasingly angry army of laden rainclouds.

Below, the trees were swaying more briskly in the gathering breeze, leaves waving a warning of the oncoming storm.

"Well, I hope we make it back before that storm sets in," Verity said, eying the weather ahead.

The pair had spent the journey catching up with exactly what had happened whilst their father occasionally whimpered and moved his head with a groan. Whatever dreams he might have been having in his drugged haze, Verity hoped they were pleasant ones.

Eventually, the four-wheel drive, expertly driven by Ethan, came into the main thoroughfare through the ruins. Dusk had arrived, and, with it, rain. And not just a drizzle but a fully loaded assault, a bombardment of heavy pellets of water, pelting down from above and lashing the vehicle, the ground, the trees and the ruins.

They came to a stop at the bottom of the pyramid steps. Even in the present weather, the impressive monument to the achievements of the Maya was as awe-inspiring as ever. The greys of the stonework matched the dark hues from the early evening rainclouds above. The looming monolith and leaden clouds made Verity feel exceptionally small and remarkably powerless. A shiver ran up her spine.

As her eyes traced the steps to the summit of the ancient building, she caught sight of movement and a splash of colour. Even in the darkness that was beginning to consume the landscape, she could make out the bright red golfing umbrella that was unmistakably Alejandro's. It was something he was proud of, having his university's emblem emblazoned upon it.

"Alejandro's going up and into the pyramid," she announced.

"Yeah, that's definitely him," Ethan replied. "Let's get up there and speak to him. Let's sort this mess out."

Verity sat there motionless. Thoughts flashed through her mind like a meteor shower through the Earth's atmosphere, some breaking apart on entry, others landing with a punch.

"I...I don't know. Maybe we should go back to the camp and find some others. I don't trust anyone right now."

"I'm with you on that, but Leo's dad has to be our best bet. There's no time like the present, Verity. Let's get up there quickly before we get totally soaked."

Of course, with the rain thundering down in a deluge, there was no chance of getting five metres without being completely soaked.

Verity slapped her father around the face gently a number of times. One of his eyes opened to a slit and he mumbled something.

"Dad, we're going up to the pyramid. If you properly wake up, that's where we'll be. Don't do anything stupid."

Her father murmured something almost inaudibly that sounded like "okay".

The stone steps were difficult to negotiate, slippery and steep, high and unforgiving. It took longer than they had hoped before they reached the zenith and the dark doorway atop. Their torches gave very little assistance in the heavy rain and quickening darkness. Their sodden clothes were lead weights and their breath was ragged as they faced the black of the entrance. With the unending rain pouring from above, they felt somehow wetter than if had they been submerged in a swimming pool.

Just inside the threshold of the doorway, they gathered their senses and collected themselves. Ethan took off the hoodie he had put on and threw it on the floor. Verity simply stood there, dripping wet, in her dirty clothes that she had been so desperate to change. Oh, how she longed for a hot shower or a warm bath. Access to such comforts seemed an aeon ago.

"So, what's the plan, oh great plan-maker?" Ethan asked with a wet smile.

"Let's find Leo's dad and see what he thinks about this. I'm just not so sure, though. Something is gnawing at my mind. Something's not quite right."

"Well, the quicker we get this done, the quicker we can get back to camp and back to safety," Ethan reassured her.

Both the children looked on into the darkness that proceeded before them. Their torches dimly lit the ancient stone interior of the passageways that led into the depths of the ancient building.

"After you, sir," said Verity, her voice sounding surprisingly loud in the consuming murk, even though they could still clearly hear the thrumming of the raindrops on the outside of the pyramid.

"I guess we'd better go down the same passageway that we went down the last time we were here," announced Ethan, her erstwhile guide. There was no sign of Alejandro and they had no time to look at the glyphs and stonework that they passed, no time to marvel at the historic wonder of the building they were in. He veered off to the left-hand passageway, and the pair carefully stepped down and into the narrow walkway. There was still that musty smell with an added dampness in the air from the rain outside.

As they had done once before when they visited the pyramid without permission, they started the zigzag downwards.

Then something quite out of the ordinary happened.

Red.

Darkness.

The children froze in shocked confusion.

Red.

Darkness.

"What the...?" was all Verity could breathe.

And then again. The stonework around them briefly lit up in response to flashes of red light that struggled to find their way up the passageway towards them. Verity's heart leapt into her mouth. This wasn't what she had been expecting.

"Is...is this real? It's like the pyramid's alive." There was no denying the fear in Ethan's voice. Verity felt it too.

Indeed, it was as if the pyramid itself was pulsating, its passageways veins carrying waves of ancient and mysterious blood throughout its depths, bringing it to life. The blood of sacrifices of yesteryear. The sounds, the smells, the light and darkness, even the air, everything had a sense of otherworldliness. Every so often, the walls simply appeared out of nowhere, blood-red and eerie.

"Should...should we go on?" Ethan asked nervously.

"Um. Yes. Yes, we should." Verity's voice found a surge of confidence as she finished.

The two children slowly edged their way further downwards, with the passageway angling back on itself in a sharp zigzag. As they walked deeper into the heart of the pyramid, the lights throbbed ever more brightly. Verity noticed that as the light blinked on, it was accompanied by a low throbbing sound. This added to the intensity of the atmosphere and didn't make her feel any more comfortable at all. She couldn't tell whether it was the thrumming noise that was deafening her, or the desperate beat of her palpitating heart.

Soon, they arrived at the source of the light and sound. The two children stood in the doorway to the room that they had previously entered and had then seen jars and artefacts. They weren't in the mood to rest eyes upon artefacts that were still being dusted and labelled; there was something else that stole their attention.

It was...horrifying.

In front of them, on the podium that stood on the far side of the room, was the cursed mask that had attracted so much attention. It sat there in full glory, or more precisely, in full horror, face stretched in open-mouthed shout, pointed teeth showing from behind wide lips. In the light, it appeared black and not its usual jade green. It seemed to be hurling the throbbing noise from its mouth as the red light radiated from around its sides like an evil halo, like a sinister aura, like a terrible energy from some hellish corner of the universe.

This, this right here, *right now*, was the curse of the Maya. This was the malevolent, primaeval force that caused the end of a civilisation, the end of an entire people, the end of an era. This was danger and evil incarnate.

Except, not in Verity's world. Not in *this* world. Not in *her* world. Maybe in some other weird, alternative universe, this was a mysterious happening, an event of epic and mythical proportions. Maybe in some parallel universe, the gods of the Maya were staring down at them, angry at their interference, angry at the brazen audacity of a pair of twelve-year-olds. Maybe in some insanely different, substitute world, the gods were just about to smite Verity and her brother, full of immortal rage and wrath, divine fury and violence.

"This is not *your* world *and you are not my gods!*" she shouted at the mask, and taking her torch in her hand like a club, she strode around the edge of the beating, resonating room. She did not hesitate as she got closer to the mask. Ethan watched on as his sister became a blackened silhouette, framed intermittently by the blood-red light. The red-tinged shadow leant towards the mask, appeared to look behind it. Ethan saw the torch being lifted above Verity's head. It swung downward with brutal force.

Even above the vibrating hum, the sound of glass smashing managed to echo around the chamber. The delicate domes of powerful lightbulbs had shattered and the room was sent into darkness, save for the scant light from the children's torches.

The deep, humming noise continued to pulse its unnerving sound. Satisfied with one job done, Verity looked around with the beam of her torch and located thick wires that snaked along the floor around the base of the stand that the mask stood on, winding their dark, writhing bodies over each other, here and there. She bent down and picked up a pair of heavy black serpentine wires and gave them the largest yank she could. Over in the corner of the room, something crashed to the floor and the room went as silent as it was dark.

"Curse? Not on my watch." And suddenly her mother was alive with her in that pyramid, in her body at that moment. That was one of her mother's phrases that Verity had never before used. But it seemed to fit so perfectly, here and now.

In the strange silence that followed, with specks of dust calmly floating about the torch lights and nothing but their breathing to be heard in the room, the children's focus was suddenly shifted to the exit. An impatient and terse voice had broken the silence.

"*Hola! Qué pasa?*"

Cruzar.

44

Ethan

"Ed's not who we think he is, Ethan. He's behind all this; he's the brains behind this insanity," Verity rattled off in panicked speed.

"How do you know?"

"You know it makes sense. You know he handed you over to the guy from the compound. That was no innocent mistake. He wants to make money out of all this, somehow. He wanted the world to think that this mask was genuinely cursed, and Dad to confirm it. He couldn't fool Dad, though, and it all went wrong," she explained in quickfire – all the jigsaw pieces had fallen into place and Cruzar's grinning face was the picture.

"Er, he still might succeed. We need to get outta here. It's too dark. He could do anything!"

Before Ethan could turn and retreat back from where they had come, footsteps could be heard scuttling from within the pitch black beyond the far doorway.

With the children still rooted to their spots, a light crashed into the room through the door. The man who thundered in was barely recognisable from the one who had greeted them at the airport. His breezy smile and easy going nature had been replaced with hard lines and a cloud of menace. Cruzar, a head torch beaming at the children and blinding them, one then the other, as he looked from Verity to Ethan. His fists clenched and he seemed to grow taller as he approached, his shoulders even broader. Verity was suddenly reminded of how easily he had picked up their luggage when they had first arrived. Although he had been nothing but calm and supportive, he looked different now; she could easily imagine him picking her up just as easily as one of Dad's suitcases.

"*Sho!* What the heck is going on here? *Dios mío, patojos!*" Cruzar was not happy, that was plain to see. "You should be...somewhere else."

"You mean, at the bottom of a cliff?" Verity said, defiantly. "Where's Alejandro?" The realisation was crushing – the realisation that it was Cruzar underneath Alejandro's umbrella.

Cruzar paused a moment to stare at Verity, torch shining in her face, causing her to flinch. He then jolted forward to grab her. Verity was surprisingly quick, and dodged his grasping hands, twisting to run around the side of the chamber. Unfortunately for her, the snaking wires on the ground had other plans, and caught her feet in a predatory tangle. She fell down in a dusty heap.

Within a second, Cruzar was there, strong hands gripping both her arms, hoisting her up to her feet. With one arm wrapped around her, he quickly retrieved something from the back of his belt.

It was a knife. And a pretty big one at that; one large blade backed by a serrated edge.

"Now, *ishta*, you don't move. And you, Ethan, you don't move either!"

Ethan had not moved, but had watched the scene play out in astonished shock.

"Don't do anything stupid, Ed. Look, we're just children. Why are you doing this?" Ethan asked, pleadingly.

"You…you kids! You have almost ruined everything. We had this all planned. We still can. We can make this place huge. We can make archaeology something that the world will want to come and see. This place here, these old buildings – they will become the next *Disney World*. We will have technology and mystery – science and myth, side by side. Everyone will want to see the cursed mask. And your father has given us the key. He has given it all the stamp of approval." Cruzar was starting to sound crazed, unhinged, his voice rising in a quickfire rat-a-tat.

"Well," said Ethan, stalling for time, "Dad's down in the car, waiting for us. If we're not back in ten minutes, he's radioing the police. You know, the proper police. Er, how about we go down there and sort all of this out. I'm sure you two can come to…"

"Shut up, *ishto!* We'll go, but don't expect to live happily ever after, eh. I have too much to lose. Now you turn and go. Lead the way. But any funny business and your sister will be the latest Maya sacrifice. A knife through the heart sounds about right."

Verity let out a gasp. "No…no!" Cruzar shook her into silence.

Ethan racked his brains as he slowly led the trio back out of the room and up the walkway, following the torchlight that was shaking and snaking about the stonework in response to his trembling hands.

Much to his dismay, Ethan could not formulate anything that seemed like a decent plan by the time they reached the top. Running away would not cut the mustard. He couldn't leave Verity to whatever fate awaited her. He just couldn't.

The drone of the rain greeted them, and near-distant sounds of thunder rumbled in mutual complaint. Ethan looked out from the doorway at the summit of the pyramid, shining his torch ineffectively down to where their truck was.

Except there were two vehicles there now. And one was painted in distinctive black with yellow writing and a badge emblazoned on the side. Its headlights were on and it was facing back towards the ruins.

Yes, the police!

As he was looking down, both the front doors to the pick-up opened as well as a rear one. A policeman exited from the driver's door, possibly Alejandro from the rear and from the front passenger door...

It was unmistakeable. Only one person wore that hat.

Ernesto! No!

The men looked up and pointed, most probably seeing the torchlight and the bedraggled figure of Ethan in the doorway, Cruzar and his captive behind. The three started the long and difficult climb up the steep steps in the pouring rain.

Once at the top, Ethan's heart fell lower still as he clearly recognised the police chief who had previously chased him in the forest.

Cruzar spoke with both men in Spanish, and Ethan didn't have much of a clue about what they were saying. Even so, it didn't sound good. Indeed, he felt their chances of getting out of this situation, surrounded by three grown menacing men, were slim to none. They appeared to be trying to work out what to do.

Suddenly, whilst they were in mid-heated-discussion, Verity chanced herself and broke free from Cruzar's uncomfortable embrace, making for the doorway and past the police chief.

In vain.

The police chief grabbed her as she tried to scoot around him, and encompassed her in his own wicked left arm embrace. With his free hand, he retrieved his pistol from his holster, shouting in Spanish.

He put the pistol to Verity's temple.

Alejandro questioned Cruzar, who looked back and said "*Piensas en tu familia, en tu casa, en la granja Alejandro. Piensas en Maria, tu difunta esposa; piensas en el dinero.*"

Ethan's Spanish knowledge from school was very limited, but he picked up "family", "money", "Maria" and "house". Alejandro had a family, a house and he needed money? But this was Leo's dad...

Alejandro looked at Verity, and Ethan saw, even in the dim light, a change come over him; quite what the change was, he didn't know or understand.

The pistol against Verity's head clicked. "*Voy a matarla,*" the policeman said gruffly, announcing to the other men. "*Tenemos que terminar esto.*"

"Terminar" – that sounds like "terminate". And that doesn't sound good. He's going to kill her. Kill...her.

Ethan's mind raced in a whirl of panic and fear. However, before he could act on his emotions, Alejandro shouted, "*No puedes dispararle a una niña!*"

All of a sudden, Alejandro shot his arm out and grabbed the policeman's wrist, twisting it back. The pistol flew from the man's grasp and clattered onto the stone surface outside the doorway to sit in a wide puddle near the steps that descended below. The policeman turned, letting go of Verity, and ran towards the gun on the ground.

"*Qué estás haciendo, Alejandro, idiota?*" the man shouted, and bent down in the rain to retrieve the firearm.

Alejandro, suddenly energised and clearly angry, ran at the other man and shoved him with all of his force. The policeman tumbled over the edge of the steps and out of sight.

Ernesto, watching this play out in stony silence, decided this was his moment to step in. He charged at Alejandro and tackled the smaller man over the edge and into the darkness after the police chief.

"Vee! Run!" screamed Ethan, and he sprinted past his sister, past Cruzar, and almost jumped the first few stone steps away from the horrors and danger at the top of the pyramid.

He turned, just as he cleared the top steps, to see Verity a heartbeat behind him, a look of sheer wide-eyed terror stamped on her face.

45

Verity

Verity took a furtive glance behind her and saw, some distance back, the shining head of Cruzar. And he had something in his hand, as he negotiated the steps downwards.

It was the pistol.

Luckily, in locating and grabbing it, Cruzar had given them a head start. Through the driving rain that slammed into their faces and the gusty breeze that had picked up, the two children managed to get safely to the bottom of the steps without any slip ups.

Goodness knew what had happened to the other three men; Verity didn't have time to consider any gratitude towards Alejandro for saving her life.

There, they had a choice: the vehicle or elsewhere. A quick look in the vehicle and they were met with a surprise.

"Dad's gone!" shouted Ethan. "I don't have the key – it was in the ignition. That's gone, too!" Ethan's voice had more than an air of desperation.

The vehicles were parked on the city side of the pyramid, with the path to the campsite beyond the pick-ups behind them.

"Let's lose him in the city," suggested Ethan.

"You sure?"

But they didn't have time to discuss it. Cruzar was almost on them.

Both children, clutching their torches, spun and ran towards the ruins that were lurking in the background, ready to welcome them into their mysterious world.

"Should...should we split up? Or stick...together?" Verity panted as they ran along the thoroughfare and into the main section of the ancient city. Of course, they couldn't see where they were running very clearly and had to slow down to shine their weak torches. The beams picked up more rain than anything else, but they were able to slowly navigate the obstacles that presented themselves: logs and stones, mounds and ditches.

"No, we stick together," Ethan eventually replied. She realised at that moment how much she loved her brother and was more than thankful that they were not going to be split from each other once more.

Ethan had a few metres on Verity and steered them towards the two large stone slabs, ornately covered in inscriptions that were presently unobservable.

Ethan swerved in and out of the two monuments and into the unknown; Verity was not so fortunate, and her elbow clipped the first big piece of jutting masonry. Her torch flew out of her hand and into the undergrowth to be snuffed out like a candle in the wind.

Verity winced and grabbed her arm. She had instinctively stopped to check her arm and to try and find the torch but soon realised the uselessness of her task; it was a needle in a haystack. In the dark. In a thunderstorm.

Glancing back, she saw Cruzar not far behind her. She could just about make out the corner of the building in front of her, covered in dripping wet foliage. Ethan's torch was bobbling further in the distance. She had to hide. Verity reached the corner and flattened herself against the soaking wet wall on the other side, edging into the vines and assorted leaves that covered it, trying to blend in with her natural surroundings.

And she waited.

After what seemed an age but was probably some thirty seconds, she leaned forward to peek around the side of the building and back towards the pyramid.

There was no one there.

No torch.

No Cruzar.

Verity ducked back behind her wall.

Crack.

Despite the monotony of the pounding rain, she heard it. Not from out in the open where Cruzar was supposed to be, but near her, from behind the building.

"Ahaa! Got you, you little..."

Cruzar pounced on his prey, having crept behind the building and flanked her. He wrapped her in a bear hug and dragged her out from behind the wall, out into the open. She kicked backwards at his legs, scratched at his arms but it made no difference. He threw her down onto the ground.

Verity sprawled in the undergrowth, getting grass in her mouth and goodness knows what else, for she could barely see a thing.

Cruzar switched his powerful head torch back on and zeroed in on Verity, lying flat and vulnerable on the muddy ground.

"You *will not* ruin everything. You will ruin *nothing anymore.* Ever."

And with that, he took the gun that had been secured in his belt and, for the second time in less than an hour, for the second and possibly last time in her life, Verity had the cold, merciless barrel of a gun pointed at her head.

"Now you will die."

46

Ethan

Ethan saw a flash of colour and movement. He was running and stopped. Cruzar and Verity were behind him – *What could that be?* There was definitely something there. In front of him, over to his right. In the undergrowth. He was sure. Or was he?

He looked back over his shoulder to see where Verity was.

But she was nowhere.

And nor was Cruzar.

Still, in this moment of desperation, Ethan felt like he was being watched. He shone his torch back over to the embankment where he had seen something, but only vines and trunks, branches and bushes, all awash with heavy rainfall, met his hasty search. He looked back towards where Verity should surely have been and then decided to extinguish his torch. He didn't want to alert the predator to his prey.

He could see the two stone monuments faintly silhouetted in the headlights of the police truck that was facing their way. Then, he heard a muffled cry and a scuffle. He saw a body being hurled to the ground and Cruzar's head torch lighting up. Something shone silver in the beam of the torch.

Gun. That's a gun. And it's pointing at Vee...

Something moved Ethan, some primal urge, to protect his sister. He was the only thing that could come between his sister and certain death. There was no thinking. There was no doubting. There was no time.

Before this holiday, Ethan had experienced genuine heroism only once. He had been at the beach and had seen a child, younger than himself, get into trouble in the water, throwing their hands in the air for help. He had been the closest other person, digging trenches in the sand. He had been valiantly fighting off the onslaught of the waves and the inevitability of the tide. He wasn't succeeding much, but people rarely did when trying to fight the might of a sea with a small plastic spade and a pair of cupped hands.

He had spied the child in distress and had immediately, without thought, dived in and swum towards him. He was a six-year-old just out of his depth. It turned out he could swim quite well and had just fancied imagining what it would be like to drown, pretending he was in trouble and being saved by a superhero.

Ethan had been the superhero, but he had not really been needed. "Don't cry wolf!" he had told the boy, disdainfully. In principle, Ethan had been heroic, even if it was ultimately pointless. At least, he described it as heroism to his family, over an ice cream.

There was absolutely no chance here that Verity *wasn't* in distress. Her life was genuinely in mortal danger. Like a flame, her life could be snuffed out in a second.

Putting his torch in his cargo shorts pocket, he set his shoulder lower and ran as fast as he possibly could.

Ethan's rugby tackle hit Cruzar plumb in the midriff, his shoulder smacking into the man's soft underbelly, catching him completely off guard. Cruzar, even given his larger frame, was thrown sideways. A large *bang!*

sounded from the pistol as it fired off into the night sky, thankfully clear of Verity.

Judging by the "Oooff!" that Cruzar exhaled, he was badly winded. Ethan felt something on his shoulder and span round, adrenaline coursing through him like electricity. It was his sister's hand. She helped pull him up.

"Come on!"

They could not risk doing anything else with Cruzar whilst he still had a gun in his hand.

"Great," complained Ethan. "More running..." He took his torch back out and turned it on.

The pair wheeled on the spot and darted off back towards the ruins. Ethan had a rough working experience and memory of the main city area, but in the dark, in the rain, in a panic and fearing for his very life, nothing looked the same. Indeed, he could barely make anything out at all. Dark greens and blacks, raindrops and flashes of vegetation, whizzed in front of his field of view, a kaleidoscope of confusion for his senses.

Ethan scanned about him for an idea. He stole a glance back to see Cruzar on his feet and making his way towards them. Tired, sodden and almost out of hope, he grabbed Verity by the arm and pulled her on.

"C'mon, keep up!" he breathed harshly.

He took her over a mound that hid goodness knew what archaeological treasures, and down again, round a large boulder, through a pair of columns and suddenly out and into a more open area, from what little he could see.

It must have been the Maya ballcourt that they had heard about and were due to visit. His puny torchlight could just about make out stone inclines here and there, walls to enclose the players, walls that would once have had a rubber ball bouncing off them, but now had rain and torchlight doing so. Ethan knew that the court was in the shape of a capital "I" as the Maya sports game was one of the few things he had researched.

The pair scrambled up a rising stone side and they were on the second level of sorts. Cruzar was still about twenty metres behind.

"Vee, I'll give you a bunk up. Put your foot here," Ethan offered, indicating a sheer wall that they were all of a sudden standing next to. If she could get up there, she would be safe from Cruzar.

He, on the other hand, wasn't so sure.

He put away his torch. Verity placed her foot in his cupped and intertwined hands and he paused to muster as much thrusting strength as he could; with a shout, he flung his arms upwards and catapulted Verity towards the top of the wall.

She did well. Really well. Grabbing the edge with her hands and forearms, she was able to manoeuvre herself over the top and onto the raised platform there above.

"Ethan!" she called as she lowered her arm for him to grab and haul himself up.

Except there was no chance he could reach her outstretched hand. No chance at all. He was stuck. With no where to run.

This was one of those rare occasions, where in years to come (if he lived that long), Ethan could thank his lucky stars he spent so long watching endless streams of online videos of things like parkour. Parkour, oh sweet parkour, the urban gymnastic negotiation of buildings by very athletic people, jumping and twisting, spinning and balancing, to the very best of their human capabilities.

He had to try.

He had nothing to lose.

He had everything to gain.

But he had only ever *watched a video!*

A flash of lightning lit up the court in an intense moment of white light. In that moment, everything became visible. The grey stonework, the overgrown vegetation, the nearby trees, and something else.

Eyes. White- and black-lined eyes. And colour. A hint of yellow, mottled with black. Thunder broke, crashing around them everywhere, answering the call to its twin; sound to its light; yin to its yang.

In the split second he had before he launched himself, Ethan knew he was being intently watched from behind a clump of vines and branches that overhung some nearby ballcourt masonry.

Ethan couldn't afford to devote any time to worrying or thinking about it, though. He took a couple of steps back to face the corner where the two walls met and bounced on his calves before taking a few vaulting steps and launching himself to his left. His left foot hit the wall about a metre up and his leg jettisoned him back the other way so that his right foot planted on the other wall. He was then able to thrust back to the left so that, in a three-step move, he was able to catapult himself towards the platform.

To his utmost relief, Verity grabbed his arm and managed to cling on to him and use all her surprisingly Herculean might to haul him up to safety.

The two children lay there exhausted and elated with their trials and tribulations, rain smothering their upturned faces as they breathed the night time forest air deeply into their rapidly gasping lungs.

"Hey! You! Get down here!" Cruzar desperately shouted from below, powerless all the while he couldn't see them. "I'll shoot!"

Ethan crawled about at the top of the stone platform, covered as it was in moss and greenery.

He found what he was looking for: a large enough rock that could be used as a weapon. "I'm, going to lob this at him," he explained to his sister.

"No, he'll shoot you. Better idea: I'll distract him." She picked up another stone, smaller than Ethan's, and from out of sight, threw it against the adjacent wall below. Ethan took that moment to stand up, hoping that Cruzar was indeed distracted, and took rapid aim with his stone. Like a medieval trebuchet, he swung the rock up and down onto the man below.

Direct hit.

The rock careened down like a meteorite on the unsuspecting Cruzar, hitting him on the shoulder. He crumpled and fell to the floor with a cry of pain. Despite this, the man twisted and with a roar of anger, levelled the gun directly at Ethan.

And then a majestic and terrifying, and quite unexpected thing happened.

Out of the undergrowth somewhere below, a swift and silent shape, with grace and agility, sprang out, finding its moment of opportunity.

"What the...?" was all Ethan could manage.

Verity poked her head over the edge. With Cruzar down on the ground, a body with feline grace, poise and lethality had recognised an instance of weakness. It pounced and landed on top of the prostrate man.

"It's a...jaguar!" said Ethan in utter amazement.

The muscled body of the spotted cat flashed into view with another flash of lightning and the erratic swinging of Cruzar's head and torch. He was screaming, but perhaps more in fright than any pain yet.

Bang!

A shot rang out from his gun out to the side as his gun flew out of his hand, his arm pinned by a large padded paw of the jaguar.

This was enough to send the jaguar warily back to its hiding place.

Cruzar, torch now blackened in the action of hitting his head on the ground, was feeling around for his side-arm in the pouring rain and ancient city darkness, to no avail.

A deep, chesty cough of a roar was emitted from out of sight, and something like a hiss. Cruzar looked back towards the sound, and decided now was not a good time to restart the fight.

He turned and fled, out past the ballcourt, and out of the very short sight of the watching children. Some sense of self-preservation prevailed.

"Oh my days..." whispered Ethan, to no one in particular. "Oh my days. That...that was mental."

"Totally. And I'm not moving until daylight."

The two children sat on top of the platform for some time, in the soaking rain. Ethan looked towards his sister and shivered, rain washing down his face, his arms, his back, his everything. He scuffled over to Verity on his bottom and put his arm round her.

"Well done, sis. You were awesome."

"You too, Ethan. You too." And he sensed a warm, wet smile in the thunderous darkness of the Guatemalan forest.

***

Not long after, the bright lights of a four-wheel drive lit up the ballcourt. There was some trepidation as to who might be driving, but this turned to elation when the children worked out it was their father.

269

It turned out he had a bruised and bloodied police chief handcuffed with his own cuffs in the back of the truck. The man was dazed from a head injury.

Ernesto, they found out, had escaped. He had driven off in the police truck to who-knew-where. Alejandro had had some kind of crisis of conscience, it appeared, and was seated next to Daniel. Their dad had taken care of the groggy policeman and had come straight out to find them, though it took some coaxing to get them down from their heights. Who knew what dangers were still lurking in the undergrowth?

Cruzar had run off, perhaps chased by the jaguar, certainly scared witless.

For the time being, though, they were all safe. There, in the headlights of the truck, the three silhouettes, one tall and slightly bent in discomfort, the other two shorter, limping and tired, came together; the Hume family reunited. And it was, even given the pouring rain, their mud-covered clothes and still slightly unnerving environment, the most wonderful moment of Ethan's life, though it lacked one missing piece. The only missing piece of the four-piece jigsaw was his mother.

Ethan broke down and cried. He cried and cried and cried. But he was not alone in that. Not alone at all.

There was some serious explaining to do back at camp, and the police needed to be contacted (after all, they needed to investigate their own man in the back of the truck), as well as the British embassy. The media would no doubt be arriving in the morning anyway, what with all the hullaballoo caused at the press conference and with the internet postings.

The media, of course, would get a whole lot more than they had bargained for. A whole lot more.

The mask, cursed or not, had spread out its insidious influence and touched them all, and would leave its many scars for lifetimes to come.

47

Verity

Helicopters and trucks full of news and media teams buzzed to, from and around the ruins over the next few days like flies around a recently deceased carcass. This was exactly what Cruzar would have wanted and yet wasn't able to see or appreciate. Although the media were now understanding the ruins and the part the mask played in the whole story more truthfully, they were presently revelling in everything that this site provided for them. They were devouring every last morsel of information, every scrap of truth and half-truth, picking rumours off historical bones, extracting every last piece of newsworthy nutrition. Soon, there would be nothing left for them. The place would be stripped clean of interest and scandal, story and myth. Then, after weeks, or perhaps months, the site would most probably return to what it always should have been: a place of huge interest for those people who had huge interest in it, for what it was worth as a historical artefact.

"We'll be live in five, Mr Hume, so you just stand here, and your children can stand here and here," said the pretty woman with long blonde-brown hair, dressed in "adventurous outdoor clothing" but still managing to look all made-up and picture-perfect.

Two days had passed since the night in the pyramid. A British diplomat from the embassy in Guatemala City had almost immediately come to assist the Humes as they came to terms with what had taken place. He had even stayed in a tent in the camp the previous night. The family were to stay another day before being flown back to the UK. Daniel Hume's job here was done, as far as he was concerned. Despite the truly magnificent wonder of the ruins, he wanted to get his family safely back home without further ado.

Daniel had agreed to a couple of interviews and the family were preparing for their first one, with the American news broadcaster CNN. The reporter, one of their South American correspondents, was Stephanie Ismene, and she was particularly excited about the interview. The story had certainly captivated the news crews and their audiences. The term "curse of the Maya" had been bandied around quite liberally.

Daniel was less than impressed with this.

"There is no blasted curse! We have a pretty good idea as to why the Maya disappeared," Daniel had complained to his children. "New information is coming out all the time. We don't need to play up to the media and try and turn this into a money-making enterprise. This is history. This is science. The real answers are, for me, more interesting than those myths that we create to excite people."

Despite his protestations, the media were still intent on concentrating on the myth and excitement that was the cursed mask.

"One minute until we're live," Stephanie said in her American accent that to the children sounded foreign and yet so familiar. In a time of watching so many movies and streamed TV shows from all around the world, they lived with American accents almost every day. But there was something rather exotic about hearing it live, and especially surrounded by TV cameras and production crews.

"Thank you, Rebecca," Stephanie said, speaking to a microphone and looking directly at the camera. "I'm here in the depths of the Guatemalan forest at some spectacular, newly found Maya ruins. Surrounded by these wonderful ancient buildings that have stood untouched for a thousand years, I am accompanied by three members of a British family who have become embroiled in a tale of deceit, adventure and danger. Luckily for them, they are here to tell their story…"

Much of the interview of her father was a blur to Verity, who was rather overwhelmed by the whole occasion. What undoubtedly took only a minute seemed to take a small age. Before long, Stephanie turned and smiled at Verity and Ethan, speaking into her microphone and thrusting it towards the children.

"So, you to seem to have become overnight heroes. How does that feel to you two young holidaymakers?"

Without even the merest thought, Verity replied both confidently and a little impatiently: "We're not holidaymakers, we're truth-seekers."

This seemed to throw the interviewer, who was no doubt a seasoned expert.

"Wow! Well, that told me!"

The rest of the interview went in a heart-hammering haze of questions and answers that, afterwards, Verity could barely remember. Well, they had both had their fifteen minutes of fame, as people often said.

"This has been Stephanie Ismene, in the heart of the Guatemalan Forest. Back over to you, Rebecca, in the studio."

After it finished, Stephanie took her small earplug attached to a coiled wire out of her ear and announced,

"Well, that's a wrap. Thanks guys. You were great." She then proceeded to speak to the children's father for a good twenty minutes. The two were deeply engaged, talking about everything that had happened and the work that Daniel did. The children waited patiently, barely absorbed in nonsense small talk.

"Well, it's been an absolute pleasure talking to you, Daniel. I hope we can keep in touch. You sound like a truly fascinating guy and I'd like to learn more about what you do. You've got great kids, there, too."

And with that, she started fumbling around in one of the pockets to her cargo pants and retrieved a small white business card. She twirled it around her fingers and then looked at Daniel.

"Look, here's my card. If you ever have any other interesting story you want to share, you know how to get hold of me. Make sure you say goodbye before you go."

She took the card and gently tucked it into Daniel's shirt pockets and patted his chest. Looking at him intently, she gave him a wink, turned and walked away. Daniel, flustered and incredibly awkward, didn't quite know what to do. Verity thought that she saw him try to wink back. However, Stephanie had already turned around, and in any case, his wink turned into an uncoordinated blink from a scrunched-up brow. He really was out of practice.

This all left rather an odd feeling in the pit of Verity's stomach. This was the first time for a long time that she had seen her father speak in any way, other than for work purposes or through polite acquaintance, with a woman. Of course, this immediately brought on memories of her mother. Something just didn't feel quite right. She dismissed any such feelings by changing the subject and asking her dad to take them back to camp for a refreshment break.

When talking about the interview over a cup of hot chocolate back at the camp, the two children congratulated each other.

Ethan looked admiringly at Verity and said, "I loved it when you said 'We're not holidaymakers, we're truth-seekers'. That was really cool."

"I loved it when you vaulted up that wall. I *think* cool and you *look* cool. *That's* teamwork." Verity smiled but then suddenly happiness drained from her face. "What do you think will happen to Leo? I can't believe his dad was in on this, too."

The smile evaporated from Ethan's face as well. "Yeah, it's a shocker. Poor Leo. I don't think his dad was involved as much as Ed and Ernesto. I don't think he realised it would get as serious as it did. Maybe because of his son, he will escape a sentence. I hope Leo will be all right. I heard he's going to stay with his grandparents on that farm he talked about. I guess it's not as happy an ending for him as his dad was hoping."

Verity nodded. "I guess every crime has innocent victims. Leo is definitely an innocent victim. He is a really nice boy who doesn't deserve any of this. Selfish decisions made by selfish people."

As if on cue, Leo walked into the central area of the camp.

"Hey guys," he said, a look of deep sadness on his face. "I'm going with my uncle soon. I've come to say *adios*."

"Leo!" both children gushed in unison.

Verity stood and ran to him, with Ethan following. They had a group-hug before sitting Leo down next to them. "Leo, we know your father was involved in this, but we are so grateful, so thankful that he did what he did. He literally saved my life. I hope this means they will be kinder to him."

"I am so sorry for this. I hope they will be kind also. He wanted to get money so my uncle can keep farm and we can keep house. It has been tough after *mamá* die. *Papá* not think good. He make bad choice."

The three children engaged in meaningful conversation for another ten minutes before Leo had to leave. They hugged again and said their goodbyes.

"I really hope everything works out for him. He doesn't deserve all this," Ethan muttered.

Having long drained their hot chocolates, the children readied themselves for their next television appearance.

A couple of days and a good dozen interviews later, the children and their father were whisked off back to the UK.

Quite simply, their lives would never be the same again.

Epilogue

Dad pulled the car onto the drive and turned the engine off. Unusually, there was silence. All three members of the family stared at the front door, too tired and drained to speak. Ethan was the first to open the door. Taking only his small rucksack from the footwell, he plodded over to the front door, the glinting knocker on the shiny black paintwork reflecting the afternoon sun as it fought to break through the clouds. He waited there, expectantly, for his father to turn up with the key.

When the door opened, Ethan bundled through, dropping his bag to collapse, comfortable on the sofa in the lounge. Verity came in last, shut the door, and leaned against the wall in the hallway. She looked around at all the furnishings, the pictures, her mum staring smilingly at the camera. All the signs that she was home. *Home.*

"I'm making some tea," Dad said to no one in particular.

Verity took in a deep breath and appreciated the smell of their own house. It was good to be home. Better than that, it was good to be home safe. Better still, it was good to be home safe with family. And with that thought, she walked through into the lounge, knelt down next to the sofa, and gave Ethan a huge, tight hug.

To her surprise, and enough to bring a tear to her eye, he hugged her back.

A few minutes later, their father walked into the lounge with a steaming cup of tea.

"Okay, kids, a couple of things to say... Firstly, your mum would have been so proud of you over the last few weeks, she really would have. There is so much of her in you, that it sometimes makes me double-take when I see you talking, or doing things. It's wonderful to think of her being here, with me, and in you."

The twins were suddenly tired, or there was dust in the air, and there was the odd, surreptitious finger to the eye to remove whatever it was.

"Secondly, (and you may or may not appreciate this), but you know the last few weeks was technically work?"

"Er, yeah...?" said Ethan tentatively, wondering what could be coming next.

"Well, I had, before we left, secretly booked us on a holiday. To Egypt. In a week's time."

"What!?" they both chorused.

"Well, I could cancel it?"

Ethan looked at Verity. Verity looked at Ethan. There was some kind of connection going on between the pair of them, because they both turned back to their father:

"No way, José!"

"This is it! This is my chance to find out about the curse of the pharaohs. More pyramids! (Actually, I may need to think about that...) Man, this will be epic!" Ethan turned to Verity, who was rolling her eyes. "OMEG!"

"What?" she asked, perplexed.

"Oh. My. Egyptian. Gods."

Verity felt like her eyes would never be returned to their forward-facing position.

MISSING ARCHAEOLOGIST
INVOLVED IN CURSE SCANDAL
FOUND

Guatemala City – Police and search teams have finally found the missing archaeologist thought to be at the centre of the "*Curse of the Maya*" scandal that rocked Guatemala last month, involving a British family.

The Hume family hit the news when they were innocent victims at the centre of a scheme to make money out of a newly-found ruin and a mask that was claimed to be the cause of the end of the Maya civilisation. The man at the heart of the illegal plan was chased into the forest by a jaguar, according to the children, twins Verity and Ethan Hume.

Unfortunately for Edwin Cruzar, he was not to survive on the run, apparently dying from lack of drinking water and food in the hot summer forest. Guatemala has been suffering something of a drought in the last month as rains have not hit the country since the night of his disappearance.